"Say my name again," Thomas said.

Tears threatened to overflow. "Don't make this harder than it already is. Do you think this is easy for me?" Jessica stepped away from him.

Her voice sharpened as she spoke. "I've dreamed about you my whole life, wanted to be with you, even when I didn't believe in relationships. No one compared to you. And when I finally got you, I put my career before you. Clearly we are not *bashert*."

He frowned. "Buh-what?"

"It means 'meant to be.'"

Stepping forward, he closed the terrible distance between them, at least physically, by taking her in his arms and kissing her. Still holding on to both her hands in his, he thought for a while.

"I like that word," he said. "You see, I think we are *bashert*."

Dear Reader,

I've had so much fun writing this series. When I started writing *Home for the Challah Days*, I never expected it to find a home at Harlequin, and I never imagined they'd want me to make a series—Holidays, Heart and Chutzpah—out of it.

I've loved diving into the world of Sarah and Aaron, Caroline and Jared, and now, with *Deadlines, Donuts & Dreidels*, Jessica and Thomas.

This book was tricky because in addition to the usual conflicts between two people who are meant to be together but probably don't realize it, there was the additional issue of different religions. Throughout the years, intermarriage in Judaism has been a touchy subject, but with so many people actively making it work and producing thriving families that love and celebrate multiple cultures and beliefs, I wanted to tackle it.

I wanted to show how love between two people, regardless of circumstance or religion, can be a beautiful thing. And rather than take away one person's identity, it can amplify it and allow everyone to thrive.

I hope I've done it justice, and I hope you love Jessica, Thomas and the entire Browerville community. Thanks for joining me on this wonderful, miraculous ride!

Jennifer Wilck

DEADLINES, DONUTS & DREIDELS

JENNIFER WILCK

Harlequin

SPECIAL EDITION

ISBN-13: 978-1-335-40207-3

Deadlines, Donuts & Dreidels

Harlequin Enterprises ULC
22 Adelaide St. West, 41st Floor
Toronto, Ontario M5H 4E3, Canada
www.Harlequin.com

Printed in Lithuania

Recycling programs for this product may not exist in your area.

MIX
Paper | Supporting responsible forestry
FSC® C021394

Jennifer Wilck is an award-winning contemporary romance author for readers who are passionate about love, laughter and happily-ever-after. Known for writing both Jewish and non-Jewish romances, she features damaged heroes, sassy and independent heroines, witty banter, yummy food and hot chemistry in her books. She believes humor is the only way to get through the day and does not believe in sharing her chocolate. You can find her at www.jenniferwilck.com.

Books by Jennifer Wilck

Harlequin Special Edition

Holidays, Heart and Chutzpah

Visit the Author Profile page at Harlequin.com.

To Gail, my amazing editor—this series never would
have come into being without your incredible support.
Thank you so much for all you've done for me!

Chapter One

"**I**'m sorry, Jessica, but there's nothing I can do."

Jessica dug her nails into the palms of her hands and tried to slow her pounding heart. Her short hair stuck to the nape of her neck as sweat popped along her hairline.

Her boss could not fire her. Not now.

The silence inside the office surrounded her like fluff, muting all the other sounds outside the glass walls—the phone chatter, keyboard taps, office-chair squeaks and TV monitor voices of a busy newsroom. *You wouldn't think it would be this busy right before Thanksgiving.*

"Alice, I apologized to everyone, and I printed a correction. There must be a way to fix this."

Her boss and the executive editor of the *Brooklyn Daily Herald* shook her head. "The Macadoos are major advertisers with us and our parent company. Your error made them look bad, and you have no idea how hard Harvey and I worked to convince them not to withdraw their support from not only this paper and the website, but everywhere else they advertise. By the time the call ended, Harvey was fuming."

Jess could picture Harvey's face, purple and pulsing with anger. As the publisher of the media company, he was responsible for three local papers in New York and New Jersey, their respective websites, four cable channels and a bunch of syndicated radio shows in the tri-state area. The story she'd written, about how Terrence Macadoo had embezzled funds to support a second family, was a terrific story. Who knew there were two men with that exact name? And it was her luck the *innocent* Terrence Macadoo happened to be their biggest advertiser. It had turned into a colossal mess, with lawsuits and divorces threatened. But she didn't want to lose her job.

"Please, Alice. I love this job. Isn't there anything I can do?"

Her throat thickened and she pulled at her Star of David necklace as she swallowed. She'd worked for the *Brooklyn Daily Herald* since college graduation. It was her first and only job and, for the past ten years, she'd loved everything about it. She loved the rush of meeting deadlines, the adrenaline surrounding a juicy scoop. How could one mistake ruin everything?

Alice, polished as usual, sat across the desk from her and stared at her with a mixture of sympathy and disappointment.

"Look, it's out of my hands. Harvey doesn't want you here…"

That was it. Jessica's stomach dropped. As much as she wanted to stay, Harvey was the boss. The big boss. The one who all the bosses reported to. If he said she was gone, she was gone.

She rose. "I understand."

Numb with shock, she left Alice's office and returned to her desk. Examining ten years' worth of stuff, she wondered what she was supposed to do with everything. In movies, when people were fired, they left with their stuff in a box. Who kept boxes near their desk? Was there some "box department" she should call? And how to pare down a decade's worth of stuff into one box?

Sinking into her chair, she opened her desk, pulled out small personal items, and stuffed them in her bag. From on top of her desk, she added the photos and mug she'd kept there for as long as she could remember. Plus the award she'd won for a story last year.

With nothing else of value to take, and no boxes having

miraculously appeared, she returned to Alice's office to turn in her badge and key card.

"I'm sorry it worked out this way," Alice said.

"Me too."

In a daze, Jessica left her office for the last time and returned to her apartment. The cold Brooklyn streets were busier than usual, the subways packed this day before Thanksgiving. Her building lobby was empty, though. As she let herself into her apartment, she paused in the entryway. She'd worked weekdays and weekends and, other than the occasional sick day or vacation, she rarely saw this place in the light of day. Dust motes floated in the air, the refrigerator hummed, but otherwise everything was still and silent. She dropped her keys in the Jersey Shore souvenir dish on her cabinet in the entryway, placed her large leather bag gently on the floor next to it, removed her sneakers and walked in socks into the living room. With a sigh, she plopped onto the sofa and closed her eyes.

What now? She was supposed to go home tonight for Thanksgiving with her family. The candied yams she'd promised sat in the refrigerator. But the thought of telling her parents she'd been fired horrified her. Her brother Brandon and his wife would be there too. What would they think of her? Tears sprung behind her closed lids, and she grit her teeth to fight them. She wasn't going to dissolve into tears. With deep breaths, she tried to invent an excuse to skip the event, knowing it was useless. No way would her parents allow her to miss it.

How could she tell her family she'd lost her job? Her parents were proud of her career, saving every article she wrote, *kvelling* every time she called to tell them about an upcoming subject she'd researched. They'd be devastated. Her brother was always supportive of her, so he wouldn't say anything. But what would he think? And after he and his wife left, what would they say about her?

She buried her face in one of her sofa cushions.

The ring of her cell phone made her jump. It was Alice.

She stared at the phone a minute, a sliver of trepidation running along her spine. They couldn't fire her again, so she shook off the dread in the pit of her stomach. "Hello?" Had she forgotten something in her haste to leave?

A loud sigh greeted her. "I feel bad I had to let you go, so I have a proposition for you."

Jessica pulled the phone away from her ear. Alice often called her at all hours about assignments, but she no longer worked for the woman. What proposition could her former boss have now that she hadn't had earlier?

"Yes?"

"A story just came across my desk. A museum rededication and awards ceremony. Apparently, the town wants to award a firefighter for rescuing an elderly man from a fire. How about you cover the story? Get it right, and I'll see if I can convince Harvey to give you a second chance."

This was ridiculous. "I'm an investigative reporter. A hometown event isn't my beat."

"You don't have a job. I'm not sure what you have to complain about, Jess."

Jessica winced at the well-placed barb. "Why are you giving this to me?"

"You're from Browerville. The museum rededication is in your hometown."

"But we cover Brooklyn."

"Yes, but Harvey wants it for his regional paper, the *Tri-State Sentinel*."

And if she went home to cover it, they wouldn't have to pay her travel expenses. Now it made sense.

"Are you serious about giving me my job back?"

Alice sighed. "Let's call it a sabbatical. Cover this story well. Interview the firefighter—his name is Thomas Carville—and interview the guy he rescued. Give it the full treatment. The ceremony is in two and a half weeks. Cover it as well. In the meantime, Harvey will have time to cool off and I'll have a better chance to change his mind. I like you, Jess. We've had a great history together. I'd love to give you a second chance. Your mistake was bad, but everyone deserves a second chance."

Jessica ran a hand through her short hair, half listening to the rest of Alice's conversation.

Her thoughts zoomed in to the firefighter.

Thomas Carville.

The object of her crush since…forever. He lived next door with his parents and siblings. She'd heard he was a firefighter. Her mom had called to let her know about his accident, but until April had given her his name, she hadn't made the connection.

Math had never been her strong suit.

She remembered how giddy she'd been every time she'd seen him. She'd followed him and his friends around, waiting to be included. She'd posed in her bathing suit and shorts on her front lawn, hoping he'd notice her. She'd always wanted him to ask her out and she'd been devastated in eighth grade when he'd left for college.

It had been years since she'd seen him. What did he look like now? She remembered his blond hair and crooked smile. When he'd turned it on her, she'd practically drooled. From the glimpses she'd seen, he'd filled out and grown taller. But how had he changed? Was his hair darker? And his voice—had it deepened? A flicker of interest warmed her.

This story was out of her area of coverage. But if it landed her in the good graces of her boss, she'd save her job. And a chance to catch up with her secret crush could be fun.

"Okay, I'll do it," she said.

With renewed determination, she rushed to pack her clothes and make her train home.

* * *

Thomas Carville pulled into his driveway and shut off his battered blue pickup's ignition. He rolled his neck, his skin tight from burn scars, and climbed out. The late November wind made his open jacket flutter, and he pulled it tighter around himself as he locked his truck door. The church where he'd attended his AA meeting had run out of the good coffee and all he wanted was a drink of water to get the taste of burnt grounds out of his mouth. He wanted something stronger than water, but he always did. He no longer gave in to those desires.

Jogging up his front flagstone walkway jingling his keys, he stopped short at the sight of a note on his door. The yellow Post-it fluttered a little in the cold breeze. He pulled the sticky note off the door and read it.

Hi, Thomas,
Not sure if you remember me, but I used to live next door.
I'm in town for the rededication ceremony and would
love to talk to you about your heroic rescue. Call me.
Jessica Sacks

At the bottom, she'd listed the name of the newspaper and her phone number. He clenched his teeth and crumpled the note. No freakin' way. He was no hero and he refused to talk about that day—especially to a reporter, no matter how who she was.

He looked over at her parents' house. Of course, he remembered her. Younger than he was by about four years, she'd had a crush on him. It had been cute when she was a kid. He'd let her follow him and his friends around, once in a while giving her attention. His parents and hers moved in different circles. His with their church friends and hers with others he didn't know well. But they were neighbors.

He remembered braces that gleamed in the sunlight when she'd smiled and big eyes that had stared at him out of a thin face.

He also remembered how kind Jessica's mother had been when his mom had gotten sick. She'd brought over meals and baked goods and donated to their church when she'd died. And after his accident, she'd sent a note and flowers to the hospital.

He shook his head. Neighborly was one thing. Humoring Jessica as a kid was fine. But now? No way. It was his fault the old guy had almost died in that fire. He'd barely made it out himself.

Though healed, the burns on his neck and back itched; a potent reminder of the disaster he'd caused. At least his hair had grown back. He didn't talk about it to anyone. She'd have to find another story.

Tossing the note in the trash, he went into the kitchen to make himself lunch. Reggie, his German shepherd, followed him, sitting at his side. As he ate, he reviewed his plan for the rest of the day. The key to his sobriety was to keep busy and avoid his former triggers. He'd made it eight months, three weeks and six days. His sponsor was great, and the meetings helped. He refused to mess things up. Therefore, he stuck to his plan.

Since he'd left the fire department, he'd cashed his disability checks and been renovating his parents' house. Scratch that, his house. With his mom gone, his dad had moved to Arizona, where it was warm, and his brothers and sister were married and in homes of their own. This house was his, and it needed a lot of work.

He'd gutted and redone the kitchen first—a man needed to eat, and he liked to cook. At the firehouse, the guys had loved it when it was his turn to cook. Sure, the meals were the easy, big-group kinds essential to fire departments, but they were fresh. His lasagna featured homemade noodles and sauce. His chili incorporated fresh ingredients and nothing from a can.

As a single guy living alone, he made smaller meals for himself, but they were still healthy, fresh and tasty. The few times he'd brought dates home for dinner, they'd loved the meals he prepared for them too.

After changing into work clothes, he surveyed the living room. With the kitchen modernized, he'd quickly moved on. Again, he'd gutted the room down to the studs and installed brand new Sheetrock, wood trim and a simple mantel and hearth around the fireplace. He'd added high-hat lights in the ceiling. All that was left was sanding the floor and painting.

He put on protective gear and got to work with the sander. Except, every so often, movement out the window caught his eye and made him stop.

Since Jessica had arrived home, there'd been more activity at the neighbors' house. He shouldn't care since he didn't intend to let her interview him. But every time a car entered or exited, or the garage door rose or fell, it reminded him she was there and wanted to speak to him.

What was she like now? She had terrible taste in careers, but he couldn't get those huge eyes out of his mind. They'd been too big for her face then, but the bright emerald green wouldn't let him ignore them.

Not that he'd ever thought of her as anything other than an annoying child.

He groaned. She was probably still annoying, just less of a child.

Manual labor didn't prevent him from his wandering thoughts, no matter how hard he tried to focus. When he forgot to turn off the sander and kept it in one place too long, he swore before yanking the plug from the wall.

No way would he ruin the floor because of her.

He stalked upstairs, grabbed an extra bedsheet and returned to the living room. Pulling tacks out of the container on the windowsill, he affixed the sheet over the glass, darkening the room, but giving him peace. Problem solved.

* * *

Jessica glanced for what seemed like the one hundredth time at Thomas Carville's house. It was only the seventh or eighth time that day, but as she waited for a response, each stare seemed to multiply. Since she'd arrived home for Thanksgiving last week, she'd hoped to catch him, but he never seemed to be home.

She'd left the Post-it note on the door yesterday. She'd heard Thomas's truck pull out this morning and seen him pull in a half an hour ago. Yet still her phone didn't ring.

Staring out the window of her parents' living room, she remembered the days when she used to wait for Thomas to leave his house so she could follow him, hoping he'd pay attention to her. Even now, her heart raced when she remembered how his cowlick whorled on his forehead. His brown eyes had glinted when he was happy, and she'd waited with bated breath for him to turn them on her.

She scoffed. Such silly childhood dreams. She remembered how he'd once let her tag along when they'd gone to play Frisbee in the park. It had probably meant little to him, but to her, it had been everything.

She'd dreamed of him asking her to be his girlfriend—ignoring how her parents wouldn't have allowed her to date someone four years older than she, or of a different religion. In her perfect childhood dreamworld, however, she and Thomas would overcome all the obstacles, dance in the moonlight, run away together, and live happily ever after.

Her real world was far from perfect.

At twenty-eight, she didn't believe in happily-ever-after, no matter how wonderful her parents' or brother's marriages were. She'd been on too many bad dates and seen too many college friends enter into terrible relationships for her to believe her Prince Charming would appear at midnight, whether or not she lost a shoe, ate an apple or fell asleep. While she didn't count it out, she wasn't silly enough to think her childhood dreams would come true.

It was time to put all romantic thoughts aside. If she wanted to save her job, she needed this story.

She'd hoped a friendly note on his door would be the way in, but either he'd grabbed it without reading it or he hadn't felt the same urgency she did. She'd give him the rest of the day before she moved onto plan B.

"Whatcha staring at?"

Jessica jumped as her mother snuck up behind her. She gasped and spun around.

"You startled me. I was hoping to see Thomas."

Her mother raised an eyebrow. "You could go knock on his door like a normal person."

"I could. I hoped he'd see my note and stop by."

Her mom looked at her with sympathy. "Well, in the meantime, want to go into town for lunch?"

"As long as it's Isaacson's Deli. No matter how great New York's deli scene is, there's something about Isaacson's that I can't get enough of."

After bundling up for the cold, Jessica and her mom drove into town and parked in front of the deli. Inside, they placed their sandwich order and sat at one of the tables to wait.

"Have you told Sarah you're in town?" her mother asked.

Jessica looked around. Her stomach sank. If she called Sarah, she'd have to explain why she was there. But if she didn't, and her friend found out—which she would since Aaron Isaacson, owner of the deli, was her boyfriend—she'd be hurt. "I'll give her a call." She'd have to figure out a way to keep what had happened a secret.

She sighed. She already kept the secret from her family. What was one more person?

Her mother nodded. "I'm glad you two have reinvigorated your friendship."

"Me too."

Aaron brought over their sandwiches. "Hey, Jess. Hi, Mrs. Sacks. Nice to see you both. Good Thanksgiving? Sarah know you're home?" he asked Jessica.

"Yes, it was, and I was telling my mom I need to call her."

"She'll be thrilled to see you. She said the three of you are due for a girls' night."

Jessica nodded. A twinge of guilt marred her pleasure. She hated keeping secrets from friends. "We are. Which reminds me, I need to call Caroline too." What would her friends say if they knew she'd been fired? For that matter, what would her parents say? Shame heated her cheeks and she reached for her drink.

Before she thought about that any more, the bell on the deli door jingled and Caroline walked in. Aaron turned toward her and smiled.

"You must have heard us talking about you."

Caroline started to make a face at him but stopped in the middle. "Jess, you're home!" She rushed over and gave her a hug. "Hi, Mrs. Sacks."

"Hello, dear. How are you? How was Thanksgiving?"

"I'm well, and it was great." Caroline turned to Jessica. "What are you doing here? How long are you here for? When can we get together?"

Jessica swallowed her bite of sandwich before she answered. She'd hoped for more time to invent a plausible reason for her visit home. "Wow, you ask more questions than I do. I came home for Thanksgiving and now I'm to cover the rededication ceremony. Not sure. And soon, I hope."

Caroline frowned. "But I thought... Never mind. I'm glad you're here."

Aaron interrupted. "I've got to get back to work, but it's great to see you, Jess. Caroline. Mrs. Sacks." He nodded to everyone and returned behind the counter.

Jessica's mom pointed to an empty chair. "Caroline, join us?"

Caroline sighed. "I need to place my order and return to the Jewish Community Center. We're planning all kinds of Hanukkah programs at the JCC, and I have a ton of work to do."

Jessica took another bite of her sandwich as Caroline checked her phone.

"How about you come over tonight? I'll see if Sarah's available." Caroline looked at Jessica. "Around eight?"

Jessica looked at her smartwatch. Until she heard from Thomas and scheduled an interview, she was flexible. "Sure. It'll be great to catch up. I'll bring the wine."

"Perfect. See you tonight," Caroline said. "Great to see you, Mrs. Sacks."

"You, too, Caroline." She turned to her daughter. "I'm happy you're getting involved. It'll be like old times."

Well, minus the crush on Thomas.

Chapter Two

Thomas sat behind the wheel of his pickup at the stoplight in the middle of Browerville that afternoon, music from Blink-182 blasting. He'd received the all-clear from his doctor. His burns had healed, his range of motion was decent and, from a medical perspective, he was free to return to work.

Mentally, though, was another story. He couldn't imagine returning to the job he'd once loved. Just the idea of a visit to the firehouse today nauseated him.

He glanced at the passenger seat, where his medical release rested next to his resignation papers. The chief was going to be pissed. As were his friends.

But they wouldn't be if they knew the truth.

He'd wanted to avoid everyone, to email his resignation and mail his paperwork. He was many things, including a recovering alcoholic, but he was not a coward.

Not anymore.

His phone rang and he glanced at the screen, groaned, and hit Ignore. He wasn't talking to the man he'd rescued, no matter how many times he called.

With a sigh, he pulled his truck into the station driveway, parked in the back and entered the building. The blast of heat hit him in the face after the cold outdoors. A faint smell of sweat mixed with the aroma of chili cooking on the stove greeted him as soon as he'd opened the door.

"Tommy-Boy, how the hell are you?" Rick whooped as he walked in and clapped him on the back. "Man, it's good to see you. I've tried to call you a few times."

Thomas nodded. "Sorry, Ricky. Good to see you too." He acknowledged the three other men who'd looked up when Rick announced his presence. "Chili on the menu?"

Ed laughed. "Fourth time this week."

"Someone ought to suggest a new recipe," Thomas said. For as long as he could remember, chili was the food of choice at the house. No matter what he did now, he'd never cook chili.

"Good luck," Rick said.

Thomas nodded. "Chief in?"

Rick tipped his head. "In her office."

Before anyone extended the conversation, Thomas walked to the chief's office. He knocked on the wooden door and entered when he was summoned. Inside, the air was fresher.

"Hey, Chief."

Chief Gordon rose from behind her desk, leaned across and shook Thomas's hand. "Good to see you."

"You too." There was a lot Thomas could say, but the words stuck in his throat. All he'd ever wanted was to be a firefighter. And it was about to end. He swallowed and handed her the papers.

She pointed to a seat across from her desk and he sat while she riffled through the papers. Her gaze was disappointed when it met his. "Are you sure this is what you want? I hate to see you go."

It wasn't a matter of what he wanted. It was a matter of trusting himself. Besides, even if he got there, the rest of the department wouldn't. Not if they ever learned the truth. "It's what I need."

She stared in silence at him for a few moments. Older than him by about ten years, Chief Gordon was one of the few female fire chiefs in New Jersey. She was tough but fair, and

Thomas respected her. It was one of the reasons he needed to leave the department—he didn't want anything he had done to reflect on her.

Finally, she gave a terse nod and signed off on the medical paperwork. Then she slipped the other envelope into her desk drawer.

"I'll hold on to these for a while, in case you change your mind."

He rose. "Thanks, but I won't."

"Don't make any hasty decisions."

Hasty? He'd thought about it for more than eight months. He stared at her.

"Oh, and Thomas? One more thing."

All he wanted to do was to leave, but he forced himself to remain. "Yes?"

"Not that I want to lose you, because I don't, but the academy needs instructors. I think you'd be great."

Great. Yeah right. He wanted to scoff, to ask her if she was crazy. But he didn't. Instead, he nodded and left her office, closing the door behind him.

With a wave to the guys in the room, he strode to his truck, walking fast to give the impression he didn't have time to talk. Truth was, he didn't want to remain one more minute than necessary. Someday he'd have to tell them, or at least inform them of his resignation. But he couldn't do it right now, and the chief's request to reconsider gave him the out he needed. The idea of explaining his situation while inside the place he'd once loved made him break out in a cold sweat.

Once in the driver's seat, he gripped the steering wheel until his knuckles whitened, took several deep breaths and rested his forehead on his hands. Goddammit this hurt. But how in the world was he supposed to do his job when he couldn't trust himself?

That's why he'd resigned. With a snort of disgust, he pulled out of the parking space and returned home. Climbing from his truck and hunkering into his jacket against the cold, he walked up the front path to drown his sorrows with a big tub of strawberry ice cream.

"Hey, Thomas!"

He jerked at the sound of his name, his muscles tightening. He groaned. Jessica Sacks stood at the edge of her property, arm raised in a wave. He was in no mood to be friendly. Neighborly was beyond him right now.

He returned the wave in the hope she'd leave him alone.

No such luck.

He'd barely lowered his arm when she walked over to him. He swallowed. She'd been cute as a kid, but now? Sexy shouldn't enter his mind, not when she was his former next-door neighbor and a dreaded reporter. Yet it did. Tall and willowy, the top of her head reached his chin. And her eyes? Those bright green orbs would draw him in if he let them.

"I don't know if you remember me, but I'm Jessica Sacks. From next door?"

He scanned her from the short brown hair that framed her face, to the navy parka that made those damned green eyes glow, to the jeans that showed off every curve. He remembered her alright, but she'd looked nothing like this.

Heaven help him.

The Jessica he remembered had been scrawny with braces and annoying as hell. She'd followed him around, peppered him with a million questions. It had been cute at first, tiresome later. But since he'd been four years older than her at the time, he'd left home when she'd hit high school and when he'd returned, she'd been in college. Their paths hadn't crossed in a while.

Now he wished they had. Because, physically, she was beautiful.

"I remember you."

Her smile showed off orthodontically perfect teeth. "Oh, good. Did you get my note?"

Any desire to get to know her better fled.

"Sorry, I don't talk to reporters."

Her mouth trembled and he once again got a glimpse of the disappointed young girl who couldn't join him and his friends. Letting her have her way had been harmless back then.

Now?

Now, there was no way he'd humor her.

"But what you did was amazing," she said. "Rescuing a man from a burning building? You're a hero!"

"No, I'm not." He used all his restraint not to yell at her.

"A few minutes, Thomas. Please? For old time's sake?"

Old time's sake? It was more than he could bear. "It was bad enough you followed me around like a lost puppy years ago. I won't talk to you now."

And before he gave her a chance to say anything else, he spun away and stalked into the house.

But not before devastation ravaged her face.

That night as she approached Caroline's house with a bottle of chardonnay, Jessica still wanted to sink into the ground. Embarrassment and anger warred with each other, giving her heartburn even her mom's delicious cooking hadn't cured. She couldn't get over Thomas's rudeness. He'd taken her memories, crushed them like the glass under the wedding *chuppah* and stomped them into the ground. He'd also shone a light on cute childhood behavior and warped it into a humiliating moment. Was a childhood crush supposed to haunt her forever? How stupid was that? Did he plan to hold it against her every time they saw each other?

Not that they'd cross paths often. She didn't live here. She only visited. Although this visit's explicit purpose was to cover a story where he was the hero.

She huffed. Some hero.

So much for him living up to her memories. See? Another reason why happily-ever-after only existed in fairy tales.

He might look like a hero with his broad shoulders, tight ass and chiseled jaw, but his attitude was more like a villain. Or the town grump.

Somehow, though, she didn't envision her editor appreciating that angle of the story. The investigative side of Jessica wanted to dig deeper, to find out what made him think he wasn't a hero for saving a man from a burning building. It was a much more interesting story than the fluff piece Alice had assigned her. But Jessica was on such shaky ground, she didn't dare diverge from the assignment. This job was her life. If she lost it…she couldn't bear to think about what would happen.

Despite the fact she hated having to deal with Thomas, and her desire to throw in the towel, she needed to continue. She needed to write this story to win back her job. And she had to put up with his *mishigas* until she finished the story—which she couldn't write if he wouldn't talk to her.

Squaring her shoulders, she knocked on Caroline's door. She'd pursued more difficult subjects before. Thomas's antics wouldn't stop her.

"You look like you're ready to fight someone, and I hope it's not me," Caroline said as she greeted her friend. Her light brown hair was pulled into its usual ponytail, and her workout outfit of choice today was black leggings with a black-and-white sweatshirt. "I think you need the entire bottle of wine for yourself. Come inside and tell me what's up."

Jessica swallowed. She couldn't tell her friends about her current employment woes. It was too humiliating. Besides, if she made a success of this story with Thomas—provided she could get past today's humiliation—her dismissal might prove irrelevant, and she wouldn't have to confess anything.

Jessica hugged her friend. "Nothing important. Is Sarah coming?"

The doorbell rang.

"That's her now," Caroline said.

"Jessica!" Sarah cried as she entered the house. "It's good to see you."

Her friend looked the same as always: chic, her long brown hair shiny. Like Jessica, she wore jeans and a top, only hers was pale pink while Jessica's was blue. It was a far cry from Sarah's previous black-only wardrobe, and Jessica approved.

Sarah turned to Caroline. "We are long overdue for this night." She lifted another bottle of wine.

Jessica smiled. "I've missed you all. And Caroline mentioned wine."

The three friends hugged in Caroline's foyer; the same one she'd entered countless times as a kid. Every time Jessica visited, it was like stepping back in time. She missed this, longed for the old days when they'd told each other everything, when things had been simpler. A part of her longed to confess what had happened to get her fired. Another part didn't think she was ready to air it in public.

Jessica and Sarah followed Caroline into the kitchen.

"Where's Jared?" Jessica asked.

Caroline's boyfriend had returned to town with his young niece months ago, and the three of them spent their time between her house and his apartment.

"He's with Becca at his apartment. This is a girls' night." She pulled out wineglasses and poured for the three of them.

"But how are you guys?" Jessica continued.

The glow on Caroline's face said it all. "We're good. He moved out here after quitting his job and has taken time off to settle in. I think he'll start his job search after the first of the year. In the meantime, we spend lots of time together, either here or at his place. I spent Thanksgiving with his family, and we've planned a trip together, just the three of us."

Jessica gave her a brief hug. "I'm happy for the two of you."

They took their glasses and sat in Caroline's living room. Caroline had grown up here with her mother and had kept the house for herself after her mother died. Although inseparable growing up, the girls hadn't hung out here as much due to Caroline's mother's illness. Jessica spotted personal touches Caroline added here and there—recent photos of the three friends, new accent pillows on the sofa, and three large, framed photos from her summer vacation to Greece, Bosnia and Herzegovina.

"Those are beautiful," she said to Caroline.

Caroline's expression took on a faraway look. "Every time I look at them, I'm transported to my vacation again. I can even smell the food."

"Have you decided where the three of you are going yet?" Sarah asked.

Caroline blushed. "I think we might go skiing in Vermont in January."

"That's wonderful!" Jessica's pulse quickened and she reached for her friend's hand. "I'm thrilled for you. And what about you, Sarah? How are you and Aaron?"

"We're great. And since his brother helps with the deli, we have extra time to spend together."

Her expression was bright with happiness, and Jessica's heartbeat quickened. How nice would it be? She squashed the momentary envy. Sarah and Aaron had gone through a lot. She was happy for her friend.

Caroline looked at Sarah, who nodded. Turning to Jessica, both girls leaned forward.

"And we're worried about you, Jess."

"Me? Why?" Her heart thudded in her chest.

Caroline squeezed her hand. "Because you haven't seemed

yourself in months. You've been stressed and evasive, and the spark has gone out of your eyes."

Sarah nodded. "You're not your usual sarcastic self. What's wrong?"

Jessica darted her gaze away. "It's nothing." Her friends had noticed her anxiety and shame mixed with sadness, and a lump formed in her throat.

"Don't tell us it's nothing," Caroline said. "Unless it's us."

Jessica's mouth dropped. "Of course, it's not you guys. I love you!" She didn't want anyone to know. Yet she'd never want her friends to think they were the problem. She tried to swallow past the lump in her throat.

"What's going on?" Sarah asked.

Jessica rose from the sofa and paced the room, unable to remain still any longer.

These two were her best friends. Once upon a time, she'd told them everything.

Before she'd been fired.

Her heartbeat increased. *How do you tell anyone, much less your best friends, you'd screwed up and been fired?* If she didn't tell them the truth, though, they'd be hurt. She wrapped her arms around her waist.

"You know you can tell us anything, right?" Caroline asked.

She hung her head. She couldn't keep it a secret, but she didn't know how to start, or where, for that matter. Anxiety, embarrassment and anger built up, weaving together like Aaron's challah.

Fisting her hands at her sides, she turned away from them. "I was fired from my job." She held her breath and waited for their reactions.

"What?" Caroline and Sarah spoke at the same time. They rushed to Jessica and wrapped their arms around her. Relief poured through her. She took a shaky breath, overwhelmed by gratitude. Her fears had been groundless.

"They're crazy," Sarah said.

"Who would want to fire you?" Caroline added. "You're amazing."

These women always backed her. Jessica would be a happier person if she remembered that.

She let herself bask in their comfort for a few seconds. She wanted to succumb to their sympathy. But to save her career, she needed to be strong.

After a few moments, the three women returned to the sofa.

"What happened?" Caroline asked.

Briefly, Jessica described the fiasco with the article she'd written.

"How come you didn't tell us?" Sarah asked. "We've been worried about you."

"I know, and I'm sorry," Jessica said. "But I'm embarrassed and angry and trying to remain strong. I don't want sympathy because it won't help me do what I have to do to get this story and save my job. I still haven't told my parents. Or my brother."

Caroline looked hurt. "I get your need for independence. Trust me, I of all people do. But you should know we'd never have gotten in your way."

Jessica nodded. "I know, and I'm sorry. I was embarrassed."

Sarah nodded. "If I could own up to my mistakes of shutting all of you out, you can tell us your bad news without embarrassment, Jess," Sarah said.

"You're right," Jessica said. "I'm sorry. Again."

Caroline refilled everyone's wine glasses and raised hers in a toast. "To us. To our friendship, our support, and our loyalty."

"Throughout the good, the bad, and the ugly," Sarah said.

"L'chaim," Jessica said, and they all clicked glasses.

They settled into the sofa cushions again.

"It sounds like your new assignment should be easy," Sarah said.

"In fact, based on the type of article, I think Alice wants

you back and will be able to convince the publisher to keep you on," Caroline added.

Jessica shrugged. "I thought so, too, but since Thomas won't speak to me, I'm not sure how easy this assignment will be. And Harvey has always been mercurial in who he wants to hire and fire, but the advertisers I offended are big. I'm not sure this article will help me keep my job as much as it will give Alice an easy way of covering the story. I'm sort of free labor at this point."

Sarah wrinkled her brow. "Somehow it doesn't sound fair."

"No, it's not. I said yes because I was caught off guard. It's not the usual type of story I cover, or that I enjoy, but I figured if I was easygoing, maybe she'd keep me on." Jessica paused. "I hate to play the 'simpering female card' though."

Jessica grabbed her hand. "You're not a simpering female. You're a consummate professional. And you'll show them what they'll miss if they fire you. You'll cover this story with your usual professionalism and abilities. If they offer you your job, you still have the option of saying no to them and finding something better."

For the first time since being fired, Jessica didn't feel powerless. "True. The decision *is* in my hands. I never thought of it that way." She paused. "I'm not sure what I'd do if I didn't work for them."

Sarah drained her glass. "You'll find something better with someone who appreciates your talents and dedication."

Jessica gave them a hug. "You guys are the best. I don't know where I'd be without you."

"You'll never have to wonder," Caroline said, and Sarah nodded. "Our friendship has helped us through lots of crises in our lives, and it will continue to do so. Nothing will separate us."

"Nothing," Jessica and Sarah echoed.

* * *

Thomas clipped a leash on Reggie, his hands shaking. He had to get out of his own mind. The German shepherd needed a walk and, despite the biting cold, it was the best way Thomas could think of to clear his head. Other than drink, which he wasn't about to do. He wouldn't lose his sobriety over a woman.

"Come on, Reg, let's go."

Tail wagging, Reggie bound across the porch and down the stairs. The dog's eagerness forced Thomas into a brisk pace as they headed deeper into the neighborhood. The longer they walked, the clearer his thoughts.

He was an ass.

Not for refusing Jessica's interview. No, he was entitled, and nothing would change his mind. But he could have found a kinder way to say no.

As he replayed yesterday's conversation in his mind, his cheeks burned. He'd been rude. He'd yelled at her, and he'd humiliated her about something she'd done as a child.

The wind blew and he raised his collar to protect his neck. His actions weren't cool. Certainly not heroic.

See, I'm not a hero.

He had to apologize. That meant he'd have to search her out and talk to her. He groaned. He knew where she lived. Or at least, where she was staying. But since the fire, he'd done little "searching out" of people. He'd been too busy working on himself.

God, he sounded selfish.

His phone rang and, once again, he let the call from one of his firefighter buddies go to voicemail. Another selfish act, but one he wasn't ready to address. The last thing he wanted right now was to talk to anyone from his old life. Not when he didn't have answers.

He blew out a breath and watched it fog in front of him. His "self" needed a lot of work. After eight-plus months, he felt like he had a handle on his sobriety. Not that he wasn't tempted to drink. Not that he could picture a time when it wouldn't be a struggle. But he'd reached the point where he understood his triggers and how to avoid them. And he knew how to ask for help when he needed it. That part was trickier. He was used to helping others. Accepting help? Well, he had a group and a sponsor and a therapist and a plan.

He wasn't about to mess up the plan because of a woman. Not even a beautiful one.

And wow, Jessica Sacks had developed into a beautiful woman.

She was no longer the gangly teenager who'd mooned after him. She'd cut her hair. The thick, rich brown emphasized her the heart shape of her face. Those mooning eyes? They were better now—big and green and framed with the darkest, thickest lashes. More than that, there was a light behind them, one that not only glowed but appeared to see everything. Scary—and fascinating—as hell.

She had breasts now, and an enticing figure. No one would ever call her awkward. Hell, she was the kind of woman he'd fall for if he let himself.

But no matter how pretty she was, he wouldn't agree to her interview.

However, he had to apologize. He just needed to figure out a way to do it without giving in to her request.

As he and Reggie looped around the block, a squirrel shot out in front of them. Reggie started to pull, but Thomas tugged the leash in time.

"Come on, Reg. You know you can't chase it."

Reggie snorted, as if in response to him.

"Yeah, I know. Discipline sucks sometimes." Thomas scratched Reggie's neck before he continued their walk home.

As he approached his house, Reggie's steps quickened. So much for delaying the inevitable. With a sigh, he diverted Reg to the neighbor's house. A Colonial, like his, the Sacks' home was painted yellow, had black shutters and a big white front porch. He jogged onto the porch, knocked on the red door, stepped back with Reggie and waited on the steps.

Mr. Sacks opened the front door. "Hey, Thomas, how are you?" The older man's voice was strong and deep.

"I'm well, Mr. Sacks."

"You know you can call me Mitch."

He said this all the time. Thomas would never be able to do so. "Is Jessica home? I need to talk to her."

"Sorry, she's out. I can let her know you stopped by when she gets home if you'd like."

Thomas nodded. "Thanks, I'd appreciate it."

Inside his own house, he filled Reggie's water bowl and made lunch. He was calmer now than he'd been when he'd set out on the walk, but he didn't like having to postpone his apology. He'd thrown away her number when he'd gotten rid of the Post-it note, otherwise he'd call.

His phone rang and a familiar number showed on the screen. In the past, he'd hated seeing his dad's name on caller ID because it had meant the man had been checking up on him. Now, however, he enjoyed talking to him.

"Hey, Dad, what's up?"

His father loved the heat of Arizona and didn't miss the snow. After spending Thanksgiving with him, Thomas had understood why. His dad had made friends and was happy out west. Thomas was thrilled for him.

And maybe a little jealous.

"I got an invitation to attend the rededication of the Browerville Museum. It says you're being honored. How come you never mentioned it when you were here for Thanksgiving?"

Shit.

"It's not a big deal, Dad."

"Sounds like it is from the description."

He swallowed. "It's nothing."

"The town sent out engraved invitations, son. How is it not a big deal?"

Thomas gripped the phone in is hand. "It'll be cold and snowy. Plus, you're already coming for Christmas. It's not necessary for you to fly all the way out here for a five-minute ribbon-cutting ceremony."

"Mmm-hmm." His father's grunt spoke volumes, and Thomas waited with trepidation for him to continue.

"You okay?" he asked.

Thomas expelled a breath of relief. He never liked to talk about himself, but he'd take this over the rededication ceremony any day. "Yeah, I am. You okay?"

"I'm old and creaky, but fine."

Thomas laughed. The release of tension lightened him, gave him a chance to catch his breath. "Glad to hear it. I'll see you for Christmas."

"Looking forward to it! It'll be nice to see the whole family. And I want to see all the changes you've made to the house."

Thomas swallowed, relieved his dad was taking those changes well. "It's been a while since we've all been together," he said. "I can't wait."

Deep in his gut, Thomas realized it was true. He'd pulled away from his siblings and dad after the fire, but now, he'd started to miss them. The banter, jokes, roughhousing, were all things he'd missed. Not to mention his nieces and nephews. It was something to look forward to. He hadn't been ready to be with his entire family for Thanksgiving, or at least he hadn't thought he'd been. Plus, visiting his dad had given the two men some much-needed time together. But Thomas had missed the rest of his family, so on Thanksgiving Day, after the turkey but before the second football game, he'd FaceTimed his siblings and invited everyone here for Christmas.

After a little more small talk, Thomas hung up the phone,

glad he'd convinced his dad the rededication was a nonstarter. Why the hell his father had received an invitation was beyond him, but his father hadn't pressed him too much.

The house needed work if his family was coming for Christmas. He'd better get moving.

Chapter Three

"Do you guys ever see the Carvilles?" Jessica asked. She'd spent the day relaxing and putting together an outline for her story, figuring out what she needed to research and who she needed to speak to. She leaned against the counter and watched her mom prepare dinner. Her dad set the table. Just like countless times from her childhood.

"Not since Thomas Senior moved to Phoenix," her mom answered. "We send him a holiday card. He loves it out there, and he's made a circle of friends. I've lost track of where the kids went, other than Thomas Junior."

Jessica remembered Mr. Carville packing his golf clubs most warm weekends. While the two families weren't close, the adults had gone out to dinner once in a while when Jessica was young. She'd always wanted to stay with Thomas and his brothers and sister, but her mom had always hired a babysitter, much to her chagrin.

She nodded. "I'm glad he likes it out there." She paused and tried to make sure her voice didn't convey anything but passing curiosity. "What about Thomas?"

"Coincidentally, I ran into him today," her dad said. "He was looking for you."

Jessica's muscles tightened. Maybe he'd changed his mind. "Did he say why?"

If he agreed to the interview, it would save her the hassle of pursuing him.

"No idea." Her dad's body language indicated he didn't think anything of it.

Her mom, however, paused in her preparations and stared at her. "Mitch, he didn't give you any idea what he wanted?"

Her dad frowned. "It's not a big deal, Renée. He asked for her, I said she wasn't here. End of story."

Her mother huffed. "After the way Jess had such a years-long crush on him when she was younger, I don't know how you can say 'end of story.'"

"Mom! You knew?" Jessica's face heated in embarrassment.

"Honey, the mailman knew about it." Her mom cupped her fiery cheek. "It was an adorable childish thing. It wasn't going anywhere—they're Catholic and we're Jewish—but it was cute and harmless. You've outgrown it now. There's nothing to be embarrassed about. It's not like you two are dating, God forbid."

Jessica paused. Her parents had always wanted her to date someone Jewish, but her mom seemed a little strident in her thinking. She shook it off. It's not like she and Thomas had a relationship. Her only worry was the humiliating way he'd treated her and the idea everyone knew about her crush. *Ugh.*

"I don't remember any crush," her dad said.

"What? Mitchell! Of course, you do. Don't you recall our conversations about it?"

Her dad held up his hands in surrender. "I tried not to think about my baby with boys, so no, I remember nothing."

Laughter bubbled in Jessica's chest at her dad's attitude. Another reason why her social life benefitted from living away from her parents. The last thing she needed was either of them meddling in her affairs or going all protective of her. She studied them as they exchanged looks, followed by a touch of hands. Her parents' marriage was wonderful. But they were two different people. They liked different things and, sometimes, Jessica wondered how they managed to get along.

Even her brother, who'd married last year, didn't appear to have a lot in common with his wife. In fact, while she'd never confess this to anyone, she'd never believed the two of them would last. So far, thank goodness, they'd proved her wrong. She hoped they always would.

Jessica was too practical for that kind of a relationship. If she got married, and it was a big if, it would be to someone who meshed with her in all ways. She'd made a checklist, and the guy would have to meet a lot of requirements before she entertained the idea of "love." So far, the guy didn't exist.

That was also why she couldn't believe she'd ever crushed on Thomas. They were different, and not only because of their religious beliefs. He didn't meet any of the requirements on her list: he wasn't Jewish, he lived out here in the suburbs, he didn't have a sense of humor, based on their previous conversation, and he wasn't as financially stable as she would like. And he was rude, which was worse than any of those other things.

Before the conversation with her parents could go any further, she cleared her throat. "Relax, you two, I'm sure he wants to talk to me about the story I'm here to write."

As the three of them ate dinner, she filled them in on her assignment. Unlike with her friends, she kept news of her being fired to herself. Her parents loved her, and she didn't want to worry them unless it was necessary. She'd been given a second chance to prove herself. With any luck, she'd never have to mention her mistake.

Her mom finished chewing. "It's a wonderful assignment, Jess, but how does it fit into your beat?"

Jessica clenched her fist beneath the table. She didn't want to lie to her parents, but she wasn't ready to discuss what had caused this predicament. Not yet anyway.

"Well, since they know I'm from here, they assumed I'd have connections." It wasn't a lie, she reassured herself. And she'd come clean at some point. If there was the slightest chance of her getting her job back, she wasn't going to mention anything.

Her dad nodded. "I'm sure it's what your editor wanted. Can't wait to read the article, and I'm glad you'll be around for a little while."

"Me, too," she said. She pushed her plate away, her stomach in knots over her secret. "This was delicious, Mom." She rose to clear the table, staying her parents with a wave of her hand. "I've got these, don't worry."

Her mom reached for her husband's arm and grinned. "I could get used to this."

"It's temporary," Jess said with a laugh. "But it'll be nice to celebrate Hanukkah together."

"It'll be like old times!" Her mom's face glowed with warmth. "I'll make chocolate gelt, and we'll have donuts. Now, if I could convince your brother to come over one night..."

The prospect of being home for a while didn't seem as bad as it had a day or so ago.

"I'm sure it will be different once he and Shelly have kids," Jessica said.

"I know," her mom said. "For now, I'll send him a care package of latkes, along with a Hanukkah gift. Don't worry, I'm sentimental. At least I got to see him for Thanksgiving."

When Jessica finished clearing the table, she wiped her hands on the cornflower-blue dishtowel and hung it on the oven door.

"Thomas didn't leave his phone number, did he?"

"No, but I don't think the house number has changed." Her mother winked.

Too easy for him to hang up on her. "It's not late. I'll run next door and see if he's busy. Worst case, I'll get his cell number for later." This time, she'd be prepared for him closing the door in her face.

Pulling on her winter jacket and slipping her feet into her

leather boots, she walked next door. The yard was emptier than she remembered, the bountiful flowers Mrs. Carville was known for dormant. But the grass was clipped close for the winter, the beds mulched and covered. The wooden siding was worn, and there were swaths of paint in shades of gray, beige and white. It looked like he was testing colors.

She jogged up the recently repaired steps and onto a porch that was also newer than the rest of the house. Thomas was renovating.

She knocked on the door. Barking echoed. After a few minutes, it opened, and he stood in the doorway, holding a dog by the collar. Holy cow! He'd always been nice to look at, but now? She clenched her teeth together to keep from drooling. Firefighting agreed with the man. Powerful neck and shoulders filled out the gray sweatshirt. Brown hair trimmed close to his scalp showed off his cheekbones and the planes of his face. And whatever cologne he wore made all her girly parts jump to attention. It was unfair for a jerk to be handsome, and her traitorous body would have to get over him. ASAP. Realizing she'd stared a tad too long, she swallowed.

"Hi, you wanted to talk?"

Thomas stared at the woman on his front porch and reminded himself Jessica was his bratty little neighbor from childhood. Except, while he didn't know if she was still bratty, she wasn't little anymore. His body stirred in ways it hadn't in ages.

Terrific.

He nodded and retreated from the doorway, letting Jessica enter, and telling Reggie to be good. The last thing he wanted was the big dog knocking her over. The top of her head reached his chin. As she passed him, a warm, floral scent surrounded her, but whether it was the shampoo she used in her short brown hair or a perfume, he couldn't tell. When she was younger, she'd doused herself in something strong enough to make him sneeze and alert him to her presence way before she showed up. But she'd become more subtle now, and for that he was thankful. Tempted, too, if he were honest with himself.

"Hi." *Brilliant, Tom.* "Thanks for coming over." It was usually at this time he'd offer someone a beer. "Can I get you something?"

She rose from where she'd been rubbing Reggie behind the ears and stuffed her hands into her jacket pockets. "No, thanks, we just ate dinner."

"Right." He cleared his throat. "I wanted to apologize. I was rude yesterday. I shouldn't have been. You didn't deserve it."

Her stance relaxed. "A lot of people are surprised when reporters want to talk to them."

That was nice of her. She didn't have to let him off the hook. The tension in his neck eased.

She looked around the room. "You're renovating your parents' house? That must be complicated."

He scoffed. Complicated? Being around Jessica was complicated. His memories of her as a child slammed into the reality of her as a beautiful woman and were twisted by her identity as a reporter.

"It's not theirs any longer, and it's either renovate or have it collapse around me."

She laughed. The musical sound somehow appealed to him. He squashed the thought as soon as it entered his mind. She was here for him to apologize to. That was it.

"I'm glad you kept your mom's garden outside," Jess said. "She always grew the prettiest flowers."

"Yeah, Mom loved flowers." He cherished the memory of his mother on her knees with dirt on her cheeks, planting and humming to herself. He cleared his throat. "I added a vegetable garden in the back, for tomatoes next summer. If the critters don't eat them first."

She laughed again and a part of him drew great satisfaction from the accomplishment.

The other part of him warned him to keep away.

"Anyway, I'm sorry again for being rude," he said.

"I appreciate it. I can see where being in the spotlight can make people uncomfortable. And I didn't realize you possessed such a green thumb."

It was more than discomfort in the spotlight, but he appreciated her attempt, once again, at understanding, and her quick forgiveness. He leaned against the stair railing in the hallway. She didn't seem to take his hint to end the conversation and, for some reason, he was kind of glad. He wanted to talk to her, but he shouldn't. They were no longer neighbors, and he was barely able to handle his solitary life as it stood now.

Still, he didn't want to be rude twice.

"I didn't know about my green thumb, either. I won't know for sure until those tomatoes come in. I'm better with construction."

"What parts of the house are you working on? What kinds of vegetables are you growing?"

She'd always peppered him with questions. It was no wonder she'd become a reporter. And while he hated questions about himself, the house he could talk about. "Herbs, tomatoes and peppers. I worked on the outside of the house in the summer and moved on to the kitchen and living room now that it's cold."

"Have you decided on a color for the outside?"

She was pretty observant. "Not yet."

"Can I see what you've done?" She blushed, and the rosy glow made her even prettier. "I'm sorry, I don't mean to be nosy."

"It's okay. I've worked hard. I don't mind showing it off." He led her through the front foyer to the kitchen at the back of the house.

"This is beautiful." She turned in a slow circle.

Her admiration pleased him. "Thanks. I switched out the light oak cabinets for modern shaker ones, replaced the tile countertops with stone slabs, and updated the appliances. Plus, paint."

He looked around at his work as he tried to envision it from her perspective. He'd always been handy with tools. His free time had given him plenty of opportunity to design the kitchen to his liking.

She walked around the room, ran her hands across the counters, and nodded. "This could be in a magazine."

Her hands on things he'd built created an unexpected intimacy, and he didn't know what to do with the thoughts in his brain. Clearing his throat, he searched for something to distract her. And himself. "You sure I can't get you anything? Water, beetroot juice, carrot juice, green tea—"

"Beetroot juice?" She raised her eyebrows in surprise.

His hand itched to trace the arched line, and he made a fist at his side. "You'd be surprised how good it is. Add a little apple juice, celery, cucumber and fresh mint…" He kissed the tips of his fingers. "Delicious. And healthy."

"I'll take your word for it."

Shaking his head in mock disappointment, he folded his arms and pinned her with his stare. "Too bad. The Jessica I remember wasn't afraid of anything."

She bristled. "I'm not *afraid* of beetroot juice. I don't get the appeal."

"Sure, sure. If you tried it, you'd understand. But, you're chicken."

Another flush crept across her high cheekbones. "Chicken? You think I'm a chicken because I won't try some crazy juice from God knows where?"

"It's juice from a beetroot," he said. "I thought it was self-evident."

She rubbed her temples, as if she had a headache. He remembered the migraines he'd gotten when first sober. Thank God, he didn't get those anymore.

"I know the juice is from a beetroot," she said through gritted teeth. "I meant… I don't know!" She threw up her hands and groaned.

Thomas hid a smile. He liked to goad her. He remembered doing it when they were younger, but always having to be careful not to upset her too much. His parents wouldn't have allowed him to be mean to her. Since she was an adult, he didn't have to worry about that any longer. She could take care of herself. Although, he still didn't want to be mean. He kind of liked the new Jessica.

"I made it myself," he said, trying to coax her to taste it.

She stared at him and he wondered what was going through her mind. Heck, he wondered what was going through his mind. He'd intended to apologize and be done. Instead, he'd invited her to stay and try his homemade juice.

"Is that supposed to reassure me?"

The sparkle in her eye made him think she enjoyed their banter too.

"Yes. I'm good in the kitchen." He extended his arms around the room. "It's why I redid this room first."

"I assumed it was because you like to eat."

He chuckled. "I do, but I also like to cook."

"And you consider making beetroot juice cooking?"

"No, there's no cooking involved. It's mixing. I told you so you'd know it wasn't weird or poisonous."

"Except it has beets," she said.

"Beets aren't poisonous."

"But they're weird for a drink."

"So that's a no?"

She nodded.

"Too bad." He reached into the refrigerator and pulled out

the pitcher. He poured himself a glass and took a long drink. "It's delicious."

He didn't know why he egged her on, or flirted with her, except that this was the most fun he'd had with another person in months.

He shifted from one foot to the other at her stare, unsure why she didn't turn away. Then he remembered she was a reporter. She was probably studying him for the story he wasn't about to help her write. He put the glass on the counter harder than he'd intended. Luckily, it didn't shatter.

Now he was stuck. He'd invited her over to apologize. He'd done so. Now what?

She walked to the sliding door overlooking the backyard. It was dark and quiet now, but when he was a child, it was the site of more flag football games than he could count. He could still hear the grunts and calls of his friends and family as they'd played.

"I remember watching you and your brothers and sister and dad play football and wishing I could join you," Jessica said.

What, was she a mind reader now?

"I remember those days," he said.

She'd wandered over to the glass doors first. Speaking his thoughts wasn't as much a surprise as he'd thought.

He glanced at her. "You would have gotten smashed to bits if you'd joined us."

She laughed; the sound of it pleasing. "Probably. But, oh, was I jealous of my brother getting to join you."

He huffed. She'd been a small pain then. He suspected her to be a much bigger one now. Still, she'd changed in the last four years or so and he didn't know how much of a pain she'd be. What he did know was she was a lot prettier now. He remained silent, staring at their reflections in the glass, wondering what she'd do if he asked her out.

"What made you want to become a firefighter?" she asked.

He stiffened and all thoughts of how pretty she was melted away, like plastic when exposed to fire.

"I think it's time for you to leave," he said. "I've got things to do."

He ushered her toward the front of the house, using his size to force her in the direction of the door.

"Thomas—"

"I told you I don't talk to reporters and I won't answer your questions. I meant it."

He opened the front door wide and gripped the doorknob until his fingers ached.

She opened her mouth as if to speak but shut it again.

Good.

With a nod, she left the house.

So much for apologies.

Once again, he'd shut Jessica out. She clenched her teeth as she returned to her parents' place, more confused than ever. She wasn't acting as a reporter. *I mean, sure I asked a question, but normal people do that, too, right?* It was part of the get-to-know-you process. In fact, until she'd asked about fire-fighting, he'd been pretty talkative.

She'd—dare she say it?—liked him.

She wanted to turn around and argue with him, or at least question him about his behavior, but she refrained. He'd practically lifted and carried her out of his house. He wouldn't open the door to her again. Not now, anyway.

She stomped home and slipped inside her parents' house.

"Hey, dear," her mom said. "Did you find out what Thomas wanted?"

"Nothing important." Explaining his apology-that-turned-out-not-to-be-an-apology was too complicated.

Her mom gave her a quizzical look and Jessica bit her lip. *Please don't say anything! Please don't say anything!*

Her mom sat at her desk in the family room paying bills but pushed away from her task at Jessica's response.

"For that long?"

Her face heated. She'd have to give a better explanation. "He wanted to apologize to me and asked me to come inside."

Her mom raised an eyebrow. "For what?"

"For being rude to me earlier. We had a nice conversation." *At least for a bit. Maybe that is the key to getting him to talk to me.*

"Well, I'd hope so. You're both grown adults. I hope you don't get too caught up in each other. You're different people."

"Mother, I can't believe you'd think that!"

Her mom held up her hands. "Being with someone requires a lot of compromise. Look at me and Daddy. We're different people and worked hard to make a life together. Brandon and Shelly needed to adjust to a relationship and marriage too. In addition to personality and age differences, when you add a different religion into the mix, it makes things harder. It's all I'm saying."

Jessica caught herself before she rolled her eyes. "I know, Mom. But you're jumping waaaayyy far ahead here and making assumptions you don't need to make. He's our neighbor and the subject of my article. That's all. I'm not marrying the man or dating him."

She thought about her teenaged self and sent her a silent apology.

Her mom brushed her hair out of her face. "I'm sorry. You're right. It's just you had such a crush on him your entire life. To find out you're talking to him now… I jumped the gun."

"I loved Elmo as a kid, too, but I don't want to date him, either. Besides, I need to interview Thomas for an article. He doesn't want me to interview him. I thought if I were friendly, it might soften him up. But he kicked me out as soon as I asked him a question. It wasn't an interview question. I was making conversation."

Her mother stared at her over the rim of her blue reading glasses. "Honey, I love you to pieces, but your idea of conversation is a little like being in the hot seat of an interrogation."

"It is not!"

Her mother stared at her. Jessica opened and closed her mouth. Even if—and it was a big if—she sometimes got carried away with questions, this time, with Thomas, she hadn't.

"My question wasn't any different than yours would have been."

Her mom quirked an eyebrow and turned her focus to her work. "If you say so."

She could say a lot of things but refrained. Instead, Jessica jogged upstairs to her childhood bedroom. She opened her laptop and studied the list of sources she wanted to talk to for the article. But unless Thomas agreed to speak to her, the other sources were meaningless. He'd been nice and open when they'd talked about food. Humor had shone from his eyes, giving them a golden glint. His smile—slightly crooked— reminded her of his younger, carefree version. She'd liked it. Her neck heated as an idea percolated in her mind. Maybe, if she worked him from that angle—the "hey, let's be friends" one—she'd be able to loosen him up enough to talk to her. He needed to see she wasn't some evil reporter but a real person. Plan B was a go.

Chapter Four

Thomas left his AA meeting the next day and drove to the diner on the edge of town where he and his sponsor met every week. The coffee was better—a special blend he still couldn't find anywhere else—and he didn't care what time of day it was, he drank at least a cup.

It wasn't like he'd had a good night's sleep anyway.

Sliding into his usual booth, he nodded at his usual waitress and raised his hand to greet his sponsor as he entered.

"Just a key lime pie slice for me," Carl said.

The waitress nodded and left, and Thomas stared out the window as he sipped from the mug.

"You seem troubled today," Carl said.

The man wasn't much for small talk, which was why Thomas liked him. He wasn't big on it, either.

"The damn reporter keeps bugging me." His phone rang and he silenced it. "So do the guys from the firehouse."

"I thought you told the reporter no. And at some point, you'll have to answer them."

He shrugged. "I did tell her no."

"What happened?"

"I needed to apologize."

"I'm confused."

"She's my neighbor. Or was. Followed me around everywhere when I was in high school. Now she's returned to write about me. But I was rude, and I needed to apologize. And she came over."

"She."

Thomas met Carl's stare. "It's not like that."

In his mind, Jessica's sparkling green eyes mocked him.

"You sure?"

"Her gender has nothing to do with it. I was rude. I apologized. Would have done it for a man too. But then we talked." And it had been fun. Despite his dislike of small talk, he'd always been a sucker for easy banter, and theirs was easy. Too easy.

"And?"

"I dropped my guard. She asked about the fire." Technically, she'd asked why he'd become a firefighter. But only an idiot couldn't have foreseen the conversation's direction.

"What did you say?" Carl asked.

"I made her leave."

Carl scoffed. "So much for apologies."

Goddammit. "It wasn't like the first time. I wasn't exactly rude."

He sure hadn't been nice, though. His mom would have been horrified. A bitter taste filled his mouth and, as much as he wanted to blame the coffee, he couldn't.

"But you weren't your charming, debonair self."

Thomas frowned at the weirdo across the table. "Have you met me?"

"Yep. It's why I know you owe her another apology."

"I don't want to talk to her again."

Although he wouldn't mind seeing her again. She'd grown into a sexy adult.

He ran a hand over his brow. Next thing he knew, he'd follow her around, like a role reversal of the worst kind. He sighed.

"You know I'm right."

"Maybe it would be better if I wait her out," Thomas said.

"She's leaving soon, especially if I won't give her the interview. We're better off avoiding each other."

The waitress returned with more coffee and the biggest slice of key lime pie Thomas had ever seen. Another reason he liked this diner, even if it was ten minutes outside town. Carl dug into his pie, and Thomas knew better than to distract the man.

When the plate was clean, his sponsor returned his attention to Thomas. "You could ignore her, except your hero-to-the-rescue complex won't let this go. And it will weigh on you, and you're not gonna be able to let it go. Do us both a favor and get it over with."

Carl gulped a glass of water. "And call your buddies back. They might surprise you."

Thomas drank his coffee and fumed. Carl was a pain in the ass, especially when he was right, which was most of the time.

Wiping his mouth, Carl pinned Thomas with another look. "You know I'm right."

Damn it.

Thomas waved to the waitress and asked for the check. "You're a pain in the ass, Carl, you know that?"

The man smirked. "But I'm your pain in the ass."

That afternoon, Jessica approached her former high school and stared at the old cement building. This was where she'd developed her passion for writing and journalism, thanks to her amazing English teacher, Dr. Nelson. She scanned the teachers' lot for the familiar VW Bug and smiled at the rusty blue car that looked older than she was. After parking in one of the visitor's spots, she walked to the front doors and rang the security bell. After school hours, someone in the office monitored the building until five pm.

"Can I help you?" a random voice asked.

"I'm here to see Dr. Nelson."

"Come on in."

The door buzzed and she entered the vestibule. A security guard met her with a visitor's badge, which she affixed to the belt loop of her jeans, and followed the guard through the labyrinthine hallways to Room 201D.

Stepping into the classroom was like stepping back in time. Her mind filled with the memories of the noise from the hallways as students passed, the announcements over the loudspeakers, and the smell of the Givenchy perfume her English teacher wore.

She cleared her throat and Dr. Nelson looked up. Now in her seventies, she was still tiny, with deep brown eyes. Like her grammar, her posture was firm and uncompromising.

Her face, with a few more wrinkles, brightened.

"Jessica Sacks! Come in!" She rose to her four-foot-nine height and grasped her in a tight hug. "It's good to see you."

"It's great to see you, too, Dr. Nelson."

"Pfft. You can call me Maureen."

Jessica scoffed. "Nope. Not happening."

The older woman shook her head. Her salt-and-pepper afro—mostly salt—was close-cropped, as usual, and her large gold hoops dangled with the movement. She pointed to the chair beside her desk. "Sit and tell me about your life. I've read your articles, and they're wonderful."

Jessica's chest tightened. What would her mentor think if she knew the truth about her latest career news? "Thank you."

"So? What are you writing these days?" Folding her arms in front of her, the older woman's red nails shone against her navy cardigan sleeves.

Jessica fisted her hands in her lap. "The museum rededication and awards ceremony."

"I didn't think it was your beat, but I assume it's because you're from here?"

That worked. "Yes, and it gives me a chance to spend some extra time home for the holidays."

Dr. Nelson smiled. "How wonderful. How is your article progressing?"

"I'm still looking for the 'piece of humanity' you taught me, but it's getting there."

"I love how you've taken my advice to heart. It means a lot, and I'm proud of how well you've done. What do you like best about your job?"

That was easy. "I love the writing—boiling down everything to its most simplistic form, yet at the same time finding the right words to convey the news."

With a nod, Dr. Nelson reclined in her leather chair. "You do it well. And you avoid the sensationalism many of your colleagues fall prey to. Good job."

Jessica flushed. "Thank you."

"If you have time, I'd love to have you speak to my class about your career. My seniors would be interested in what you studied, how you got where you are, what your future plans are, and any advice you could give them."

Her stomach dropped. She doubted they'd want to hear how she had been fired. "I'm not sure how much time I have while I'm home now, especially with your Christmas break coming up, but maybe in the spring? It's easy enough for me to come home."

"You're right, we don't have too many free days before the students are gone. However, if you don't mind being flexible, let's leave the possibility open. Otherwise, why don't you call me in February, and we can schedule it."

Jessica nodded. Silence would allow her to give Dr. Nelson what she wanted without commitment. A sour taste rose in her mouth. She hated lying to people she cared about, and although this wasn't a lie per se, it wasn't the truth.

With an abrupt change in subject, she asked about Dr. Nelson's family. The older woman's face brightened. "My youngest daughter had a baby."

"*Mazel tov!* Congratulations. Do you have pictures?"

A look of incredulity flickered across her mentor's face. "What kind of grandmother would I be if I didn't?" She pulled her phone out of her purse, swiped a few times, and handed it to Jessica. "She's three months old now."

Affection poured from Dr. Nelson even with those brief words. Jessica oohed and aahed over the adorable baby. In one photo, she slept in a crib, arms and legs splayed. In another, she lay in her mother's arms. Her head was covered in dark curly hair and her brown eyes were huge. The last photo was with Dr. Nelson. Grandma and granddaughter were nose to nose.

"She's beautiful," Jessica said. "This is your third grand-baby?"

"Fourth. Maurice and his wife have five-year-old twins, Charlotte and her husband have a three-year-old son, and now Amelia and her husband have Giselle."

"I love that name," Jessica said. "Sleepovers at Grandma's house will be fun."

"Yes, they will. I'll spoil them rotten."

"And read them the best stories."

Dr. Nelson nodded. "Including yours when they're old enough."

Jessica flushed. "Thank you." She looked at the time. "I have to go. It was wonderful to see you."

She rose and gave her mentor a hug.

Dr. Nelson hugged her and then held her at arm's length. "I hope you'll try to visit my class while you're home this time, because I'd love to see you again."

"I'll try."

She left the classroom, wondering what she'd say to the class. She didn't want to disappoint anyone and, somehow, she didn't see how she could avoid it.

That night, Jessica climbed into the back seat of Caroline's old car. Despite its age, Caroline kept it spotless.

"So where are we going tonight?" she asked Caroline and

Sarah. Caroline sat in the driver's seat and Sarah was in the passenger seat. She stared at the blue painter's tape covering the other back door's door handle. "And when are you getting a new car?"

Every time something broke, for as long as Jessica could remember, Caroline covered it with duct tape until it needed to be fixed. At this point, only one rear door worked.

"We're going to Mama Mia's," Caroline answered. "And since I've taken a vacation, the car is the next thing on my wish list. Of course, Jared wants to buy me one, but I said no."

"What?" Sarah squealed. "You never told me."

"I didn't tell anyone." Caroline pulled onto Main Street in Browerville. "I appreciate his generosity, and I understand his refusal to let Becca ride in here, but I want to be able to afford my own car. Despite how it looks, it's fine for short trips around town."

"Hmm," Jessica said as they pulled into the parking lot of the Italian restaurant. "If you two are as serious as you seem, you might want to reconsider refusing his offer. But, regardless, make sure you stay safe."

"I will," Caroline said. "And someone has to let you out, because only the outside door handle works."

Jessica and Sarah both groaned. After letting Jessica out of the back seat, the three women entered the restaurant.

"You know, one of these days you'll get stuck in your own car and they'll need the Jaws of Life to get you out," Sarah said.

Laughing, they gave their information to the hostess, who seated them at a cozy table next to the fireplace.

"Any luck with the elusive Thomas Carville?" Sarah asked.

Jessica sighed. "Nope. I think I need to play up the friend angle in order to get him to talk to me. Of course, we were never friends, so this might be tough."

Thinking about her last encounter with him filled her with disappointment. It had all gone well until he'd told her to leave.

And she hadn't asked him about the fire, just about his career choice. Her cheeks burned at how much she'd enjoyed their easy conversation until then.

"Oh, she has a look," Caroline said to Sarah. "Think maybe she'd like to do more than talk?"

Sarah gestured while Jessica tried to get them to lower their voices.

"I'm not a kid with a crush anymore," she said, although Thomas had grown even more handsome as he'd aged. "Besides, he's not Jewish. My parents have always expected me to marry someone of the same faith as me. My mom's already on alert."

"No one's talking about marriage, Jess," Sarah said.

"Yeah, if anyone's talking about marriage, it's Sarah," Caroline said.

"What? Aaron and I aren't getting married any time soon," she said.

"But you're thinking about it," Jessica said.

Sarah's cheeks reddened. "Don't change the subject. Tell us about you and your crush on Thomas."

Jessica gulped some of the wine the waiter had brought over while they'd spoken. "I don't have a crush on him any longer. Even if he is gorgeous."

"Master of the understatement," Caroline said.

Jessica stilled the butterflies that started to flutter when she thought about his smile. "Maybe. But seriously, my biggest issue right now is getting him to talk to me. My entire career depends on it. Not to mention, I kind of lied to Dr. Nelson."

"What? How could you do that?" Sarah asked.

Jessica rested her chin in her hands and told them about her visit today.

"I think you should talk to the class," Caroline said. "You'd be great at it."

"Right, because they want to hear from someone who's lost her job."

Sarah reached across the table and squeezed her arm. "It's real-world experience. And, besides, lots of people have similar experiences. It would help them to learn how you deal with it."

Jessica paused. She hadn't considered that angle. "Maybe."

The waitress came over and took their orders. Mama Mia's made the best Greek food in town, and the three women ordered souvlaki, spanakopita and dolmades. When the waitress left, Sarah continued. "As for Thomas, I think befriending him is a good idea. At least give him a chance to see the real you."

"I agree," Jessica said. "He asked me over to apologize. We talked and everything was fine, until I asked why he became a firefighter."

Caroline and Sarah looked at each other. "Were you interviewing him?"

"No, I was making conversation." She thought about how much fun it had been to banter with him. So much fun, in fact, the question had slipped out. "I shouldn't have asked him. Next time, I'll have to be stealthier."

Sarah and Caroline looked at each other. "It's a fine line you're treading," Caroline said. "You don't want him to think you're befriending him to get the story."

Sarah agreed. "No, you're not manipulative."

"You're right," Jessica said. "I will be careful. And while my ultimate goal is to write the story, I want to use the personal angle to show him talking to me isn't as bad as he thinks it will be. I'm trying to soften him up, not be sneaky about it."

"That works," Caroline said. "How much time do you have?"

"My deadline is right before Hanukkah. Whatever I do, it has to be fast."

The three women paused to taste the food their waitress brought. Greek music played in the background.

"Here's the real question." Jessica swallowed a mouthful

of spanakopita. "How is this in comparison to what you ate on your vacation?"

Caroline took another bite of her dolmades. "Good. Not the same, but I still like it here. Plus, the smells and the photos on the walls elicit great memories." She took a sip of wine. "Returning to Hanukkah, which theme do you like better— lights and love, food and family, or dreidels?" Caroline asked. "I need to decorate the JCC senior center."

"I don't know," Sarah said. "I'm always partial to food, thanks to Aaron. Maybe the seniors would like to include their family recipes in a display or something?"

"My mom always collects recipes," Jessica added. "How about a cookbook?"

Caroline's face lit up. "What a great idea! Would you help me while you're here? I know you're on an assignment, but in your spare time..."

"Sure, if I have time."

"Great," she said. "With Hanukkah almost here, I have the seniors working on decorations, and I need volunteers to hang them."

Jessica sighed with relief. "No problem. What are we decorating?"

Caroline paused as the waitress refilled their water glasses. "The senior center. If you're free tomorrow, want to come with me to take a look?"

"Perfect," Jessica said. "As is this food." She brought a forkful of souvlaki to her mouth and moaned with delight.

"I'll bet if you made those noises, Thomas would talk to you," Sarah said with a wink.

Swallowing quickly to avoid choking, Jessica glared at her supposed best friend. "Not funny."

Caroline held up her thumb and forefinger. "Maybe a little."

With her two best friends laughing, it was hard to stay straight-faced, and Jessica's mouth quivered.

"See," Sarah said. "You think it's funny too."

"Like old times," Jessica added.

Well, minus the crush on Thomas.

Thomas grimaced as he strode the crowded sidewalks of Browerville. He hated to shop. He hated to shop after Thanksgiving more. But with his family coming home to celebrate Christmas with him, he had no choice but to brave the crowds to buy presents for them. Gritting his teeth, he maneuvered his way through shoppers who'd somehow lost their ability to walk and carry packages at the same time.

As he was about to turn around and go home to order online instead, he reached his destination. The Gift Horse. The purple horsehead sign hanging out front swayed in the breeze as the jingle bells on the door announced his arrival. Upon stepping over the threshold, cinnamon, cloves and spices assaulted his nose. He swallowed. It's not that he didn't like those fragrances. He did. But they overpowered the small shop, though they didn't appear to bother anyone else. With a sigh, he unzipped his jacket and meandered around the store, gift list open on his phone.

A shelf on the wall to his right caught his eye. Bookends of all types were on display, and he reached for a set with images of iconic women. His sister loved to read and was a feminist. Perfect. He continued his search and selected a set of whiskey glasses with the letter *L* for his brother, Liam. Silk scarves for his sisters-in-law, and a carved oak cheeseboard for his other brother, and he was finished with his siblings.

He got in line to pay for his purchases. Next to the checkout stood a small child and a woman examining the Christmas cards.

When the young boy looked at him, Thomas smiled. The boy returned it before he tugged on the woman's arm.

"Mommy, what's wrong with that man's neck?" he whisper-yelled.

The mother turned toward him, her face rosy with embarrassment. "Justin!"

Thomas leaned forward. "It's okay," he said to the woman. Lots of people, especially children, were curious about his scars. "I got them in a fire," he said to the boy.

The boy's eyes widened. "You did?"

Thomas nodded.

"We learned about stop, drop, and roll in school," the boy said. "Is that what you did?"

Before Thomas had a chance to answer, the woman nodded. "You're the hero firefighter who saved the man from the burning building, aren't you! I recognize you from the *Browerville Sentinel.*"

Thomas' stomach dropped. He didn't mind if people noticed his scars. But he was no hero. His heartbeat increased and his body heated. He needed to get out of there, but he also needed to purchase the presents. If he left them, he'd have to return. What if the mom and the boy were here again? Or other, more curious, people? His thoughts started to swirl in irrational patterns in his mind. The mother and son gave him a strange look. He swallowed.

"Can I help you?"

The question startled him until he realized it was the saleswoman behind the counter, waiting for him to pay for his purchases. Forcing himself to focus on his task, he grunted, placed his items on the counter, and reached into his back pocket for his wallet. By now, the woman and boy had moved on, but his discomfort remained.

"Would you like me to gift wrap anything?"

The woman was trying to be helpful. But all he wanted to do was to get out of the store and into the fresh air before rushing home. Shaking his head no, he took his package and walked for the door.

On the sidewalk, the biting air made him shiver. He strode away from the store, not paying attention to where he was headed. He just knew he needed to go. Somewhere. Anywhere. A few more blocks and his steps slowed. The roaring in his ears gave way to the hum of car engines, the chatter of other shoppers, and the muted sounds of music coming from the stores.

Looking around, he realized he'd walked toward the firehouse. His firehouse. His chief still held on to his resignation papers, but he'd be damned if he went inside there today. A flash of red caught his eye and he turned toward the bright color.

Jessica Sacks.

Not now.

He turned, but not fast enough.

"Hi, Thomas."

He nodded to her and hoped he could leave without a conversation.

"Are you going inside?" she asked.

He shook his head. "I'm on my way home."

Her expression was curious, but he wasn't about to stop long enough for her to ask her questions.

"I was—"

He couldn't do this. It was hard enough when the little boy drew attention to his burns, making his mom recognize him and praise him for something he didn't deserve. If Jessica started in with him, he would lose it. "I'm sorry, Jessica, but I have to go."

Turning around, he walked as fast as he could without running away from her. The last thing he wanted to do was to discuss her hero worship, or her story, or anything.

Chapter Five

Jessica squinted at Thomas's retreating figure. Now he couldn't bear to be around her? He'd pushed past her and rushed away. What was up with him? Did he think she'd interview him in the middle of the street? *I mean, I could, but it wouldn't fit with my "get to know you first" plan.* The man was a mystery. A sexy mystery, but a mystery, nonetheless. Because his winter jacket couldn't hide the way his jeans hugged his ass and thighs.

No, you can't drool over him. Been there, done that. Do not need any more T-shirts. Or embarrassment.

The wind picked up and she shivered. It was too cold to stand in the middle of the sidewalk without moving. Not to mention, the holiday shoppers would run her over. Stuffing her hands in her pockets, she waited for the light to change before she crossed the street to the firehouse. The doors to the garage were up and, inside, firefighters washed their trucks. She pulled out her old press pass, ready to flash it if necessary.

"Jessica Sacks?"

The voice came from the back of the garage and Jessica squinted to see who it belonged to. Booted footsteps approached and a tall Asian man appeared.

"Jay Song?" Jessica greeted her friend from high school English class with a hug. "I didn't know you worked here," she said.

He nodded. "For a few years now. You home for a visit?"

"I'm home to cover the museum rededication and awards ceremony."

Jay nodded. "Right, you're a reporter. You always said you wanted to be one. Congratulations on making it."

She swallowed the bile in her throat. Her dream job might be coming to an ugly end.

"Thanks. Speaking of which, do you know who I can talk to about the fire?"

He looked around, gesturing. "The full company responded, so any of us. But it's best to speak to the chief first. She's in her office." He pointed to the front door. "Inside, first door on your right."

"I will. Nice to see you again."

"Same."

She waved and entered the firehouse. The spicy scent of chili wafted toward her. Her stomach rumbled and she wondered if it was possible to get an invite to dinner. Following Jay's instructions, she knocked on the chief's door.

"Come in," she called.

Chief Gordon was in her forties, with light brown hair pulled into a sleek bun. She looked up, removed her glasses and pointed to the chair in front of her desk. "May I help you?"

"I hope so," Jessica said. "I'm a reporter with the *Tri-State Sentinel*, and I'm writing a story on the rededication of the Browerville Museum. My name is Jessica Sacks. Is there anyone I can talk to about the fire?"

She handed her credentials to the chief, who examined them before returning them to her.

"You can start with me," the woman said. She looked at the clock on her desk. "I have about ten minutes right now."

"Great." Jessica sat across from the chief and crossed her legs. She pulled her laptop from her bag and opened it. "What can you tell me about the fire?"

The chief reclined in her chair. "It was a bad one. The building was closed for the night. It burned awhile before anyone noticed. Luckily, there wasn't anyone inside, other than the janitor, Eric Payne."

"Can you tell me about his rescue?"

The chief nodded. "He was in the basement, putting away his supplies, when the smoke filled the space. Overcome, he passed out. Officers Thomas Carville, Jay Song, Mira O'Malley and Julie Stern were the first on the scene. They spread out to search the building, and Thomas found him. Part of the building collapsed as they were on their way out and resulted in Officer Carville suffering severe burns on his neck and torso. He's been out on medical leave since. He blocked most of the falling debris from hitting Mr. Pierce, though."

"So, he's a hero," Jessica said.

"I'd say so, yes."

Jessica typed furiously. "Didn't the building have smoke alarms?"

"Yes, but it spread. It took about an hour to put it out, and we kept an eye on hot spots for another couple of hours. The building was badly damaged."

"How did it start?"

"Faulty electrical panel. If you need to talk to the investigator, I have his number."

Jessica nodded. "Great." She looked at her notes. "Do you have contact information for Eric Payne?"

"Yes." The chief tapped the keyboard of her computer and gave Jessica the phone number.

"Which firefighters can I speak to?"

"Any of the ones I mentioned," the chief said. "Although, good luck speaking with Officer Carville."

Jessica smiled. "I know. I've tried multiple times without any luck."

Chief Gordon nodded. "Most of our guys look upon what

they do as part of their job. It's the public who considers them heroes, and I think, for some, it rubs them the wrong way."

Jessica rose and stuck out her hand. "Well, thank you for speaking with me. If I have any more questions, do you mind if I follow up with you?"

The chief shook her hand and walked her to the door. "Of course. Leave a message for me and I'll get back to you."

Just then, the station alarm went off.

"I've got to run," the chief said.

Jessica stood to the side in the lounge area and tried to keep out of everyone's way. Perusing the bulletin board, she noticed a colorful flyer, stepped closer, and smiled. Browerville's Annual Holiday Decorating Contest. She remembered all the years she and her family had spent driving through neighborhoods admiring the holiday lights. Why not decorate for Hanukkah? Determined to get her parents to agree to enter the contest, she photographed the flyer to show them when she got home. If she had to spend the holidays here, she planned to enjoy herself.

Outside, her phone rang.

"Hi, Alice."

"How's the story coming?"

Jessica stomped her feet to keep warm. "I spoke to the fire chief, although I may need to follow up with her. The alarms went off."

"That'll happen in a firehouse."

Jessica chuffed at the woman's sarcasm. It was one of the reasons they got along well. Or at least, they'd used to. "Yeah, funny how that works. I'll talk to the old man who was rescued."

"What about the firefighter?"

Jessica sighed. "He's being difficult."

She imagined Alice's ears perk like a Chihuahua's. "Oh, why?"

"I don't know. He doesn't want to talk about it."

"Maybe there's more to this story than we thought. Find out why."

Jessica squirmed. In the past, a difficult subject challenged her. This time, it made her uncomfortable. "I don't think it's that kind of story, Alice. He's my neighbor—"

"Perfect, you'll have no trouble dogging him."

Alice hung up before Jessica could say anything else, like maybe there wasn't any story behind Thomas's reluctance. Maybe he was a private person. She stared at the phone, a pit in her stomach. She didn't think talking to Thomas would be as easy as Alice thought. Especially if she planned to ease him into the idea. But she couldn't give up. Not if she wanted to keep her job.

Thomas woke the next morning to slobbery kisses on his hand from Reggie. He groaned. Reggie took the noise as the signal to move onto his face because, all of a sudden, he was awash in dog drool and breath worse than his.

"Oh, man," he groaned, pushing the dog away while he scratched Reggie's ears to show him he loved him anyway. "You are a hell of an alarm clock."

Checking his phone, another missed text alert from one of his firefighter buddies flashed across his screen. He left it unread. After he washed his face and brushed his teeth, he slid on a pair of jeans and a sweatshirt, stuffed his feet into his work boots and grabbed Reggie's leash.

"Make it quick," he said. "I need coffee."

He yawned as he waited for Reggie to do his business. Glancing over at his neighbor's house, the sight of Mr. Sacks on a ladder drew him up short. The older man was hanging something. Jessica stood below him, giving directions.

She was gripping his lower legs, and Thomas scoffed. As if she could prevent him from falling off the ladder. If the man lost his balance, the only thing she'd do was maybe break his fall.

Walking Reggie back to the house, he glanced again at his neighbor. He shouldn't be on a ladder.

Stop trying to be the hero, Thomas.

Except, if something happened that Thomas could have prevented, guilt would consume him. With a heavy sigh, he fed Reggie, ensured the door closed behind him, and walked across the yard. He made sure to make noise and not to startle anyone.

"Need any help?"

Mr. Sacks's face creased in a smile while Jessica's flattened into neutral. A wave of guilt struck him. She hadn't experienced the best, or better, side of him since her arrival. He needed to fix things with her—and have a long talk with himself.

"Thomas!" her dad called. "We didn't disturb you, did we? Jessica's pretty particular in her vision here, but we tried to keep quiet."

Jessica's face reddened. It was cute. Unless, of course, she was angry and that was his sign to run.

His mood lightened at the picture in his mind of her chasing after him. But he thought of how fierce tiny dogs could be against large ones and he sobered.

"No, you didn't disturb me at all. But I'm happy to get on the ladder and help you both. What are you doing?"

"We're entering the town holiday decorating contest," Jessica said. "But you don't have to help. You've made it pretty clear you want to be alone."

Her father's expression turned quizzical, and Thomas closed his eyes. "Yeah, you caught me at a bad time. I'm sorry for my actions in town."

She paused, as if considering whether or not to forgive him.

He held his breath, unsure why he wanted her forgiveness so much, but he let it out in a whoosh when she nodded.

"You're entering the contest?" He'd never seen them decorate before; at least, not outside.

Jessica's voice returned to its usual animated state as she explained. "Yes! I convinced my parents to do it. It'll be fun."

"She, who doesn't have to wrestle with lights, says," her father said good-naturedly.

"The Star of David lights are adorable, Dad. We have to use them."

Thomas looked at where Mr. Sacks had begun to hang them. Each star was outlined in miniature white lights. Strung from the roofline, it would be festive and cheerful.

"Okay, I have lots of experience hanging lights," Thomas said. "Why don't you let me do it?"

"It's not necessary," Jessica said. "We're okay."

He didn't like the idea of Mitchell Sacks on a ladder, not when he was around to help. "Please," he said, "I climb ladders for a living."

He cringed. Giving Jessica an opening to ask him about his job was the last thing he'd wanted to do. Yet, for some reason, she didn't bite. Maybe she was too focused on the decorating. He didn't know the reason, but he was grateful.

Now he needed Mr. Sacks to agree so he could get the man off the ladder.

"Alright," he said. "Thank you."

Thomas heaved a sigh of relief and helped Jessica hold the ladder steady while the older man descended. Taking the lights and brackets from him, Thomas ascended the ladder and strung the Star of David lights to Jessica and her father's specifications.

"Could you fix that one?" Jessica pointed to one halfway between the front door and the living room window.

"Sure."

When he'd finished, he descended the ladder and the three of them surveyed his work.

"Nice job," Mr. Sacks said. He started to walk away but paused. "Can we treat you to lunch as a sign of appreciation?"

"For getting on a ladder?" Thomas asked. "It's not necessary."

Mr. Sacks raised a brow. "Are you sure?"

"Positive."

As the older man walked away, Jessica spoke. "Thanks for your help. It was nice of you to take care of it, so my dad didn't have to be on the ladder for long."

Thomas nodded. "You're welcome. And thanks for not holding my rude behavior earlier against me."

Once again, she stared at him, and he wondered what was going through her mind. Part of him wanted to ask. Another part said to leave. But that was the part that had gotten him into trouble with her before. He waited and tried not to fidget.

"You didn't used to snap at me as often," she said. "Of course, you didn't talk to me, either, so what do I know." She shrugged.

He couldn't tell if she was letting him off the hook or not.

"We've all changed," he said. "Although I'm more of a work in progress." He blew out a breath and looked once again at her decorations. "I don't recall you ever hanging lights outside for Hanukkah."

Jessica's eyes lit up. In fact, he'd swear she swallowed one of the lights he'd strung. Her skin glowed. Her lips stretched in a smile. *Whoa.*

"There's a first time for everything. Have you entered?"

He barely heard what she said; her pure happiness transfixed him. What must it be like to be carefree?

"Entered?" He couldn't stop staring at her. He needed to say something to not look like a dummy. Her joy inspired him and the old Thomas wished he could get some of it. This new Thomas? He wasn't sure. But he wasn't against it.

"The Browerville Annual Holiday Decorating Contest?"

She stuck her phone in front of him and he looked at the photo of a flyer. Of course, he knew about the contest. The firehouse competed against the police station and public library. Last year, the library had won with an unbelievable book display, but the year before, the firehouse had won with an electric light display of Happy Holidays pouring out of the firehose from the top of an engine. This year?

"Guess I forgot."

"You should enter," she said. "In fact, I challenge you to a contest between our houses. Loser has to give the winner a holiday present."

"A present?" Geez, how could one smile from her make him forget how to string complex sentences together?

"Whichever of our houses places higher in the contest wins."

"But I helped you hang your lights," he said.

"You provided additional labor," she said. "We came up with the design. Plus," she added, moving closer to him, "you're the one who volunteered."

She stood in front of him, their toes touching. Narrower and shorter than he was, her wool hat tickled his chin. What would she do if he slung her over his shoulder? Forget her reaction, what would he do? Or, better yet, what would happen if he kissed her?

Kissed her? What was wrong with him?

He took a deep breath and her flowery scent overwhelmed his senses. It didn't help. He cleared his throat and retreated a step.

She wanted a contest. Was she insane? "Okay, you're on."

Whoa, how did that happen? He'd wanted—intended—to say no. To turn around and storm into his house and finish the renovations necessary to complete before his family arrived for Christmas.

At her look of satisfaction, he tried to convince himself it would be okay. Hell, his family would love the house festive for Christmas. Even he would probably like it. He'd always liked the decorations his mom had used when he was a child.

"If you give me your phone number, I'll text you the flyer photo I have," Jessica said. "That way you know all the information."

Before he could convince himself of all the reasons giving her his number was a bad idea, he rattled off the ten digits.

His phone buzzed with a text and he opened the photo. "Got it," he said.

With another one of her megawatt smiles, Jessica spun around and walked to her house with her dad.

"Oh, Thomas?" she called. "I like dark chocolate, the color red, and Agatha Christie. You know, for when I win."

Jessica leaned against her front door and enjoyed Thomas's look of confusion. She hadn't meant to tease him, but it was easy. In fact, she'd meant to ignore him, but he hadn't been his usual grumpy self. First, he'd apologized for his behavior and volunteered to help hang the lights, then he'd initiated a conversation about Hanukkah decorations. Just like the other night when they'd teased each other about beet juice, he'd been fun to talk to. Maybe her plan would work.

What hadn't she expected? His ass to look fine in his blue jeans.

"Jess, what other decorations do you want outside?" her mother asked.

Her breath caught in her throat at the question and at the thoughts her mother had interrupted. She coughed. Clearing her throat, she thanked God once again that thought bubbles didn't appear over one's head and tried to focus on the question at hand.

"I have an idea, but I'm not sure if it will work," she said.

"Let me hear it." Her mom sat on the steps and waited.

"A Hanukkah menorah has nine branches, four on either

side of the shamash. If you count all the windows on our house, they add up to eight. The front door makes nine. What if we got tiny white lights and outlined each window, adding one per night, plus outlining the door the entire time? Do you think there's any chance it would kind of give the idea of a menorah?"

Her mom frowned, stood and took her hand, leading her outside. "I need to visualize," she said. "Tell me again how it would work."

Jessica pointed to each window and door. "The first night, we'd light that window all the way on the right, plus the doorway. The second night we'd add this one…"

Her mom nodded. "You know, if we also got yellow lights to put on the bottom of the windows and the doorway and kept them lit the entire time, they might look like the candle holders."

"Oh, my gosh, yes!" Jessica bounced in her brown leather ankle boots. "Mom, you're a genius!"

"Great, now you tell me, after you've moved out and I don't have anything to record you." She bumped Jessica's shoulder. "I'm glad you like the idea. Any store that sells Christmas lights will carry them. In fact, I think Mack's has it."

Mack's Fixer Upper was the local hardware store and carried, or could get, any part or tool you could need. Jessica nodded. "You're right, I'll go there."

"Wow, twice in a row. I need to keep my phone handy."

"Yeah, yeah, yeah," Jessica said. She leaned over and gave her mom's cheek a kiss. "I love you, but don't expect me to say too many 'you're rights.' I can't make things too easy on you."

"God forbid."

Her mom surveyed the front yard. "Did you and dad talk about the yard at all?"

"How would you feel about blow-up dreidels?" Jessica

asked. "We could put one or two over there." She pointed to one side of the front yard.

"It's for a contest. We might as well go all out. Besides, in addition to a prize for the winner, the charity of their choice gets a large donation. Go for it."

"Thanks, Mom."

Jessica entered the house with her, saying, "I think I should go to Mack's now. I don't want to risk his running out of anything."

Grabbing the car keys off the hall table, she went out to her car and drove into town. Alone, her thoughts strayed to Thomas once again. Why the sight of him in tight jeans caught her off guard, she had no idea. He was a firefighter, and they needed to be in top shape to carry all their equipment. He'd rescued a full-grown man. Maybe it was the ladder. That was it. He'd climbed to the roofline to hang the lights and she couldn't help but look. She gave a small sigh. Wow.

When she'd crushed on him in high school, she'd admired everything about him, including his looks, but she didn't recall him filling out his jeans in the same way. She pulled into a parking spot behind Mack's and chastised herself. It was time to focus. She was determined to win the contest. Focusing on Thomas's cute butt wouldn't help her.

The scents of sawdust and pine oil assailed her senses as she searched the aisles for the Christmas light section. Several people filled the store, all with as similar thoughts as she had. She was about to grab a few packages of tiny white lights when she realized she hadn't measured how much she'd need.

"Crap," she said under her breath.

"Problem?" A deep voice spoke behind her, and she turned.

Thomas appeared, as if by magic, in the same aisle of the same store.

"I think we're destined to run into each other everywhere," she said.

"Well, when you challenge me to a contest, I have to make sure I win," he said. His brown eyes twinkled and rendered her speechless.

She'd grown used to his annoyance; the twinkle was an unexpected head rush. She swallowed and tried to get her brain to function again.

Lights. Right.

"I don't suppose you'd know many of these I'd need for a window." Her voice sounded weak to her ears.

Get over him, Jess, she said to herself.

"Didn't you already do this?" he asked.

Oh, yes, and getting to watch him on a ladder was a bonus she wouldn't soon forget. "That was the first part," she said.

"Are you suggesting I help the enemy?"

The way he cocked an eyebrow made her breath hitch. "I'm not the enemy. I'm your challenger. There's a difference."

"Maybe so, but helping you won't help me win."

"No, but it's neighborly." She grinned at him. She asked questions for a living, yet her interview subjects had never caused this this rush of adrenaline.

"Sixteen feet." His rough voice made her heart stutter.

"Thank you." She looked at the basket on his arm. "What are you buying?"

"Stuff."

She laughed. "Trust me, telling me what's in the small basket won't make the difference between winning and losing. Besides," she said, trying to peek into his basket, which he shifted away, "don't you have decorations already?"

"Yes, but they need some refreshing since I plan to beat you. But I'll tell you a secret." He leaned toward her.

She moved closer, inhaled his spicy male scent, and willed herself not to drool.

"I'm not here for the contest."

With that, he spun on his heel and walked away.

Chapter Six

God, he was such a liar, he thought to himself as he rushed out of Mack's, his bag of compound and carpentry nails clutched in his hand. Sure, he needed those items for the work on his house, but he'd also needed Christmas lights. Thanks to his unexpected run-in with Jessica, he'd have to make another trip. Muttering to himself, hands at ten and two on the steering wheel, he drove home.

Reggie wiggled his butt in greeting and Thomas scratched his ears, tossing the bag onto the counter. "If you knew what a mess I am," he whispered under his breath. Gah. After he refilled Reggie's water bowl, he went into the basement and pulled out the Christmas decorations. All seven boxes of them.

His mother had saved every ornament and Christmas memento any of the kids had made. With the entire family here for the holiday, he'd have to decorate more than he'd intended to. Plus, the decorating contest and an unofficial competition with the Sackses…why the hell had he raced out of Mack's without the extra lights?

Not only was he a liar, but he was also a coward. Something about Jessica fried his brain every time he saw her. He didn't know what it was, but he needed to get over it. Pronto.

Since he didn't yet have a Christmas tree, he left the boxes of ornaments alone. That left four boxes of decorations to bring upstairs.

As he organized the contents and determined where to hang what, his phone rang.

"Hey, Tommy." His sister's voice over the speakerphone pierced the silence of the house.

"Hey, Brat, what's up?"

"At what point will you start using my name?" she asked.

He'd called Debbie "Brat" for as long as he could remember. It always annoyed her, which was why it gave him such satisfaction.

"When it stops bugging you," he said.

She sighed. "What do you want me to bring for Christmas dinner?"

"I haven't thought about it yet."

"Well, think, because I need time to plan and cook."

"You can cook here," he said. "I redid the kitchen. It's a chef's dream." Well, maybe not, but he liked it.

"Wait, you mean you have four burners that work?"

It was a family joke that there was always at least one burner on the stove on the fritz. As soon as his dad had fixed one, another one had acted up. But for some reason, his mom had never wanted a new stove. A wave of nostalgia hit.

"Yeah, I did. The oven too."

"Holy cow. I have to rethink my food suggestions now."

"Funny. You can bring whatever you want."

"Great, I'll bring my sweet potatoes and my spinach artichoke casserole. Are you making Mom's rib eye recipe?"

Thomas's stomach growled thinking about the savory dish.

"I heard that!" Debbie said.

"Yeah, yeah, yeah, whatever," he said. "Yes, I'm making the rib eye."

"Good." She was quiet a moment. "It'll be nice with everyone together," she whispered. "I've missed us."

His chest tightened; he'd been hard to be around when he was drinking. "Yeah, me too."

He'd already apologized to his sister, and she'd accepted it. For the past nine months, she'd called every few days, checking on him, inquiring about what he did to fill his days, and asking his opinions on things. She'd made her presence known, somehow without being intrusive, and he appreciated her more than he could ever say.

"You're buying me an amazing Christmas gift, right?" Her taunt made him smile.

"A pony, a unicorn, and bright pink nail polish." It was his annual response to her question, but he thought about the bookends.

"Excellent. I'm buying you a fire truck and a baseball bat." Her response was the same, as well, but this time his throat tightened and he remained silent a second too long.

"Tommy, when will you forgive yourself?"

Never. "I'm working on it."

"Are you? Because sometimes I wonder."

"You don't need to worry about me, Brat."

"I didn't say I worried, although I do sometimes. But not recently. But I do wonder about the guilt you carry."

"Who says I carry guilt?"

"Every line in your face and tense muscle in your body says it."

He ran a hand over his forehead and counted to ten before he responded. "I'll work on it, okay?"

"Okay."

"Anything else?" he asked. "Because I've got to get to work."

He said goodbye to her and unpacked more decorations. When he found the box of Christmas lights, he sorted through the different color options, deciding on multicolor lights for the outside of the house, green lights for the bushes, white for the lamppost and mailbox, and red for the trees. He needed more of each, and he berated himself for leaving Mack's before he'd searched the correct aisle.

"I wouldn't have known how much to buy anyway," he said to Reggie.

Reggie nuzzled his side and he gave the dog an extra pat.

He looked out the window at Jessica's house. He'd never seen Star of David Hanukkah lights before, and he wondered about her other ideas. She'd flustered him when he'd run into her, and he hadn't bothered to check her basket.

Now, driving to the store with his list, he wondered what other ideas she had hidden in her sleeve.

Jessica knocked on the door of Eric Payne's town house at the appointed time that afternoon and waited for someone to answer.

The door opened and an elderly man with white, close-cropped hair, gold-rimmed glasses and a green-plaid shirt tucked into black jeans appeared. He peered at her.

"You must be Jessica." He coughed.

She nodded. "I am. You're Mr. Payne?"

"Call me Eric." He said opened the door wider and made room for her to enter.

She stepped over the threshold into a small living room/ dining room area in shades of blue and gray.

"Take a seat." He gestured to the sofa. "Can I get you a drink?"

She wasn't thirsty, but she didn't want to be rude. Plus, her habit from her investigative reporter days of making the subject comfortable before she interviewed them was ingrained.

"Sure," she said. "Water or soda is fine."

He disappeared for a minute, returning with a filled glass and a napkin. "Hope Pepsi is okay." He placed it in front of her.

"It's perfect." She took a sip before she opened her laptop. "Can you tell me what happened the day of the fire?"

He leaned forward in his chair, a distant look on his face before he cleared his throat. "I was on the second floor when

I smelled smoke. I went to investigate because I thought it was some kids smoking. I didn't expect to see the fire in the basement. By the time I called 9-1-1, the smoke was heavy and I couldn't find my way out. I tripped over something and banged my head as I fell. Next thing I knew, I was outside in the ambulance on my way to the hospital."

"That must have been scary," Jessica said.

"It was terrifying at the time. They told me I was lucky to be alive, and I wouldn't have made it if it wasn't for Thomas Carville." He coughed.

"Why were you on the second floor?" she asked.

"I was cleaning the administrative offices. The museum pieces were downstairs on the first floor, with the staff offices upstairs."

"You said you expected the smoke to be kids, but were there often kids in the museum after hours?"

He shrugged. "I wasn't thinking. I didn't expect an actual fire, not one the size I saw."

"What happened to the exhibit?" Jessica asked, "Were any of the pieces able to be saved?"

"You'd have to ask the museum curator for specifics," he said. "But I believe special cases prevented the most valuable pieces from damage."

The Browerville Museum displayed artifacts from the Revolutionary War, as well as pieces from the founding of the town. Jessica made a note to talk to the curator, as well as to find out what was different in the new building.

"Tell me about Thomas Carville."

The older man's face brightened. "The man is a hero. I wouldn't be here today without him. I'm told he came into the basement, saw I was on the ground, and rushed me out of the building as it started to collapse. They put him in the other ambulance, and I was able to thank him when I was discharged from the hospital." He lowered his voice. "The man didn't like my gratitude, but I couldn't leave before I told him how appreciative I was." He shrugged. "Some people are uncomfortable with praise, I guess."

Jessica finished typing. Thomas's reaction confused her more since she'd heard the firsthand account of his heroism.

"I understand Mr. Carville was injured in the fire," she said. "Do you mind sharing your injuries?"

"I suffered a concussion and some smoke inhalation. Mr. Carville bore the brunt of the injuries." The older man's mouth drooped. "I feel bad he suffered because of me. I've tried to contact him a few times since, but he doesn't answer my calls."

The hardest part about being a journalist was remaining objective. The human side of Jessica wanted to comfort the man, but the reporter in her couldn't. She couldn't show her surprise, either, that Thomas didn't want to talk to him. So she nodded and waited him out. Sometimes the best nuggets came in the silence.

She sipped her soda, but the older man remained lost in thought.

"Is there anything else you think I should know?"

He shook his head. "The man's heroism belongs in the museum. What he did is part of Browerville history. Not because he saved me, but because he acted like a hero. I'm thrilled he's being honored at the rededication ceremony. I hope to talk to him again there."

Jessica finished typing and, after ensuring she could follow up with him if she thought of additional questions, she left his home.

Her investigative training told her there was more to this story. Why else would Thomas refuse to talk about it to her or to the man he'd saved? She'd have to push harder.

As she pulled into her driveway, Thomas was standing outside at his mailbox. She waved, got out of her car, and walked over to him.

"Hi," she said. "Have you figured out your decorating plans? You made a quick escape from Mack's earlier." She couldn't be sure, but she thought he blushed. Good. She liked keeping him off balance.

"We've decorated the house for years," he said.

His cheeks were redder, and she a sudden desire to run her palm over them. She clamped her hand closed. "Yes, but you've never entered the contest before, and you've never competed against me."

His brown eyes twinkled.

Why did every place he looked heat under his gaze? She shifted from foot to foot, hoping he wouldn't see her flush.

"You seem awfully sure of yourself for someone who hasn't done this before," he said. "I can't wait to see what you do." He folded his arms across his chest, his biceps straining his shirtsleeves.

She forced her gaze away from him. "I kind of wish there was a way to erect a barrier between our properties," she said. "You know, to keep the element of surprise."

Thomas waggled his eyebrows. "But seeing what we each do might also provide incentive."

"True," she said. "I never thought of that."

Thomas puffed out his chest as surprise showed on his face. "You admit you like my idea. Wow."

Better than admitting how sexy he is. "Everyone has them once in a while."

He placed his hand over his heart. "You wound me."

She patted his shoulder and admired the strength of his muscle. "I have faith in your ability to recover."

Once again, their conversation was going well. She didn't want to rush anything, but she also needed to make her deadline. Should she bring up her interview? Maybe if he knew she'd talked to the man, he'd want to share his own side of the story.

As Thomas turned to go home, she decided to take advantage of his good mood. She called out to him.

"I spoke to Eric Payne."

Thomas's entire body stiffened.

Shoot. That wasn't the reaction she'd wanted.

He paused. When he turned around, all traces of neighborly friendliness had vanished. Before he told her off, she pushed forward.

"He was filled with gratitude and complimentary things about you. Why won't you talk to me? Or to him? You saved him from certain death." She kept her voice friendly and tried to show him this wasn't an interrogation. She hoped he'd respond to her tone.

"I did my job. You don't need me for your article, and he's already thanked me."

He hadn't stalked away, though. Progress. She pressed on. "You're getting an award. Maybe if I understood why you're reluctant about this article, I could help you feel better about it, or make sure to frame the article in such a way to make you more comfortable with it. And, as for Mr. Payne? Maybe he'll make you feel better too."

He folded his arms across his chest and widened his stance. "I don't deserve any award, and I don't need to feel better about anything."

They were engaged in conversation. This was headway. "Sounds like you do to me. You saved him. I understand modesty, but…"

He frowned. "You're entitled to your opinion. Doesn't mean I have to be a part of it, though." He started to walk away.

"Thomas, please." She chased after him. "You're going to avoid me? I've enjoyed getting to know you, and I think you feel the same."

He spun around. "As a person, yes. But you're a reporter.

I don't talk to reporters. Especially ones who are trying to be friendly in order to further their own interests."

She groaned in both frustration and embarrassment. He wasn't right, but she couldn't say he was wrong, either. She bent around and looked at him. "I'm sorry," she said. "Truly. But we're neighbors," she countered. "And no matter what you think, getting the information for my article isn't the only reason I've been nice to you. Can't we be friends?"

He stuffed his hands in his pockets. His breath came out in white puffs as the temperature dropped. He stared off into the distance before returning his focus to her. "Okay, we're friends. Happy now?"

"I don't believe you. In fact, I don't think *you* believe you."

He frowned. "And why would you think that?"

She bit her lip. "Because I think you're saying it to shut me up."

His mouth twitched, like he was trying to suppress a smile. Good. Progress.

"Fine. Come over tonight and I'll cook dinner."

Her breath caught. The teenager she used to be jumped for joy. "You're going to give me whiplash," she said. "Did you invite me on a date?"

"No, I offered to feed you. It's what neighbors do. Seven o'clock." And without saying another word, he stalked into his house and left her more confused—and excited—than ever.

What the hell was his problem? Thomas shut the door harder than necessary, which scared Reggie. "Sorry, bud." He scratched the dog behind his ears and, mollified, Reggie trotted to his water bowl. After slurping, he flopped on the kitchen floor and stared out into the backyard with a sigh of contentment.

If only Thomas could be as easily placated.

What was it with him? Every time he went near Jessica, random stuff came out of his mouth. His body went hot and cold. And, somehow, he was reduced to an awkward teenager at puberty. He was tempted to look in the mirror to make sure acne hadn't sprouted on his face.

She wanted to interview him for the *Brooklyn Daily Herald*, he'd said no, instead, inviting her for dinner. One he cooked. Tonight.

Maybe he could fake an illness. Shame filled him. During the height of his alcoholism, he'd done that when the hangover hadn't worn off in time for his shift. Never again.

And it meant he had to go through with the invite.

Damn it.

He opened the fridge and stared at its contents. What the hell was he supposed to cook for her? She didn't like beetroot juice. She'd probably hate whatever he made.

He called his sister again.

"Hey, Tommy, everything okay?"

"Yes. No. Why wouldn't it be?"

Her voice oozed with concern. "We already spoke today, and you don't call me this often."

Crap. Would she ever not worry about him? Guilt pummeled him. "I'm sorry. I need a recipe."

"A recipe? What kind?"

"Dinner. Jessica Sacks is coming over—"

"Jessica Sacks? Little Jessica Sacks who mooned over you our entire lives? Next-door Jessica Sacks?"

He was starting to think calling Debbie had been a bad idea. "Yes."

"You asked her out on a date?"

"What? No." Why would his sister think that?

"When you ask a woman to dinner, a dinner you cook, it's a date."

His heart sank. Jessica had thought so, too, until he'd corrected her. Unless she hadn't believed him.

He didn't intend to date anyone.

"Does she keep kosher?"

"I have no idea. Why?"

"Because she's Jewish, and you're cooking for her. It's something you should know."

Thomas wracked his brain. He didn't think the Sackses kept kosher, but he couldn't be certain. Damn it, again.

"Wouldn't she have told me?"

"I don't know her as well as you do," Debbie said.

He didn't like the snide tone of her voice. "I don't know her well at all." And that made his reaction to her all the more puzzling.

"Well, you might want to ask her."

"Fine, but let's say she's not."

"Do you know what food she likes?"

"I have no idea. But she hates beet juice."

His sister laughed. "Most normal people do. Points to her. Well, best to stay away from shrimp, in case she does keep kosher. Not to mention, isn't tonight her Sabbath?"

Thomas smacked his forehead. He should have asked more questions.

"I think so, but wouldn't she have said something when I invited her if it was a problem?"

"Probably," his sister agreed. "How about salmon? I have a great recipe for it."

He didn't have any in the house, but he could run out and buy some. "Can you email it to me?"

"Done," she said. "Have fun tonight and be nice!"

Her singsong voice grated on his nerves. He grunted his thanks and hung up the phone. And he stared at it. Should he call Jessica and ask if she kept kosher? Or if there were any foods she didn't like?

Gah! She wasn't his girlfriend. He was being neighborly, that was all. If she didn't like the food, she didn't have to eat it, and he'd know for next time. Except there wasn't going to be a next time.

* * *

By the time she rang the doorbell that night, he'd put more effort and worry into a simple salmon and rice meal than he'd ever put into anything he'd cooked for the firehouse. His sister's voice rang in his mind. *Be nice to her.* Mentally warning his sister to back off, he opened the door.

Jessica stood there in jeans and a silky green shirt, sparkly things in her ears and holding a foil-covered plate.

"Hi. I brought brownies." She held the plate up extra high so Reggie wouldn't get it. "I figured anyone who enjoys beet juice might have some interesting opinions on dessert. It was safer to bring my own. Plus, being neighborly and all."

He burst out laughing, something he hadn't done in who knew how long. He couldn't help it. The combination of her sarcasm, sparkling eyes and teasing made it impossible to do anything else.

Still chuckling, he moved out of her way and let her enter.

"Smells good," she said, bending down to pet the dog.

Her stare burned a hole in his back as he led her into the kitchen.

"Thanks." He took the brownies from her and placed them on the counter. "I made salmon and rice, as well as a salad. I hope it's okay."

"Perfect," she said.

He warmed at the praise, though there was no reason to. She stole a peek into the living room.

"You finished." She pointed to the painted walls.

The blue-gray color was peaceful, something his sober self craved. He'd added stone sculptures—the kind found in Zen gardens—on the shelf below the picture window and on the fireplace mantel. The comfortable sofas in navy blue had arrived yesterday, the gray wood coffee table and end tables were to be delivered in about a week, and by the time his family arrived, it would be sufficient.

He nodded. "My family is coming for Christmas, so I have a deadline." He cringed at the word *deadline*, but she merely nodded. Relief spread when she didn't use it as a segue into the minefield he was trying to avoid.

"It's always easier to accomplish things with a due date—at least, for me. Otherwise, it goes into my 'someday' pile and 'someday' has never arrived."

"Yeah, I've yet to see it, either." Any reference to her job or his recovery was off limits, at least for now, and he breathed a sigh of relief the word hadn't fazed her.

He brought out the dishes and motioned for her to sit. "I should have asked if there was anything you didn't like to eat," he said as he pulled out the loaf of fresh-baked bread.

"Salmon, rice and bread," she said.

Again, he laughed, and this time, she joined him. Her voice might be sharp and inquisitive, but her laughter was musical. He liked it. And he liked how she used her sense of humor with intent. It made things easier.

"No," she added. "What you made is great. Provided you didn't add beets."

"After the fuss you made? It wouldn't be neighborly of me, now, would it?"

"Probably not," she said. She took a bite of the salmon and he waited while she chewed and swallowed. "This is delicious."

"It's my sister's recipe."

"Geez, does your entire family cook?"

He nodded. "My mom made sure of it."

Jessica's expression softened. "She did a good job. How is your sister and the rest of your family?"

"They're okay, thanks." He didn't add, *Now that I'm sober.* He still dealt with guilt over the pain he'd caused with his struggles, and the last thing he wanted was to air those issues to her.

"How are your parents?" he asked. "Although we're neighbors, I don't see them often."

"They're great. Both still working and busy with friends and the temple. My mom is on the temple board and my dad is president of the brotherhood."

"So that means…?"

Jessica paused. "Other than the annoyances of running a temple?" She smiled, and he thought, once again, about how pretty she was. "The temple board members are lay leaders responsible for how the temple serves its community. The brotherhood is the men's group."

"Ah, now I understand. My dad did something similar in our church when we were young."

"He's out west now?" She rested her cheek on her hand and turned her full attention on him.

Every once in a while, he forgot she was a reporter. Then a moment like this arrived and he reminded himself this was what she did for a living.

"Arizona."

"Everyone talks about how nice it is out there. Have you visited?"

He'd spent three months of his recovery out there, but no one knew. He wasn't about to tell her.

"I have. The desert is amazing. So vast, it makes you realize how insignificant you are."

She looked like she stared right through him, and her voice turned reflective. "It's funny how everything we do can seem important, but something happens and we realize how wrong we were."

He stiffened. She couldn't know what had happened to him, could she? He'd told her they could be friends, and he wanted to go through with it. Inhaling, he ran through many of the ways she could have dug up his past, but if she'd contacted any of his friends, they'd have warned him. He decided to do a little investigation of his own.

"You sound like you speak from experience," he said.

Whatever she'd thought disappeared. She lost the dreamy quality and, like a switch turned on, she snapped back to the present.

"Can I help you clean up?" She grabbed her empty plate and his.

Part of him relaxed as he realized she hadn't been hinting at his life or probing for his secrets. She'd been talking about herself. Another part of him empathized with her. He didn't like people who questioned him about his past. He wouldn't turn the tables and do it to her. No matter how strong his curiosity might be.

"If you'd like," he said. "Stack everything on the counter. I'll deal with it later."

"I like later," she said. "I'm a big fan of it myself."

They cleared the table together.

"Oh?" he asked. "You're a big procrastinator."

"The worst." She beckoned him closer.

A light floral scent teased his nostrils.

"I'll tell you a secret," she said.

He didn't need anyone else's secrets. He possessed enough of his own. However, she tantalized him with her wit and her smell and her smile. He'd have to be careful of her. Later. Right now, he wanted to focus on her. He leaned forward.

"What is it?"

"I'm late for everything. Without fail."

He couldn't help himself. The question escaped before he could stop it. "But you're a journalist. How does it work?"

She placed her hands on her hips. "I set my clocks ahead, I rework my deadlines so they're due earlier than they're assigned, and I've learned how to work under pressure those few times I can't play with assignments."

He leaned against the counter to put some space between them. "You weren't late tonight."

"Because I put dinner on my calendar for six thirty."

As if to prove it, she held out her phone for him to see. It was warm from her touch but, more importantly, "Dinner with Thomas" was typed in at six thirty.

"And your brain doesn't tell you not to worry? You're able to trick yourself and it works?"

"Sadly, it does. You should ask my friends. I'm late to everything. They do it too."

He opened and closed his mouth in disbelief. "I don't know how you do that."

"I've done it so long, it's second nature."

"Why not learn to be on time?"

She gave him a look like he was an amateur. When it came to her, he might be.

"I've tried, believe me," she said. "And I got tired of everyone being mad at me all the time. I figured out a way that works for me."

"If you say so."

He led her into the living room, and they sat on his new sofa, she in one corner, he in the middle. He didn't want to crowd her, but he liked being close to her. She leaned with grace against the armrest.

What would it be like if she leaned against him?

"What will you put in that space?" She pointed to an empty corner of the room.

He returned his attention to her words. "I'm saving room for the Christmas tree," he said. "I need a bigger one than if I were going to celebrate here by myself." Loneliness consumed him.

"Real or fake?" she asked.

"Real. I love the smell." He didn't tell her about the small tabletop one he'd planned to use. It was fake and kind of pitiful.

"Mmm, though it's not my holiday, I love the spruce smell at this time of year. Where do you go for the tree?"

"The local tree farm. My dad used to take us there as kids. We'd go on the weekend after Thanksgiving. The place was packed. Since I'm an adult, and not fond of the crowds, I'll go during the week or at a time when there will be a few less people."

"Sounds like fun. I've seen it in the movies. Is it similar?"

He shouldn't be surprised she'd never shopped for a Christmas tree, but he was. In his circle, everyone did it.

"You can come with me if you want." He hadn't expected to suggest it, but since he had, anticipation made his heart beat faster.

"I don't want to intrude," she said.

"You're not intruding. I'm going alone. It's not a big deal." He didn't tell her how much he wanted her to accompany him, but he held his breath as he waited for her to decide.

"Alright, I'd love to go. When?"

Gladness surged through him. "Monday." He couldn't wait to pick out a Christmas tree with her. He cocked his head. "What time do I tell you, though, so you won't be late?"

She laughed. She'd laughed with him more than anyone in his recent past, and he loved it. He wanted it to continue, to see the dimples flash in her cheeks, to watch her mouth curve.

"You're a funny guy. You don't have to make up a random time. I made it here, didn't I?"

"True." Thank God. Inviting her to dinner was one of the best decisions he'd made.

"So, you tell me what time to be ready and I'll do the magic mumbo jumbo with the time travel."

He was having more fun with her than anyone else in a long time. "You time travel, now?" She'd gotten him to enjoy her company; he wouldn't put it past her to be able to accomplish anything.

"Of course not, but my dad used to call it that and now that's how I refer to it."

He frowned. "Ah, okay. I won't ask. Let's go around one."

"Yeah, that doesn't work. I need an actual time, or I'll hold you up."

He groaned. "This is why your plan is flawed. But, fine, one-oh-three. Better?"

She play-punched him in the shoulder. He held his other hand on the spot in mock suffering.

"Why do I feel like I'll regret this?" he asked. He liked teasing her. He liked being close to her more.

"I have no idea," she said. "You're hard to read."

"I am?" He wasn't sure if it was good or bad, or why he cared. But this was the longest time they'd spent together, and he didn't want it to end.

She nodded. "I shouldn't tell you this, but I rarely have any idea what you're thinking."

She didn't move away from him. In fact, she was close enough to him, he could lean over and kiss her. He swallowed. Kiss her? The idea popped into his mind and it was all he wanted to do. What would she think? Would she mind?

There was one way to find out.

He grasped her shoulder and pulled her close. Her breath hitched. Before he second-guessed himself, he kissed her. Her lips were soft, her breath sweet, and all the reasons why he shouldn't do this flew from his brain.

She wasn't his little bratty neighbor anymore. She was a grown woman. A sexy woman. And he had no regrets.

He pulled away after a couple of seconds. He'd wanted to throw her off kilter a little, to live in the moment.

Too bad for him that he wanted more.

Her lips parted in an *O*. "I didn't expect that," she whispered.

He exhaled. "Neither did I."

Later that evening, after she'd gone home and he'd cleaned up and gotten into bed, Thomas grabbed his phone. Before he could change his mind, he sent her a text.

I had fun tonight.

He waited.

Me too.

And for the first time in months, he went to bed with a smile on his face.

Chapter Seven

Jessica lay in bed Monday morning and relived Thomas's kiss. His taste, his smell. She sighed. As kisses went, it had lasted only a few seconds. She'd played make-out with her pillow for longer as a teenager. But this kiss had been special because it was with Thomas. The boy she'd dreamed about had grown to a man and kissed her.

Willingly.

And he'd followed it with a text of his own volition. No longer did he try to escape her company.

Her body hummed as she got ready for the day. But as she drafted her article and planned her next steps her blood cooled. Her screen remained blank. Every time she tried to type, Thomas's image filled her mind. Her heart rate increased with a combination of desire and nerves. Their conversation jousted with the sentences she needed to form and created a jumbled mess.

Alice emailed to ask for an update.

Her stomach plummeted.

With a groan, Jessica threw a bunch of information into the email reply, all the while trying to put her feelings for Thomas aside. Feelings like desire and joy. But guilt ate away at her. Her stomach hurt. She didn't know if it was from the fear of not having a job, or her growing distaste for the story, or from the aggravation of dealing with Thomas. Or maybe it was her attraction to him. The only thing she did know was that it wasn't as fun as it used to be. And while she'd planned to befriend Thomas to loosen him up, she realized she was starting to like him. A lot.

Dr. Nelson's rules for journalism, which were burned into her brain, blared. Especially the one about impartiality. She wasn't impartial. Her original plan to make friends with him felt more like a manipulation than a strategy. How could she separate Thomas the subject from Thomas her friend…from Thomas who'd kissed her? What was she to do?

After she crafted a draft of her article that didn't focus on Thomas, she went downstairs to lunch.

"Where are you off to today?" her mother asked.

"Christmas tree shopping," she said. "Or choosing. Or whatever one does at a Christmas tree farm."

Her mother looked at her askance. "Please tell me you're not getting a tree to make a Hanukkah bush for the town contest."

Jessica laughed. "Of course not. I think turning our house's façade into a menorah is enough. Thomas is going to get his Christmas tree, and he invited me along."

"Oh."

She looked at her mother, who was never at a loss for words about…well, anything. One-word answers were not typical.

"Is it a problem I'm going?" she asked.

Her mother looked up from where she dusted invisible crumbs off the table. "What? No, of course not. You seem to be spending a lot of time with him, though."

"I'm trying to get to know him better, so he'll be more at ease with talking to me." Uttering those words out loud didn't make her believe them any more than her mother. She'd tried to make lots of subjects at ease over the years. None of them had caused butterflies flit in her stomach.

Her mother studied her for several long seconds. "If you're sure that's all it is."

"Of course." Another lie. Every moment she spent with Thomas made her like him more.

Somehow, she made it outside by one-oh-four. Thomas's truck sat in her driveway, engine running. Its thrum reminding her of her own vibrating nerves.

"Hi," she said as she climbed inside. Would he kiss her again?

"Hi." His voice was low and, somehow, his presence soothed her.

"Were you waiting long?" she asked.

He looked at the clock on the dash. "About a minute thirty. I didn't come to the door because I wanted to see you come outside in your own time, without my rushing you." He moved the gearshift into Reverse. "You know, so I could witness your timeliness in the wild."

His wink made her gasp. The child with the major crush on him somersaulted with joy. But Jessica the adult didn't want to start something she wasn't sure she could finish. She scoffed and buckled her seat belt.

Hands on ten and two, he reversed out of the driveway and hit the road. As he chatted about the tree farm, she studied his profile. Strong jawline, a trace of stubble on his cheeks, and burn scars on his neck that disappeared beneath the collar of his shirt. His dark hair was cropped close to his scalp, a bit lengthier on top.

When he was younger, his hair had been longer, shaggier. She preferred it now. Plus, there was less temptation to run her fingers through it.

"You're quiet," he said.

"Sorry, I remember how I would have given anything to be in a truck with you when I was a teenager."

He huffed. The sound sent tremors through her.

"About as much as I would have given *not* to have you as a passenger," he said. "Funny how things change."

Those four little words charged the air around her. They were both dancing around what happened last night. Who would make the first move?

"Brave assumption you made there," she said.

He pulled into a spot in the gravel lot of the tree farm, cut the engine and turned to her. "You trying to tell me something?"

Her face heated. The easy banter before their kiss had fled. He hadn't read her mind, had he? "Nope, but I think it's time to focus on the trees."

His laughter echoed in the truck as she let herself out. She needed to be more careful. Zipping her jacket, she adjusted her scarf and walked next to Thomas from the parking lot to the farm. His stride was long and his expression was open for once.

"Our choices are pick-ur-own, over there," he said, pointing, "or precut, over there."

"What do you do?"

His gaze turned inward and his expression softened. "When I was here as a kid, we picked our own. More recently, I've chosen precut. But I'm good either way."

"Pick your own sounds fun," she said. What kind of tree would he choose?

He nodded and they walked toward the tree forest.

"Why did you stop?" She tried to match his long strides with her shorter ones.

"Stop what?" He slowed his steps.

"Picking your own."

He stuffed his hands in his pockets. "Wasn't in the mood."

Something about the way he set his mouth suggested he had secrets, but he always seemed to react badly when she asked a question. For now, she let it go.

The scent of pine and sawdust filled the air and she inhaled. A hint of his aftershave tickled her nostrils too.

"This place smells delicious." She wasn't talking only about the trees.

He inhaled as well. "Do you do anything like this for Hanukkah?" he asked.

She shook her head. "No, my menorah was passed down to me from my grandparents. I treasure it because of the memories it resurrects."

"Cool."

"They bought it in Israel the first time they visited. We do sometimes make our own candles, though."

"Really?"

"The smell of beeswax always reminds me of the holiday."

"Sometimes the strangest things remind us of our childhood." His voice was low and filled with wonder. Around them, the outdoor sounds were muffled. She wondered what his memories were and if he'd tell her.

He must have decided to keep them to himself because he blinked before he said, "Okay, here we are."

She paused next to Thomas and looked around. To the side was a small shack with a person inside. In front of her, and all around were rows and rows of trees.

Thomas pointed to the shack. "First, we go there. Then we choose whether we want a pine, spruce or fir tree."

"Lead on," she said.

His long strides ate the distance between where they stood on the path and the shack on the edge of the trees. She raced to catch up.

A woman in a sweatshirt and hat sat on a stool behind a makeshift wooden counter. A space heater warmed the inside.

"Hi, do you want to cut your own, or mark it for us to cut?"

Thomas turned to Jessica. "What do you want to do?"

She stuffed her hands in her pockets. "Hey, this is your tree. I'm here to watch."

He thought for a moment before he spoke. "You should get

the full effect." He turned to the woman in the shack and said, "We'll cut our own."

She handed him an axe and a handsaw. "There's a twenty-five-dollar rental fee, which gets subtracted from the cost of your tree when you return the equipment."

He reached into his back pocket for his wallet and, once again, Jessica admired the view. She blinked. She needed to stop that.

Axe and saw in hand, he thanked the woman and led Jessica toward the trees. "I like the Scotch pines over there." He pointed to a line of trees on their right, and they walked over to the correct section of the farm.

"You were right." She looked around. "It's not crowded at all."

"There's a mad rush right after Thanksgiving, a lull during the week, and then it's crazier on weekends."

"What's the difference between the different types of trees?" she asked.

"Shape of the needles, color of the trees, density of the branches. Everyone has their own preferences. There isn't a right or a wrong type of tree."

"What about Charlie Brown trees?"

Raising an eyebrow, he stared at her. "For the price I pay for the trees, I'm not getting a Charlie Brown tree."

"Good thing I don't do Christmas trees. I'd want a Charlie Brown tree."

He chuckled. "What do you think of this one?" He pointed to one about a foot taller than him, making Jessica assume it was around seven feet tall. It was full, with a nice deep green color.

"Looks pretty. Will it fit in your room?"

He walked all around the tree. "Yeah. It's a good shape and symmetrical." He crouched near the trunk. "Looks healthy and sturdy." Rising, he studied the top. "And with the topper, it should be fine. Okay, I think this one is it."

Jessica nodded. "Poor tree. You're going to cut it?"

"Of course. That's why they grew it in the first place. And for each one we cut, they plant three more."

She sighed in relief. "Okay, I feel better." She ran her hands through the clusters of needles. "This has a nice feel to it."

He smiled. "Alright, stand back."

Jessica retreated a few steps and watched while Thomas chopped the tree. Muscles bunching, jacket straining, he couldn't have picked a better activity to show off his handsome body. Forcing herself to drag her gaze away, she scanned the tree farm to see if other men looked like this while felling trees, but there weren't any others she could see. And so, while he took care of the tree, she wondered if pick-ur-own was a known sexy activity among those who celebrate or if she was just the lucky one. Because watching him was almost enough to make her convert.

The tree fell over, he returned the axe and saw, and walked to where she stood, still collecting her thoughts and libido.

"They sell hot chocolate and peppermint cookies in the barn, if you want."

"Does anyone ever say no?"

He grabbed the trunk and dragged the tree behind him as he ushered her toward the barn. "Not yet, but there's always a first time."

She licked her lips. "Not from me!" She turned to look at the tree. "It doesn't get damaged?"

"Nope."

They stopped at Thomas's truck and she helped him load the tree into the bed of the pickup. He shucked his jacket before they headed for the barn and, this time, Jessica couldn't help but stare. His shirt molded to his chest and arms, showing off the muscles she'd watched him use. Whoever said firemen were sexy should win an award for understatement.

"You okay?" he asked, a twinkle in his eye.

Did he realize she was staring at him? Did he know why? Her face burned. She thought she heard him chuckle, but she couldn't be sure. She shook her head to clear it and rushed to catch up to him.

They entered the barn, where the scent of sawdust, cinnamon and peppermint greeted her. She inhaled. "It's a good thing you brought me here on the way out. I might never have left otherwise. In fact, I still might not."

He pointed to a corner where a sleigh was filled with red and white blankets. "You could curl up here if you want."

He had a great sense of humor when she wasn't trying to get him to answer her questions. "Is that a dare?"

"I remember you following me around and trying to show off," he said, his tone nonchalant. "It's not a dare. I'm pointing out a comfortable place for you, in case the seasonal smells overwhelm you and you need a place to land." His mouth twitched.

"Oh my God, I can't believe you." She took a few steps away from him, mouth open. "You saw me?"

His shoulders shook and his face flushed. "Maybe."

She'd been thirteen at the time and Thomas had been hanging out with some of his high school friends in his backyard, throwing the football and grilling. As usual, she'd been smitten and had wanted to see what they'd been doing. She'd climbed one of the trees that bordered the two properties. But in her eagerness to see him, she'd lost her footing and slipped, shrieking as she'd fallen. The branch hadn't been high and all she'd gotten were a few bruises. As she'd laid on the ground catching her breath, she'd prayed none of them had heard her. When no one had run over, she'd assumed she'd been safe.

She'd been wrong.

"I can't believe you didn't say anything," she said. "Or check on me!"

"We did. You were on the ground, and we peeked over to

make sure you weren't hurt. When you got up, we assumed you were fine. We didn't want to embarrass you."

His humor faded to earnestness. "Thirteen-year-old egos are fragile. Once we made sure you were okay, we figured the best thing to do for you was to ignore you."

Why she was embarrassed at twenty-eight about something she'd done seventeen years ago was beyond her. He'd been kind, and he was contrite now. She nodded.

"Those blankets would have been useful," she said.

This time, he nodded. "Come on, let's get you your hot chocolate."

"Yeah, it's the least you can do."

Waiting in line to purchase the hot drinks, Thomas couldn't help but remember all the family times he'd spent here. This place was special, and he'd brought his neighbor. His reporter neighbor, who filled him with emotions he wasn't used to.

The cinnamon must have addled his brain.

Although it wouldn't explain why he'd kissed her last night. Or followed it with a text. In the dark of the previous evening, kissing and texting had been natural. In the light of day, though, his inner demons mocked him. Still, he did his best to exorcise them.

She was more than a neighbor. More than a friend. Although, he wasn't ready to admit it despite his body's reaction to her every time she came near him.

Glancing at Jessica through the corner of his eye, he couldn't help but find her attractive. She'd been awkward as a teenager—hell, he'd been awkward too—but she'd developed into a beautiful woman. Her short, dark hair gleamed. A strong nose and high cheekbones made him unable to look away. Her body was softly rounded, and she smelled amazing.

He groaned. Returning her to the "neighbor" or "friend" box was impossible.

"We can skip the hot chocolate if you want." Jessica misunderstood the reason for his groan.

And despite his conflicting thoughts, he didn't want their time together to end.

"You've never picked a Christmas tree before. You need the entire experience. Plus, I don't want to hear how I deprived you of the treats afterward."

Her grimace gave him a bit of satisfaction. He loved goading her; she gave as good as she got. She kept him on his toes.

And that's why she was dangerous. He kept wanting to say something but refrained because, if she dug too deep, she might find out things he didn't want her to know.

Yet she was fun to be around. She was sexy. And as much as he might think he should keep his distance, he didn't want to. It meant establishing rules, though.

At the front of the line, he ordered their hot chocolates and peppermint cookies.

"You don't have to pay," she said.

He ignored her.

She pulled out her wallet and handed the clerk her card.

"What are you doing?" he asked.

"You did all the work," she continued. "I should at least do something." She bit into her cookie. "Wow, this is good."

The ecstasy on her face made his body tighten and he shifted from one foot to the other. He took a drink of the hot chocolate, burnt his mouth but ignored the pain. "It is."

They took their snacks and brought them to one of the tables nearby. After eating in silence a few moments, Jessica looked at him, her eyes focused, hand grasping her mug of hot chocolate. A bit of powdered sugar dusted her lip and he reached a finger out to wipe it off. Her skin was soft.

So soft.

He leaned forward and kissed her. This time, she reached behind his neck, her hand on his scars, and pulled him closer.

She tasted of chocolate and peppermint and sugar. When he pulled away, he caressed her cheek.

She leaned into him and they remained in that position, breathing each other in. If he could, he'd stay this way forever. But conversations outside made him look up as other people began to enter the barn. He pulled away and she finished the last of her cookie, crumpled the cookie wrapper into a ball, drank her hot chocolate, and rose.

"I'm glad you came with me," he said.

"I'm glad you asked."

They held hands as they walked to his truck and during the ride to his house. He pulled into the driveway, let the truck idle and turned to her.

"Did you enjoy your first Christmas tree picking?"

God, that's lame.

"Today was fun," she said.

"It was. Last night was better." Instead of worrying about all the things that could go wrong, his mind made a list of all the things they could do together. For the first time, hope took hold.

Her cheeks turned pink, making him want to kiss her again. "We haven't argued in three days," she said, changing the subject.

"You're right." He scooted closer to her.

She swallowed and scooted further back.

His hope faded.

"So…any chance you'll let me interview you for the story?"

"No." Maybe it was because he could see her preparation for this question from a mile away, but he wasn't angry she asked.

That is new.

"May I ask why not?"

He took her hand in his. She'd taken off her gloves and her hands were cold. He rubbed them between his own to warm them. "Because it's not something I want to discuss. I've told you."

She didn't pull away. "I need to write this story." Sadness darkened her eyes.

"I'm not stopping you from writing it," he said. He wished there were some other way to make her happy.

"You just won't let me interview you."

"Correct." Her request usually caused tightness in his chest. This time, it didn't. The lack of feeling didn't change his intentions, though.

"If it makes you feel any better, everyone has said you were a hero."

"Everyone is wrong. Which doesn't make me feel better for a lot of reasons." He tried not to scowl.

"Hmm."

He watched her. He could tell she was trying to figure out a way to get what she wanted. She was cute when she was determined. Hell, she was cute regardless.

"Well, at least you were nicer about it this time," she said.

Somehow, they'd lost ground. He didn't want to leave things like this but wasn't sure how to fix it. There were only so many barriers he was willing to dismantle. Part of him was annoyed—at her and himself—but the other part of him was sad. He made one last attempt to reclaim the easy camaraderie they'd shared before.

"Since you've got time off, maybe we can go out again sometime?"

Instead, a mask slipped into place. Her body stiffened. Her jaw clenched.

What had he said wrong?

"Yeah, maybe." Her voice was quiet, but her sadness dulled her eyes. "I'm not sure how much free time I'll have."

Her answer hurt more than he thought it would.

Great job, genius.

"Thanks again." She didn't look at him but opened the door

and slid out of the truck. Before he was able to try to fix anything, she shut the door and walked away.

Jessica hugged her torso as she walked from Thomas's truck to her house, eyes downcast. The more time she spent with him, the more she liked him. Normally, she'd be ecstatic at this chance to be with her childhood crush. But she couldn't only consider her personal feelings. She had a job to do. Without Thomas's point of view, her article would be incomplete. Like her life, if she didn't save her job.

She either had Thomas but no job, or a job but no Thomas.

She loved journalism. Loved talking to people, getting to know them while pursuing the story. She loved the deadlines and the puzzles she needed to solve. She loved asking questions. It might be her favorite part. She'd asked questions since she was able to talk. In fact, the lore in her family was that her first word was "why."

If she didn't get this story right—and by "right," she meant hitting-it-out-of-the-park right—and she lost her job forever, she'd be adrift. She'd be like the menorah that didn't have enough oil to burn for eight days, needing a miracle for it to last.

This story was her miracle. It must be perfect. And it meant all her attention needed to focus on the article. If she couldn't get Thomas to talk, she would figure out something else. All she wanted was to spend more time with him.

Jessica sat at her computer and studied her notes. The fire had started in the basement, where rodents had eaten through electrical wires. It had been an accident. She'd spoken to the fire department and the old man. She still needed to speak to the museum director, as well as the mayor and town council, about the rededication ceremony. It would be easy.

The problem was Thomas. Everyone said he was a hero, but

he insisted he wasn't. She didn't think he was being modest. He wouldn't have been rude when she'd first asked to speak to him if modesty held him back. Although he wasn't the type of guy to brag, she sensed there was something bothering him about the fire. What was the issue?

If everyone said he was a hero, but he insisted he wasn't, maybe he knew something the others didn't.

She possessed investigative skills. It was time to use them.

She called the fire inspector and left a message. She did the same with the EMTs.

She tapped her fingers on her desk. Okay, maybe there was one thing she disliked about her job—the waiting. Patience wasn't her strong suit. It wasn't part of her wardrobe at all.

"I didn't realize you were home."

Jessica jumped at her mother's voice.

"Sorry, didn't mean to startle you. How was Christmas tree shopping? Find any Hanukkah bushes?"

"It was fun, and of course not. But I did discover the most amazing peppermint cookies and hot chocolate."

Her mother smiled. "Ah, you tried the farm's specialty."

"You've eaten them before?"

Her mother nodded. "A long time ago."

"And you didn't share?"

Her mother laughed. "I didn't remember it until you mentioned it now. I'm sorry. But you're right, they're delicious."

"Probably better I didn't know about it," Jessica said. "It could be addicting."

"Oh, yes. Was it crowded?"

"No. Thomas said the weekdays are the best time to get them." She thought about their kiss, relieved no one had witnessed it. "Did you know Thomas cuts his own tree?"

Her mother looked at her like she was crazy. "Isn't it why you went?"

"Yes, but I assumed someone else would cut it." Images

of him wielding the axe and handsaw like a pro flashed in her mind.

"I'm sure they do it for those who need it, but he's a fire-fighter. I'm sure he knows how to use those tools." She looked at Jessica a moment before she continued. "You two seem to be pretty friendly."

Jessica shrugged, not wanting her mother to know how "friendly" they'd gotten. "Like I said, I need to interview him for the article." The words left a bitter taste in her mouth.

"You keep saying that. How's it going?"

"Not well. He won't talk to me about it."

"And yet you went to the tree farm together…"

"We're friends."

"Are you? Is that all?"

"Of course." They'd enjoyed their time together. She'd heard it in the tone of his voice and in his laughter. He'd relaxed around her, and she was learning her childhood crush had turned into a sexy man whose company she enjoyed. And their kisses were…like coming home. She couldn't tell her mother about those, though.

"Be careful," her mother said.

"I'm not a thirteen-year-old girl anymore, Mom."

"I know. And it's for that reason you need to be careful. Relationships are complicated enough when you both come from the same background. Look at your brother and Shelly."

Jessica nodded, though her brother and sister-in-law were different from her and Thomas—if there was a her and Thomas. Brandon and Shelly were married a little over a year, and their relationship wasn't without its challenges. But their relationship had always been rocky. She remembered how much they'd fought in college, and she'd been surprised when they'd gotten engaged. Still, somehow, they made it work.

"You and Thomas come from different backgrounds," her mom continued. "From a religious and social perspective."

Her mother sighed. "There is so much hate and anti-Semitism in the world. Add in all the Jews who were killed in the Holocaust, and the need to maintain the beauty of our religion becomes extra important."

"Mom, don't you think you're jumping the gun a little?" Jessica asked. "We're not dating, and you're talking about marriage."

Her mother pierced her with an imploring stare. "Yes, I am. But I have to, because you need to know what can happen before you start to date." She reached for Jessica's hand. "I'm not saying you can only fall for someone Jewish. My parents enforced that rule, and while I'd prefer it, I won't insist you follow it. We've never been so observant. We didn't expose you to any other cultures or religions. It would be hypocritical for me to forbid you. Not that I could, anyway."

She looked away for a moment before she went on. "I guess I want you to think long and hard about the differences in religion if you plan to pursue anything other than friendship. Add in your need to interview him for your story and…well, it adds more complication. Especially if your actions cause him to question your motives for being friendly."

"Please don't tell me you don't believe guys and girls can be friends." Part of Jessica didn't know why she encouraged this conversation. The other part of her wanted her mother's answer.

"Of course not! You can be friends with whomever you want. But if you think of him as more than a friend, I think you have to make it clear. And have some of the hard conversations early." She kissed the top of Jessica's head and turned toward the door. "But I'm glad you had fun today."

Jessica stared at the doorway of her room after her mom left. That had been the first time her mother had tried to explain her perspective. The child in Jessica wanted to rail against her mom's narrow thinking. But the adult in her understood some of her fears, even if she didn't agree with them. Her mom had been raised with the specter of the Holocaust, and where the need for complete assimilation was real. But it was different for Jessica's generation, even with anti-Semitism on the rise. Her mom didn't mean to be anti anyone else's religion. She was afraid. It had been clear in the trembling of her voice, in her beseeching tone.

She tried to look past her mom's religious argument.

And when she did, she realized her mother had made a good point. While her original goal to soften Thomas so he'd be more amenable to her interviewing him resulted in the beginnings of their friendship, Jessica wasn't a manipulative person. The thought of using him solely to get the story turned her stomach. That was why now, after kissing him, she was uncomfortable. She enjoyed their camaraderie. And she was attracted to him. However, any discussion about a relationship and respecting their different religions was premature. No matter how much her fantasies might develop, they were friends. Nothing more. Because she needed to remain objective for her article.

With a sigh, she called Dr. Nelson again. "I need to work out an issue," she said when her mentor picked up the phone. "Do you have time for coffee?"

Chapter Eight

At eight the next morning, Jessica met Dr. Nelson at the Caffeine Drip, Browerville's popular coffee place. Dr. Nelson was an early riser and, since Jessica's appointment with Caroline was scheduled for later this morning, the timing was perfect.

She tapped the toe of her black leather boot as she stood in line to place her order before she proceeded to a table in the back where Dr. Nelson already sat.

"What's this issue you need to work out?" Dr. Nelson got right to the point. Her mentor leaned forward with anticipation, focused and eager.

Jessica couldn't discuss the issue without coming clean. She picked imaginary lint off the sleeve of her black wool sweater. "First, before I ask for your help, I need to confess something."

The light in Dr. Nelson's gaze dimmed and she morphed from eager accomplice to formal mentor. "Yes?"

"The reason I'm working on this particular article, which is, as you mentioned, outside of my regular beat, is that I'm fighting for my job." She crossed and uncrossed her legs, smoothing her gray slacks.

She briefed the woman on what happened and waited for her response.

Dr. Nelson sipped her coffee before she answered. "I appreciate your telling me the truth. I thought something was off."

"I'm sorry. I was embarrassed. I didn't want to disappoint

you. And when you asked me to talk to your class, I couldn't see myself doing it when I was barely holding on to this chance to get my job back, which is why I hedged."

"And now?"

"I realized I couldn't ask for your advice and dishonor you by not telling you the truth."

Dr. Nelson nodded. "I still think you'd be perfect for my class, but we can get to that later. Now that I know everything, what do you want my help with?"

Jessica exhaled. "It's difficult to balance my growing feelings for my interview subject with my need to be objective, and I'm afraid I'm being manipulative, which is the last thing I want to be."

Dr. Nelson's lips twitched.

"It's not funny," Jessica said.

"Oh, I'm aware. But I was thinking it's a good thing I know what a bright and articulate student you were, because your sentence…" She shook her head. "Okay, back to business."

"Fine, maybe it was a little funny. But do you understand my dilemma?"

Dr. Nelson folded her hands on the table. "The role of a journalist is unique. Ideally, you want to tell your story in an objective manner—just the facts. But it can be tricky, as you're learning."

"Thomas has been reluctant to talk to me about the fire. I thought if I befriended him, he'd be more comfortable. But as I get to know him better, I find I care about him. Do I pursue the story and maybe hurt him, or do I give up and stick to the personal side?"

"You have to decide what you want, Jessica."

Jessica rested her chin in her hand. "Ugh, I hate the idea of putting a man above my career. I'm too independent."

"I don't know if that's what you're doing. If you don't like the way your editor is making you attack the story, then you're within your rights—from a journalistic integrity standpoint—to object. It has nothing to do with choosing a man over a career."

For the first time, Jessica's mood eased. "What if I give up too soon, though? And what if I don't get my job back?"

"Only you can decide. I can't help you with that. As for your job? It's a concern. But you're smart and any news organization would be thrilled to have you, as would many other employers. It might take you some time to find the right fit, but if you have the luxury of a support system behind you, you may be able to be choosy. I'd suggest you take it one step at a time. First, decide if you want to pursue this article and how far you'll go for it. Then figure out your next steps."

Jessica warmed her cold hands on the coffee mug. "You know, when I was a student, I couldn't wait to be finished with school and out in the world. And since I'm there, I'm starting to wonder why I was eager to leave."

Dr. Nelson smiled. "I think your generation says 'adulting is hard.'"

"We do, and it is!" She dropped her head onto the table before lifting it up again. "Why didn't you warn me?"

Dr. Nelson shook her head. "I doubt you would have believed me if I'd told you."

"What would you do if you were me?"

"That's not the way this works, Jessica. You have to make the decision yourself." She reached across the table and patted Jessica's hand. "But I have faith in you. You'll make the right decision for yourself. You've gotten this far. Now, about your visit to my class…"

Jessica exhaled. "Yes, I'll do it." She pulled out her phone and calendar app. "When is good for you?"

"We have availability this Friday at ten. Does it work for you?"

Her breath caught in her throat. Three days from now? "You're sure this is a good idea?"

Dr. Nelson put on her stern face; the one she'd used with Jessica any time she'd been unsure of herself. "They need to know about challenges too. I think you can do this."

"Okay, I'll be there." She'd deal with the butterflies later.

"Excellent. I look forward to seeing you."

Jessica still thought about Dr. Nelson's words when she pulled into the JCC's parking lot later that morning. She stopped at the reception desk but before she had a chance to ask for Caroline, her friend stepped off the elevator.

"Perfect timing." Caroline walked over and gave her a hug. "Come with me."

Jessica followed her friend behind reception toward the senior center.

"This is the part of the foyer I want to decorate with the seniors. The entire lobby will have some Hanukkah decorations, but since this area leads to the center, I want it to reflect this year's theme of community."

Jessica looked around. "Since when do we make such a splash for a minor holiday?"

"After those anti-Semitic events at the temple and Aaron's deli, the town pushed for inclusion, education and acceptance. The senior center entered the contest, and I thought our theme would resonate."

Jessica smiled. "I like it! There is a lot you can do with the theme too. I think the seniors will love it."

"I know, right? They were more than happy to help out."

"Alright," Jessica said. "Will you stick to traditional blue and white for your color scheme?"

Caroline nodded. "Yes, but I want to add silver and gold too. Give it a little sparkle."

The two women walked around the space, measured the windows, made note of the width of the walking areas, and pointed out surfaces they could decorate with menorahs and gelt.

Jessica stood before a bulletin board filled with daily schedules and events.

"What about asking people to bring photos from their childhood celebrations?" she asked.

Caroline's eyes widened. "Great idea!" She punched notes into her phone. "You're awesome."

"Thanks," Jessica said. "And if you'd like, I could interview any of the interested seniors about their memories from Hanukkah celebrations in years past. You could keep an oral history and play it during Hanukkah."

"I could design an entire program around it. Jessica, it's brilliant! How soon can you start?"

"Tomorrow, if you want. I can be here from nine to eleven and interview as many people as are available. I wish getting Thomas Carville to open up to me was as easy." She bit her lip. She hadn't meant to say that.

"Uh-oh. What's wrong?"

"He refuses to discuss what happened. We get along great when we do anything other than talk about the fire. As soon as I mention it, he clams up."

"Wait, what other things are you doing together?"

Jessica described their Christmas tree excursion, leaving out their kisses. "It was fun, until the end."

"Do you like him?" Caroline asked.

Jessica frowned. "Of course, I like him. Why?"

"No, I mean *like* him. Because you have a look when you talk about him."

Jessica paused. Her mom, and now Caroline, were both focused on her feelings for Thomas. What were those feelings? She was attracted to him, of course. It's why she'd kissed him. He'd gotten better looking with age. He was smart, easy to be with, and had a great sense of humor. The more she saw him as an adult, the more interested she was in the whole person. And she liked the whole person.

"I enjoy my time with him. We have fun together, and he's sexy as sin. We kissed."

At Caroline's gasp, Jessica told her about their kisses. "But, more? It hasn't been long enough." Maybe not, but her senses were heightened when she was with the man, and conversations with him were easy.

"I'm glad to see you happy again. And kissing him? Wow. What about the whole religion angle? Or is it too soon to consider?"

Jessica retreated a step. "I think it's premature, although I admit it's something we'll have to address if things keep going as is." Her cheeks heated. Dating Thomas had always been on her mind, and to pretend otherwise wasn't a good look. However, she couldn't do anything if he were the subject of her story.

Caroline nodded. "You're right, it's early. As far as I'm concerned, if you're happy, I'm happy." Caroline hugged her.

Jessica gave her a quick hug. "Thank you. I appreciate it." Since she'd never dated much, dating outside her religion wasn't something she'd worried about in the past. Now? She was an adult, free to make her own decisions. And while she'd love to be with someone Jewish, she wouldn't turn someone away strictly because of his religion.

Caroline looked once again at her phone. "I have to go to work. I have a class to teach in twenty minutes. You'll be here tomorrow—and let's get together this weekend?"

"Definitely."

After saying goodbye to Caroline, she drove to the library to research the history of the Browerville Museum, but her mind was on Caroline's comments. Of their group of friends, Jessica was the least observant. She loved her religion and celebrated the holidays, but it didn't inform every aspect of her life. If anything, it was more of a culture thing for her. While her parents might stress marrying someone Jewish, she wanted to focus on someone who was compatible with her. Their religion wasn't as important.

She swallowed as she pulled into the library parking lot. If things ever came to that with Thomas, she wasn't looking forward to the conversation she'd have to have with her parents.

With a groan, she got out of the car and turned her focus to her job.

A gray stone building near the main street of town, the library was stately and old. Inside, Jessica inhaled the scents of books, ink and dust. No matter how easy it was to find things on the internet, she loved going to the physical library as often as possible. She'd come here every weekend as a child, and the place was full of memories. In New York City, she met friends for lunch and in nice weather picnicked on the front steps of the New York Public Library or in Bryant Park behind it. She and her friends always made sure to take a trip inside afterward and explore.

Approaching the information desk off to the side near the entrance, she asked about the local history section and was directed to the second floor. Her feet padded up the forest-green-carpeted stairs as she jogged toward the correct section. Once there, she browsed the shelves, pulling out building records and architectural information. Armed with what she needed, she sat at one of the maple tables and paged through the booklets, jotting notes as she went along. Even if her story wasn't the investigative piece she was used to, she loved research.

Browerville, incorporated before the Revolutionary War, was steeped in history. George Washington and his troops had once stayed here. The Browerville Museum itself had ties to the underground railroad and the town once been home to a famous activist for women's voting rights.

The more Jessica learned, the more fascinated she became.

When she finished, she pulled her computer out of her bag and went to the museum's website. The place housed a collection of artifacts from the Revolutionary War, the Civil War and the early 1900s. Most of them had survived the fire, though the building had been damaged. She searched for the museum curator's name, found her email, and sent her a note asking to speak to her. She hoped the woman would respond soon.

In the meantime, she was free. It was weird to be free in the middle of the afternoon. She still hadn't acclimated to life without the rush of deadlines. She packed her bag and returned the books. Needing some fresh air, she decided to walk through town. Her favorite part of Browerville was the diversity of its people and celebrations.

Even without the excitement of a contest, the town was decorated for winter with extra greenery and snowflakes hanging from the trees in the main square. Asian restaurants advertised the traditional foods for the Dongzhi Festival— the Winter Solstice Festival. Many stores in town displayed decorations for Christmas, Hanukkah and Kwanzaa. Indian businesses and restaurants had hung multicolored lights for their recent celebration of Diwali. Overall, the town was celebratory and festive.

She window-shopped, looking out for Hanukkah presents for her family. They didn't give eight nights of presents, and hadn't since she was little, but they did exchange gifts on the first night. This year was the first year she'd be home for the holiday in a while, and although she hated the reason for her being here, she looked forward to celebrating with her parents.

Inside Tea Towels and Trinkets, she scanned the aisles of the cooking and gift shop, looking for something for her mom as the aromas of cinnamon and spice swirled around her. She paused in the hostess gift section and admired the bottles of fancy olive oil and homemade vinegars. At one time, she would have considered them as a gift for her boss, but now? She didn't want to look like she was begging for her job, nor was she in the mood to provide the woman any additional holiday cheer.

She bit her lip, unhappy with the bitter thoughts that flowed into her brain. With a mental shake, she resolved not to let the situation depress her.

Smiling, she sifted through the plethora of dish towels with seasonal themes and matching potholders. Snowflakes, candy canes, latkes and cute sayings tempted her, but her mom probably owned enough of them.

"Can I help you find anything?" the salesman asked.

Jessica turned to the tall man with tightly coiled hair. "I need a Hanukkah gift for my mom. Something not too Hanukkah-y, if that makes sense."

The man gave her a thumbs-up. "Skip the latke-making sets and the dreidel sculptures."

"Not that I don't love them," she said. "I love so much in this store. But I want something for my mom she can use all the time, not only for eight days."

He led her across the store. "I'm glad you love this place," he said. "It's mine. And I know what you mean. Does your mom like to cook?"

Jessica raised a brow. "Did I mention we're Jewish?"

"It just means she'll arrest you if there's not enough food. It doesn't mean she likes cooking."

"You get it."

He nodded. "I might not be Jewish, but my mom's love language is food, so, yes, I get it."

"To answer your question, yes, she likes to cook. Although she doesn't do it as much as she used to."

"Okay, what about this snack set?"

He showed her a set of stacked ceramic snack bowls, each one a different color with flowers and birds painted on the sides. "A local artist makes them, they're dishwasher safe, and can be for snacks or to hold ingredients while she cooks."

"They're beautiful! She'll love them."

With a knowing smile, he grabbed a set of four and brought them to the front counter. As Jessica paid, he wrapped them for her.

"Thank you," she said. "I'll be sure to return."

"Happy Hanukkah," he said with a wave.

On the street, her phone rang and, as if her thoughts had conjured her up, it was her mother.

"Hi, what's up?" she asked.

"Any chance you can grab potatoes and onions for me for latkes? I want to make them early so I can get the oil smell out of the house, and it will be warm enough this weekend for me to open the windows."

Jessica loved latkes but hated the oil smell. "Great idea. Sure, I can pick them up. And I'll help cook if you want."

"Sounds good."

She said goodbye and banged into a body. Her phone fell out of her hand, but she clutched her bag tighter so it wouldn't fall too. The body knelt to retrieve her phone.

Thomas. Looking sexy as hell in his usual blue jeans and an Arizona sweatshirt.

"Sorry." She wished she could stay in his arms and disappear for a while.

"My fault." His deep voice bore a trace of humor. "I wasn't looking where I was going."

He handed her phone to her. "No worse for wear, I don't think."

She looked at it. It was a little dusty, but otherwise fine. "Thank goodness. Doing anything interesting?"

"I went to a meeting," he said. "You?"

"I met with Dr. Nelson from school, then my friend Caroline to help her with decorations at the JCC. I researched my article, and now I'm Hanukkah shopping." Why she'd told him that, she didn't know, since too many specifics would make him shut down again. Maybe it was the shock of banging into rock-hard muscles.

"You have a lot of shopping for eight days." He looked at her bag.

If he wondered about her research, he didn't bite. "No, we don't do eight days of gifts. At least, not anymore. How about you? Have you started your Christmas shopping yet?"

"It's also why I'm here." He pulled out his phone and showed her the list in his notes app.

"Whoa, that's long," she said. "I'd better not hold you up."

He shuffled from one foot to the other. "It's been a while since we all celebrated together. I don't mind."

"You don't always celebrate Christmas with your family?" She carried this Norman Rockwell vision in her mind of entire families gathered around the Christmas tree, singing carols and opening presents.

His expression saddened. "Not for a while. But we'll make up for it this year."

She probably shouldn't ask what was different about this year, at least not in the middle of the sidewalk.

She sidestepped around him, ready to continue on her way.

"Mind if I join you?" he asked.

Once again, the thirteen-year-old inside her cheered while the adult part of her filled with conflict.

"Sure." They walked along the sidewalk. "I researched the Browerville Museum earlier," she said. "It was fascinating. They have artifacts from the Revolutionary War and the Underground Railroad."

"Uh-huh."

"We're lucky they didn't burn in the fire. I can't wait to see them at the ceremony."

"Umph."

On the scale of reactions to a journalist, she supposed grunts were better than curses. But she wanted more.

"Did you ever visit the museum?" she asked. "I seem to recall a field trip there in elementary school, but I don't remember much about it. Do you?"

Was it her imagination or did he sigh? And if he did, was it a good sigh or a bad sigh?

"My fourth-grade class with Mrs. Hamm went there," he said. "The only thing I remember about it was running around outside before and after. At the time, I wasn't into history."

"And now?"

"Now I can't seem to get away from it."

He couldn't blame anyone but himself for her array of questions. He'd asked to join her because she'd looked happy, and after she'd left his truck looking sad, he'd wanted to see the joy in her again. Being around her lightened him. That, and she looked adorable in her winter hat and coat. Her cheeks were red, her eyes sparkled, and he was a goner.

Now, he wished he was gone. Anywhere but here. Because she was asking questions again.

"Get away from what?" she asked.

He'd just returned from his AA meeting where one of the other people had spoken about confronting their past. It had made him think and realize he needed to confront his as well. But if he answered her question, told her about his past, what was to stop her from printing it for all to see?

"Some things I'm not proud of." He hoped manners, or recognizing they were in public, or a brain blip, would make her stop asking questions.

She looked sideways at him, and he held his breath.

"We all have those moments in our past, I think. The key is to learn from our mistakes and not repeat them. And, maybe, to forgive ourselves."

He scoffed. "Easier said than done."

"All the good things are."

There was a pause, and he weighed whether or not to continue this line of conversation.

As if trying to give him an out, she changed the subject. "Speaking of good things," she said, "I want to run in here to see if they have anything for my dad."

It was a men's clothing store; a place where he often shopped. He followed her inside, and while she looked for a gift for her dad, he looked at clothes for his own father. A few sweaters caught his eye and he grabbed two.

Jessica held two flannel shirts. He walked over to her.

"Which do you think my dad would like better?" she asked.

It seemed like an intimate question, the kind you'd ask a boyfriend or spouse. He wasn't, either. But he knew her dad, having lived next door to the man for his entire life. He looked at the green-striped shirt and the denim-colored one.

"They're both nice."

She frowned. "Ugh, you're not helpful. I'll get the green. That way he can wear it with jeans."

"Why can't he wear the other one with jeans?"

"He can, but he has to be careful what color jeans he's wearing."

"He does?"

She hadn't heard him, or if she had, she wasn't bothering to answer, instead walking toward the checkout counter at the back of the store. He followed her.

She paid for her gift, requested a box, and moved aside so he could check out.

"Would you like a box?" the saleswoman asked.

He nodded. "Please."

He handed her his credit card.

"You're the fireman who saved the elderly man, aren't you?"

Shit. It had happened more than nine months ago. Why the hell was she bringing it up now?

"Just doing my job."

He hoped she'd drop it, but luck was against him today.

"That was way more than your job, that was heroic," the saleswoman gushed. "You put your life on the line for a stranger. Not many people would do what you did. I hope we'll see you at the ribbon-cutting celebration. They're giving you such a nice award. You must be proud."

He mumbled his thanks as she handed him his bag, not making eye contact. His stomach churned and he rushed outside.

On the sidewalk, he gulped in large amounts of air, ready to forfeit the rest of the day and retreat to his house alone.

A hand on his elbow made him pause and he spun around. Jessica.

"Are you okay? What happened in there?" she asked.

The last thing he wanted was to deal with her questions. Now. Ever.

"I wish you'd talk to me about why you're dead set against this award. Maybe discussing it would help you."

His pulse pounded in his ears. Why couldn't everyone leave him alone?

"I don't want to talk about it, to you or to anyone." He tried to keep his voice from carrying on the wind to the people who walked along the street. "This is my business, no one else's."

Unable to stay in one place any longer, he turned and stalked away.

Jessica watched Thomas's retreating figure and burned with frustration. No matter how she phrased it, no matter how much concern she showed him, he still wouldn't answer her. This time, she hadn't tried to interview him. She'd showed concern for him. Her professional side hated that she couldn't get him to answer her questions. Her personal side, however, sympathized with him. There were things she didn't want to discuss, either. The difference was that she was a reporter and needed his information for her story. Her growing feelings for him, though, made it harder for her to demand he answer her. Plus, she was starting to think it was her turn to apologize. Or at least to make sure he was okay. It was one thing to ask objective questions. That was her job. It was an intrusion, though, to suggest his talking to her might help him overcome whatever bothered him. They didn't have the relationship, and she'd overstepped.

She still needed to shop for Hanukkah, but her enjoyment fled. She planned to buy gifts for Sarah and Caroline, but she'd never find the right thing if her heart wasn't in it. Turning around, she walked to her car, the chill in the air that had once invigorated her now left her cold. She shivered, jacked up the heat, and drove home.

Thomas's truck sat in the driveway. Had she ruined his day too?

Her parents weren't home, so she hid their presents in her bedroom closet, squared her shoulders, and prepared to own up to her mistakes.

She walked over to Thomas's house and knocked on the door. He didn't answer. She knocked again. As she was about to knock a third time, he swung the door open, his face hardened in anger.

"I told you I didn't want to talk to you."

He started to close the door, but she swung her arm and pushed it open. His surprise was the reason she'd succeeded.

"I'm not here to talk to you," she said. "I'm here to apologize."

The only change in his expression was a quick frown before Thomas smoothed his features into a mask. But his tight grip on the door belied his fake calm. His wide shoulders and broad chest blocked the doorway. In her imagination, she hadn't pictured apologizing on the porch. Heck, she hadn't imagined any details of what she'd say other than a broad outline of what would happen. She'd show up, he'd hear her out, all would be forgiven, and he'd agree to talk to her. Well, maybe not the last part.

But he didn't seem amenable to hearing her out, based on his posture. In fact, while she'd stood there, he'd edged the door closer and closer to being shut in her face.

She took a step forward to prevent the door from moving again. His breath was loud, like his anger was physical. She met his gaze and waited for his response. His glare sharpened right before he opened his mouth.

"I don't need you to apologize."

"Yes, you do."

His mask slipped.

"Why?"

"Because apologies are important to you. You apologized to me when you were rude."

"You weren't rude."

She rested a foot on the threshold. "True, but I assumed a level of trust that wasn't there. I tried to force you to confide in me to make yourself feel better, and I shouldn't have done so. I'm sorry."

She tucked a curl behind her ear, and his eyes tracked her move. All of a sudden, the space between them became charged.

He swallowed, his Adam's apple bobbing. "You think you know me," he said, his voice low.

She nodded.

"And you'll use the knowledge to get me to agree to an interview."

"No." She'd considered it at first. But that wasn't the kind of reporter she wanted to be, which was why she was there to apologize. "I won't."

"Prove it."

His expression was hard, his body tight.

She stepped forward, until there was an inch of space between them, stood on tiptoe, and kissed him.

He inhaled in surprise.

"I don't kiss my interview subjects."

He grabbed her with one arm, drew her against his chest and returned the kiss times ten. A hundred. A million.

Clasping her arms around his waist, she leaned into him while he ravaged her mouth, nipping and licking and plunging inside with his tongue. Kissing him was like riding a roller coaster. She hung on, enjoying the feel of his lips on hers. His grip was tight, his body hard, and all her childhood fantasies disappeared.

Reality was better.

But as she raised her arms to stroke the back of his shoulders, he pulled away.

Panting.

"You won't interview me now?"

She blinked, trying to marshal her thoughts and sound coherent.

"Right now, no. I'm still processing your kiss."

He lifted her chin and stroked her cheek. "You started it." His eyes crinkled as he smiled.

"I'm good with that," she said.

"Me too."

"Do you want to come in?" This time, he swung the door wide. Reggie raced over, wagging his tail.

"Might be a bad look if I kiss and run." She stepped over the threshold and gave the dog a pat on the head.

His chuckle was warm as he put an arm around her. He closed the door, bent his head and kissed her again. But this time, he took his time. She melted into him as they explored each other's mouths. Their tongues wrestled for control, and she looped her fingers around his belt loops, her fingers skimming his jeans. His whiskers pricked the skin around her mouth, but his lips were soft. She sighed. He skimmed his hands down her body and behind her knees, lifting her so they were chest to chest. She wrapped her legs around his waist as they deepened the kiss, getting to know each other by touch and mouth and breath. Just as she was sure she couldn't take any more, he pulled away and rested his forehead against hers. Now they both were panting. She ran her fingers along his neck and over his close-shorn hair, studying him by feel.

"Is this real?" she asked.

"What do you mean?"

"Or is this one of my fantasies and I'll wake and be thirteen again."

His eyes widened. "God, I hope not!"

She hummed, and he kissed her again before letting her slide down his body to the ground. With feet planted on the floor, he hugged her to him before retreating a few steps.

"We should talk," she said.

He nodded. Taking her hand, he led her into his living room. They sat on opposite ends of the couch, facing each other.

"To be clear," she said, "I still want an interview with you for my story, but I didn't kiss you in order to get it. It's two separate things."

He raised an eyebrow. "You can do that?"

"Yes. And if you won't agree, I'll respect your wishes."

He nodded. "So where do we go from here? I'm attracted to you, but I'm not ready for a relationship."

She didn't believe in relationships, although a small part of her jolted at his honesty. "I don't want one."

"No expectations, no pressure…"

"Just fun," she said.

"Fun is good."

"Fun is good," she responded.

He reached for her neck and pulled her closer to him. Their

mouths came together and his hands roved her body, lighting a trail of fire beneath his fingers. He growled as she slipped her hands beneath his shirt, eager to feel the warmth of his skin. A small part of her brain registered she was with Thomas Carville, her childhood crush, but the rest of her couldn't do anything other than feel—his body, his breath, his presence.

His tongue plundered her mouth and took away her air. He pulled her onto his lap and pressed her core against his hardness. They moved fast, and she didn't want to stop. Stopping meant thinking, and Jessica was tired.

She gripped the sides of his face and arched her back, their bodies rocking against each other. Moving his hands to her backside, he held her in place. Heat surrounded her. She tugged at his shirt. With a groan, he pulled away long enough to yank his shirt over his head. She did the same with hers, and they paused to stare at each other. As he ran a finger beneath the lace of her bra, she stared at the scars that ran from his neck over his shoulders. But his fingers teased her, making it hard to do anything other than react to his touch. She arched against him, her breath stuttering.

"That's it, baby, that's what I want," he whispered, his hands at her waist and his mouth at her ear.

His knuckles pressed against her stomach as he opened the front of her gray pants. She writhed beneath his touch and grabbed for his belt. Together, they stripped each other of their remaining clothes, keeping their mouths together, like some kind of sexy reality challenge. Stripped naked, they collapsed to the floor, ignoring rug burns and table corners and thinking only of how to become one.

Where Thomas got a condom, Jessica didn't know, but when the foil packet crinkled as he opened it, she breathed a sigh of relief, wiggling against him, thinking of the release she wanted. He dropped it, and his swears mingled with hers.

Jessica reached between them and stroked him. His skin

was soft, but he was hard, and, oh, how she wanted him inside her.

He hissed at her touch, but gentled his response with kisses, running his thumbs over her breasts and making her shudder.

"I need you inside me, now," she said. Her voice was a mixture of pleading and demanding. She'd never been a big fan of begging, but she'd never been with Thomas.

After what seemed like twelve thousand years, he rose above her. His eyes homed in on hers, drew her in and made it impossible for her to do anything but look at him.

"Are you ready?" he asked.

She nodded.

"I need you to tell me, Jess."

Jess. What a wonderful sound coming from such a man.

"Yes," she said.

He plunged inside her. Not too hard, for she was ready for him—begging for him—but harder than she'd expected. But once inside, he stopped.

"Sorry," he said. "Did I hurt you?"

"No," she said. She arched her back, needing him deeper, not wanting him to stop.

With a nod, he entered further, until there was no space between them, until they were one person, one need. Her body clenched around him. His breath roughened. Together, they climbed, reaching for the peak just out of reach, until—

He touched her, and she shattered. With a cry, she tumbled over the precipice, blinding light sparking behind her eyelids. His climax followed with a roar. They held on, riding the waves of release until they were spent. Their harsh breathing eased, their damp limbs dried, but he remained locked together with her, as if he didn't want to break whatever bond they'd formed.

Without energy to much more than lie in his arms, she ran

her fingers through his hair, marveling at the attainment of her teenaged dreams.

She'd had sex with Thomas Carville, and it was amazing. When her friends heard…but no, she didn't want to say anything to anyone. Not right now. This was hers to savor without risking exposure to the reality that her well-meaning friends might present.

"Fun without responsibility, right?" Thomas whispered.

"Right." Her response was immediate.

She settled into him and, rather than push her away, he held her close.

"It was more than fun, though," he said. "It was amazing."

As she basked in his praise, and in the afterglow, a part of her wondered how long this "fun" would last.

Chapter Nine

Thomas woke the next day, grabbed Reggie's leash, and took him for a walk. The streets were quiet at six in the morning, and it was cold. But he liked the alone time to gather his thoughts.

And today, Jessica consumed those thoughts. Her kiss had surprised the hell out of him. Once he'd tasted her, he couldn't stop. For a few moments, while he'd disappeared into her smell and her sighs and the way her body fit against his, all his cares had disappeared.

He'd kissed her again, for real, unable to get enough of her. It had taken all of his willpower to remind himself and her—his neighbor whom he'd known since he was a kid—their relationship was pure fun and nothing else. Because when he'd closed his eyes and let himself feel, he hadn't been kissing his neighbor. He hadn't been having no-strings-attached sex. He'd been with the sexiest woman he'd ever known, and was loathe to let her go.

She wasn't his type. Not only was she literally the girl next door, but she was smaller and rounder than the women he was attracted to. Her hair was short and dark, not the long red or blonde tresses he typically preferred. But two kisses, and she was perfect. And after sex? Indescribable.

How was it possible?

His body craved her more than he'd ever craved the alcohol that had consumed his attention these last few years. It should have scared him, but it didn't. Because being close to her, kissing her, having sex with her, settled him.

Okay, *that* scared him.

The old him would have run as far away as possible from her. But he didn't want to run. He wanted to pursue her, to get to know her better. He wanted to learn everything there was to know about her.

He'd never felt this way about anyone before.

He pulled up short. Reggie turned his head and look at him. "Sorry, Reg."

Reggie wagged his tail and they continued to walk.

Maybe she didn't feel the same way as he did. Maybe sex had done the opposite for her, made her realize her childhood crush was over and exorcised all her desire.

His sponsor would accuse him of being dramatic.

Jessica responded to him as feverishly as he did to her. He'd been with enough women to recognize the signs, and she was into him. Still.

But she won't be when she learns your secrets.

He groaned at the voice of reason in his mind. This time, Reggie turned around and nudged Thomas's knee with his snout.

"It's okay, Reg. I'm too hard on myself." As usual.

She was looking for fun. God, how long had it been since he'd had fun? A year? Three? More?

Firefighting was fun. Until the stress had gotten to him and he'd turned to alcohol for relief. That had also been fun…until it hadn't been. He'd gone into recovery, and no one with any sense thought *that* was fun, although he was grateful for the push and his success. And now? He was sober, he followed a routine, but he wasn't having fun.

If he were honest with himself, he needed to take the next step: figure out what kind of job he would do, since he was done with firefighting. The chief's suggestion to apply to the fire academy as an instructor intrigued him. But would they want him? An alcoholic? Was it different from being an actual firefighter, something he refused to do? The chief could keep his resignation letter in her desk for as long as she wanted. He wasn't changing his mind.

He also wasn't changing his mind about talking to Jessica. Well, he'd talk to her, but not about her article. That subject was off limits.

Again, his blood pressure started to rise when he thought about his job, but thoughts of Jessica brought it right down again—until they'd started to kiss.

He smiled to himself.

At home, he fed Reggie and then, a surprising feat for himself, he answered the latest text from Ricky.

Hey, yeah, I'm good. Busy.

He wasn't an asshole, even if he didn't want to get involved with the guys. And answering the occasional text was the least he could do.

Finished, he went outside to decorate for the contest. As he hung red and green lights along the roofline of his house, he stole glances over at his neighbors'. No signs of life yet from Jessica's. Well, they hadn't left the house, at least. They might be awake. He looked at his watch. Eight thirty. He'd wait until ten and go over. Whistling, he went to work.

At ten minutes to ten, Jessica stepped outside and he tightened his grip so as not to drop the string of lights he was fastening over the garage. Wearing jeans and a navy parka, hands around a cup of coffee, she looked cold. He wanted to warm her up.

Whoa. Had it been that long since he'd been with someone? As she'd said yesterday, they were "having fun." Although

he didn't know how long she was home—he should find out—
she did live in the city. Whatever they did was temporary.

He descended the ladder and strode over to her. "You look
like you're freezing," he said. "Come inside before you catch
a cold."

She raised an eyebrow at him. "Good morning to you too."

"Good morning. Now get inside." He herded her toward his
house, not satisfied until she was inside where it was warm.

"I see you're not much for conversation in the morning,"
she said.

"There's plenty of time for conversation when I don't have
to worry you'll freeze to death."

"I have a coat, unlike you who has been outside in a sweatshirt since the sun rose."

She'd noticed him outside. He didn't know what to think.
He pushed it to the recesses of his mind and continued. "I'm
larger than you. I don't get cold as fast."

Her expression was a combination of amusement and disbelief. He also ignored it. But when she tapped her fingers,
he questioned her. "What?"

"You said we'd have a conversation once we were inside.
Well—" she gestured around the room "—we're inside."

"Good morning," he said.

"That's better. Why were you outside this early?"

"Reggie needed his walk and breakfast."

"What about you?"

"What about me?"

"Did you eat breakfast?"

It had been a long time since anyone had asked about his
welfare, disregarding, of course, people's concerns about his
drinking. Although he used to hate those questions, he found
he didn't mind Jessica's.

"I didn't."

She put her coffee cup on the table where he kept his car

keys, unzipped and removed her jacket, and walked into his kitchen. She opened his fridge and took out a container of eggs before she opened cabinets and drawers.

Leaning against the doorway, he watched her, arms crossed. "Why do we always end up in my kitchen?"

"You like food?"

"I like you too."

Her cheeks reddened, and satisfaction warmed him.

"You need to eat breakfast before we do anything else."

"We're doing something else? Good to know."

With a backward glance, she scoffed. "You're impossible. How do you like your eggs?"

"I'm partial to ones with asparagus, tomatoes, parmesan, Monterey Jack, bacon and spices."

"Perfect. Scrambled eggs coming up."

She stood at his stove, scrambling eggs. The pan sizzled and a buttery aroma filled the kitchen. Their most memorable conversations were in the kitchen. It was as if all their differences slid away, and here, in the heart of the home, they found their rhythm.

He sat at the table while she served him eggs and orange juice. Then she sat while he ate. The silence between them stretched. But not uncomfortably. It was a companionable silence. When he'd eaten with the guys at the firehouse, there was always the background noise of the TV, people chewing and razzing each other, and the alarms in the middle of a meal. But here, with her, it was quiet.

When he finished, she rose, took his empty plate and cup, and put them in the sink before she joined him once again at the table.

He didn't like her across the table from him. He wanted her closer.

"Come here," he said.

She looked at him quizzically.

"Please."

"There you go! I knew food would help." With a smirk, she came around to his side of the table.

He pulled her into his lap. Now, all was right with his world.

They sat there, again in silence, for a minute. He listened to her breath, felt her heartbeat against his chest. Her hair was soft against his cheek. He breathed in her floral scent.

"This is new," she said, her voice soft.

"This is nice." He rested his hands on her hips, giving her the chance to move but hoping she wouldn't.

"Is nice the same as fun?"

"It could be." He waited, and when she didn't make a move to leave, he exhaled.

"Shall we try this again?" she asked. "Good morning."

He liked her sass. "Good morning. What are your plans today?"

"I have to do some work—"

"How about we don't talk about that?"

She twisted her torso around to look at him. "You asked."

"What else?"

She blinked like she was processing what he'd said and how to answer. "I promised Caroline I'd interview her seniors for a Hanukkah program. And then, more decorating."

"How about something fun?"

"You said this was fun."

"It is, but at some point, one of us will have to stand up. How about we go do something fun?"

"Are you trying to prevent me from beating you in the contest? You know, by distracting me."

He pretended to consider it. "No, but now that you mention it…"

She elbowed him in the ribs.

"Oof, you've got pointy elbows."

"What's your plan? Or did my pointy elbows jab it out of you?"

"We never did finish our shopping. And it's trivia night at the diner. How about we go around three, shop, and end at the diner?"

"It will give me time to work and decorate."

"It's a date," he said.

He felt her inhale, a deep one, like the windup before a pitch, and he braced himself for what came next. But she exhaled, nice and long and slow, and she nodded and slid off his lap.

She turned to him. "I'll see you later."

"I'll pick you up," he said as she walked to the front door.

He worked on getting the inside of his house organized in preparation for his family visiting. He had a few weeks and while the house didn't need to be perfect, it did need to be livable and festive. But all the while, he looked forward to this afternoon. He kept checking the time and running different scenarios in his mind. Did she like trivia? Was she any good? He wasn't worried about their conversations. They hadn't run out of topics, or dealt with uncomfortable lulls yet.

By the time three o'clock came around, his palms were sweaty, and he rubbed them on his jeans-clad thighs as he exited his truck and walked to Jessica's front door. Her dad answered his knock.

"Hey, Thomas, how are you?"

"Doing okay, you?"

"Not bad, not bad. What can I do for you?"

"I'm here to pick up Jessica."

Her father's look of surprise disappeared as Jessica jogged downstairs and greeted him. Thomas' blue-plaid shirt peeked out from his jacket.

"Hi, Thomas. Dad, I'm going out. I'll be back later tonight."

"You look pretty," her dad said.

She covered her white sweater with her winter coat and stuffed her ID into the pocket of her jeans. "Thanks."

"So, we shouldn't hold dinner?"

"No, you and Mom have the place to yourselves."

Her father smiled, but it didn't reach his eyes. "Have fun," he said, a thoughtful look on his face.

"You didn't have to come to the door, you know," she said as they walked to Thomas's truck.

"I said I'd pick you up, and I'm not about to honk the horn at you."

He opened the door for her. "Such service," she said as she climbed inside.

He jogged around the cab, already energized by her.

"Should we park on the main town green and walk along Main Street, or do you have a particular store in mind?"

Jessica looked at the cloudy sky. "It's not that cold, let's walk."

"Tell me about your interviews," Thomas said.

Jessica's gaze sharpened and he was drawn to her. "It was great. I asked them to tell me about their favorite Hanukkah traditions from their childhoods. Some of them talked about food, some about their family members. They all possessed such interesting memories."

"And what are you doing with the information?"

"Caroline is putting together a cookbook and an exhibit with photographs and Hanukkah memorabilia from the past. That way, it's more than just decorations, and it makes it more personal for the seniors who live and go to activities there."

Thomas nodded. "Sounds great. I know my parents and grandparents always reminisced about Christmases past, and I loved looking at photographs from their childhoods. In fact, my mom preserved an entire box filled with handmade decorations through generations of our family."

Walking with her and talking about making the holidays

meaningful made him excited to spend Christmas with his family. He looked at Jessica and wished she could spend it with them too.

The thought should have disturbed him. He barely knew her. Except, the more time he spent with her, the more comfortable she made him. It felt like they'd moved past the "first getting to know you" stage.

Should he ask her to come over for Christmas? It was too soon.

As they strolled the holiday sidewalks, Thomas pointed to various stores and places he'd worked or played as a kid.

"Sweets for the Sweet candy store has been around forever," he commented. "I was one of Helen's Hooligans."

Jessica paused at the window. "I'm sorry, what?"

"I loved the candy store when I was a kid, and one day, Helen, the owner, accused me of shoplifting. She called my parents and they came in, and when she realized her mistake, she apologized. I think I was about seven. Years later, when I was looking for a job, I stopped at her store and she hired me, along with a few other teens. What I found out after I'd worked there a few weeks was that the other kids had all shoplifted from her and that, after they'd repaid her, she'd hired them in hopes they'd turn their life around."

Jessica's eyes widened. "That is the craziest thing I've ever heard. Although, my friends and I always called her Crazy Helen because of the glares she'd give us whenever we shopped there."

"I think she assumed everyone under twenty-one was a shoplifter."

"And potential sales help."

"Want to go inside? I can get some candy for my nieces and nephews."

Inside, the store looked as it had his entire life. Barrels of candy filled the center and dispensers lined the walls. The place smelled of sugar and looked like a rainbow. Helen, wearing thick glasses, with her hair dyed an orangey-purple, stood behind the counter.

He grabbed several bags and filled them with assorted candy.

"Hi, Helen." He approached the counter. It had been years since he'd been in the store. "I'm Thomas Carville. Remember me?"

"Of course, I do. You were one of my hooligans, although not really." She winked.

He grinned. "You're right." He put his sacks of candy on the counter. "These are stocking stuffers for my nieces and nephews."

She bent over and examined the candy close up. "Good choices," she said.

He turned to Jessica. "Anything you want?"

Jessica shook her head. "No, I'm good. And Sarah and Caroline would kill me if I gave them candy."

"What's your favorite kind?" Helen asked.

"Peppermint drops," she said. "Our rabbi used to hand them out at Hebrew school."

Helen toddled out from behind the counter and scooped some into a bag. "For old times." She handed them to her. "No charge."

"That's nice of you," she said. She popped one in her mouth. "Yum."

Outside on the sidewalk, Thomas walked next to her. "I would have sworn you'd say chocolate."

"There's something about peppermint drops that I love."

They continued on their way.

"How long are you in town for, by the way?" Thomas asked.

Jessica clenched her jaw and faced forward.

She turned to him. "I thought we weren't discussing my article."

"We're not."

"I don't think we should discuss anything related to my work, at least right now."

Weird. He was the one who didn't want to talk about the article, but his question concerned vacation time, not her article. Regardless, he decided not to quibble because he didn't want to mess up their agreement. He liked spending time with her when they weren't fighting. He nodded.

Jessica pointed to a workout store and they entered. "I want to get Caroline her gift. Can you hold these?" She handed him her candy.

He followed her around the store as she browsed through workout clothes, finally deciding on a mint-green top and leggings with a gray and mint-green pattern. She held them up.

"These are cute, right?"

She was. He loved her looks, but when she raised her chin, he realized he'd been silent and staring too long.

"Yeah, sure."

She rolled her eyes. "Never mind. I'll get them."

"What? I said they were."

"It's not what you said, it's how you said it."

He'd never understand women, but he was wise enough not to say anything. Instead, he stood with her while she paid for her purchase.

"You don't want to get it wrapped?"

"They don't have Hanukkah paper. I'll wrap it myself at home."

He looked behind the counter and noticed the wrapping paper. All of it was red and green.

"I never thought of it before," he said. "I should have."

"I wouldn't expect you to consider whether or not a store has Hanukkah paper. It has no effect on you."

"Well…" He didn't know what to say, so he remained silent.

After stopping in several more stores where they each purchased additional gifts for people, Thomas's stomach grumbled.

Jessica glanced his way. "Is that the dinner bell?"

"Only if you're ready to eat. I can manage a few more stores." He placed his hand on his stomach as it rumbled again.

"I think we'd better get you fed, otherwise you might not be up for trivia later. I wouldn't want to give you any excuses for losing."

"Already with the trash talk? Seems a little premature."

Her eyes danced with merriment. God, he could banter with her all day and never get enough.

"I want to make sure you put your best foot forward," she said.

"So kind," he replied. He loaded their packages into his truck before he opened the door for her.

Once they were settled, he drove them to the diner. It was the same place where he met his sponsor, but she didn't know, and he saw no reason to enlighten her. He'd seen the ads for trivia nights during one of his meetings with Carl and filed the information away for future use.

"Confession time," he said as he pulled into a spot on the side of the building.

She turned in her seat.

"I've never attended a trivia night."

"Me neither," she said. "Caro, Sarah and I talk about going, but we haven't made it yet. I didn't know they held them here," she said as she got out of the pickup. "I've heard of them at bars."

Same for him, which is why he'd been happy to see one offered here. He wasn't ready to spend several hours in a bar. Not yet anyway.

He ushered her inside and upstairs to where trivia night was held. The hostess outside the large room suggested a small table in the front, which was fine by him. They sat and opened the menu.

"There's a lot to choose from. I love diners," Jessica said from behind the menu.

It was large. He couldn't see her behind it.

"I love the idea of breakfast for dinner. When I was a kid, my mom used to dedicate one day a month to that at home." He savored the memory of him, his brothers and sisters, and his parents eating pancakes and waffles for dinner. He remembered how he'd covered his pancakes with enough syrup to float a boat, while his sister had hogged the powdered sugar.

"Sounds fun," Jessica said. "We didn't do that, but every Shavuot—another Jewish holiday—my mom let my brother and me have ice cream for dinner. It's a holiday where you eat dairy meals. It was her way of marking the occasion." She leaned forward. "My favorite holiday, obviously."

"Sounds great to me."

The waitress appeared and they placed their orders. Thomas ordered pancakes with bacon and a side of scrambled eggs. Jessica ordered the French toast.

"And to drink?" the waitress asked. "Soft drinks, beer, wine…"

"I'd order wine, but it doesn't go with my dinner," Jessica said. "I'll have water."

"We also have mimosas if you'd like," the waitress said.

"Oh, yes. Perfect. Thank you."

"Soda for me," Thomas said. He shifted a little in his seat. He and his sponsor had discussed how to order drinks with others, but this was the first time he'd done it on a date. He hoped Jessica wouldn't comment.

By some miracle, she didn't. Or maybe it wasn't as big a deal to her as it was to him. Either way, when she spoke about anything other than his drink order, he was relieved.

"Are we on the same team, or are we playing against each other?" she asked.

"I guess it depends on how competitive you are," he said. "We're already competing against each other with our holiday decorations."

"True. Maybe we should try the same team this time."

His heart warmed at the idea, though it was a game.

The waitress returned with their meals, and the trivia host walked to the dais at the front of the room.

"Okay, everyone. Welcome to Trivia Night. I'm your host, DJ Mark, and we're about ready to get started. Get your teams together now." He passed out answer sheets and pencils.

Jessica picked up the sheet. "What's our team's name?"

Thomas was terrible at creative ideas. "I think it should be your choice," he said.

Her eyes sparkled. "How about Crush."

His shoulders shook with silent laughter. "Sounds good to me."

DJ Mark took the microphone. "Alright, ladies and gentlemen. Our first round will be the 80s—Fads, Fashion and Trends. Are you ready?"

Music played in the background. Thomas smiled. "My dad played this song. Do you know it?"

Jessica shook her head.

"It's 'You Spin Me Round' by Dead or Alive," he told her. He moved in time to the music and made Jessica laugh. It was the best sound ever.

"First question," DJ Mark announced. "What fashion trend did Crocket and Tubbs on *Miami Vice* popularize?"

Jessica leaned forward. "Oh, I know this! Didn't they wear pastel T-shirts under their Italian leather jackets, and shoes without socks with their white pants?"

"Yeah, I think so," Thomas said. "How do you know?"

She smiled as she wrote their answer. "Because whenever

my dad wore loafers without socks, my mom teased him about how he looked like Sonny Crocket."

"Good one."

"Question two," DJ Mark said. "Which name was not in the top ten of baby boy names in 1981? Jason, Isaac, Joshua or Daniel?"

"Well that's specific," Jessica said. "I have no idea. Do you?"

Thomas shook his head. "Try Jason."

She wrote it on the paper.

"Question three," DJ Mark said. "Which 1983 movie inspired the fashion trend of leg warmers, tights and cut-off sweatshirts?"

"Fashion question is yours," Thomas said.

"Ugh. I want to say either *Flashdance* or *Footloose*," she said. "Let's go with *Footloose*."

The music switched and Jessica straightened. "My aunt loved 'Enola Gay' by OMD. I remember she played it in the car whenever we went out together with my cousins."

"Question four," DJ Mark said. "Which fitness guru contributed to the aerobics craze and was also known for Deal-A-Meal and *Sweatin' to the Oldies*? Richard Simmons, Denise Austin, Jane Fonda or Jack LaLanne?"

"I think we're the wrong age for these questions," Thomas said.

"Should we call our parents?" Jessica asked.

"And admit we don't know anything? No way. What's your guess?"

"I think Richard Simmons?"

"Okay, I'll agree," he said. He'd agree with whatever she said to make her happy. The thought terrified him, but he wasn't about to change anything. Not now.

"Question five," DJ Mark proclaimed. "Poison and Guns 'n' Roses influenced which fashion trend? Hair Bands, Punk Rock, New Wave or Grunge?"

"Oh, I know this," Thomas said. "Hair Bands."

Jessica wrote the answer. "Guess I'm not the only one into fashion," she said with a smirk.

"Shush." He winked.

"Question six," said DJ Mark. "Which popular car sign was made in the mid-80s to encourage safe driving?"

"Car sign?" Thomas asked.

"Oh, wait, what about Baby on Board?" Jessica asked.

He nodded. "Yeah, might work."

"Question seven." DJ Mark switched the music again. "'Don't hate me because I'm beautiful' was the slogan for what beauty product?"

"I have no idea," Jessica said, "but I like this song, whatever it is."

"We have to write something," Thomas said. "What's a beauty brand?"

"I don't know. Pantene? Was that around in the eighties?"

"Who knows? Let's try it," he said.

"Question eight," DJ Mark continued. "Violence at the post office in 1983 led to what phrase?"

"Going postal," said Thomas. "Easy."

"Question nine," DJ Mark said. "In 1985, Princess Diana of Wales danced with what American celebrity at the White House?"

"John Travolta."

Thomas and Jessica glanced at each other as they said the answer at the same time. He loved how they were on the same wavelength. She wrote down the actor's name, and he waited for the next question.

"We're getting better at this," he said.

"Maybe."

"And finally, question ten," said DJ Mark. "Which couch-jumping celebrity starred in *Risky Business* in 1983?"

Once again, they answered at the same time. "Tom Cruise."

Jessica handed Thomas their answer card. "Check it to make sure there's nothing you want to change."

He didn't want to change anything. Not the card, not tonight, not Jessica. But he scanned the card, just to listen to her. Handing it to her, he nodded.

"Okay, everyone," DJ Mark said. "Hand in your cards."

Jessica rose and Thomas watched her walk across the room, admiring her stride and the way her leather pants hugged her butt. When she returned, the DJ read out the answers.

"Answer number one. Pastel T-shirts, white linen pants, sockless loafers and Italian leather jackets."

Jessica's face beamed like a kid's on Christmas Day. "We got it!"

If it was how she'd look for every correct answer, Thomas wanted to hit it out of the park.

"Answer number two. Isaac."

Thomas' stomach dropped at Jessica's look of disappointment. "It's okay," he said. "There are plenty more answers to get right."

And, to his relief, they got seven of the next eight questions right.

"We make a great team," Jessica said.

His heart swelled. They'd worked together and done well. She was right. They were a team. His stomach rumbled and he jumped in surprise.

"I was focused on the game and forgot to eat," he said. "I don't think it's ever happened to me before."

"Whoa, I don't know whether to be impressed or to laugh at you," Jessica said.

"I think you should be impressed. It will tide me over until the nutrients kick in," he said as he took a forkful of pancakes.

Jessica burst out laughing. "Too late," she said when she'd calmed.

"All right everyone," DJ Mark said. "After Round One, the

scoreboard is as follows. In first place, we have The Bro Code. In second place, Crush. And in third place, the Legal Eagles. We'll take a five-minute break before we move on to Round Two."

He played a Bruce Springsteen song and Thomas turned to Jessica. "Second place. We did pretty well."

"I know, considering I didn't think I knew anything about the 80s. I hope Round Two isn't some crazy topic I know nothing about."

"I'm sure you know more than you realize," he said. They chatted about their favorite sports teams—she was a football fan while he liked hockey—movies they'd loved—he liked horror while she preferred thrillers—and concerts they'd attended—they'd both seen Drake and Post Malone. The more they talked, the more comfortable Thomas was around her.

"Time to start the second round," DJ Mark announced. "Are you ready? This round's topic will be theme songs. I'll play a ten-second clip, you'll write the movie or TV show it's from."

Jessica's eyes widened, the green irises like reflecting pools.

Thomas jerked. He could get lost in them if he let himself.

"This will be fun," Jessica said.

They whispered to each other for the next five minutes as they determined the ten TV shows and movies the theme songs were from. After submitting their answer sheets, they waited for the DJ to announce the correct answers.

Thomas's anticipation grew as DJ Mark replayed each song snippet and indicated the name of the show. He let out a whoop at the end. "We got them all right."

He pulled Jessica to him and planted a kiss on her lips. It was instinctual, but Jessica didn't seem to mind. If anything, she held him close when he would have pulled away. After a few seconds, they both came up for air. Her mouth was red, her chest rising and falling quicker than before.

"We did great," she whispered.

He didn't think she meant the trivia contest.

"Yes, we did." He certainly wasn't talking about the contest.

"In first place is Crush," the DJ announced. "Second place is Oldie but Goodie, and third place is The Bro Code. Last round will be in fifteen minutes." This time, he played the theme songs in full to fill the silence.

But there was no silence between Thomas and Jessica. Every time they spoke, he learned new things about her. Some, because she told him. Her favorite color was yellow, her dad had fostered her love of football, and she'd always loved writing. Others, because her emotions showed on her face. Especially when she spoke about writing. Her expression was guarded, like there was something she didn't want to discuss. He understood that better than anyone.

Didn't mean he wasn't curious, though.

"It's time for our last round," DJ Mark declared. "This round will be brain teasers. Are you ready? This time I'll tell you all of them, give you five minutes to solve, and ring the bell."

Jessica wrote down the ten teasers. Thomas knew a few of them right away, but most of them he'd have to think about. DJ Mark started the timer, and Thomas and Jessica huddled together to solve the teasers. Of the ones he didn't know, Jessica knew three. It left them four to work out together.

"Oh, I got it!" she cried with ten seconds left. She scribbled the answer and the timer beeped.

"Nice one," Thomas said.

She bumped his shoulder. "We do well together," she said.

He nodded. They did. If he possessed confidence in his ability to manage a relationship, she'd be the one he'd choose. He wasn't sure he was ready.

He turned in their answer sheet, and DJ Mark announced the answers. They waited for the rankings.

"In first place is Crush," he said.

Thomas didn't hear the rest because he whooped and grabbed Jessica in a hug. Pressed against him, she was soft and warm. He pulled away, pulse racing in his ears. But they were in the middle of a diner, and he wasn't about to embarrass her.

"Do you want to go get our prize?" he asked.

She left and returned with an envelope. They opened it together.

"It's a twenty-five-dollar gift card," she said.

"Nice. I guess we'll have to go out again to use it." He watched her for a reaction and her smile was all the encouragement he needed. This time, he kissed her longer and deeper than before, pulling her close and breathing her in. But once again, they separated before he was ready.

"Ready to go?" he asked.

She nodded, and he paid their check and walked Jessica to his truck. He held open the door for her, and when she turned toward him, he backed her against the side of the truck, tipped her chin up, and kissed her lips. Kissed her the way he'd wanted to inside. Their bodies flush against each other, his arms around her waist, hers finding their place on him. Her hands settled in his back pockets. Her scent and touch enveloped him. He hardened. He kissed along her jaw and behind her ear, and she shivered against him. The column of her neck was long and pale in the glow of the parking lot lights. She made a sound deep in her throat, and he returned to her lips, tasting them, nipping them, before swirling his tongue inside her mouth. She tasted like maple syrup and sugar. He wanted to pull her closer.

"Wait," she whispered.

He stopped, his world off kilter from desire.

She stroked his cheek. "What are we doing?"

"Having fun," he said. "Like we said."

She opened her mouth as if to respond, but closed it and nodded.

"Are you not?" he asked. "If I misread the signals, tell me." His heart dropped.

"No, you didn't misread my signals. I don't know why I asked the question."

He retreated a step to let her breathe. "Maybe you got nervous?" He got nervous all the time.

Her expression eased. "Yeah, maybe. I don't know why."

"You don't have to know. I'll stop and you set the speed. Okay?"

She nodded and he held the door wider so she could climb in. No matter how much he might want to continue, he wouldn't push her out of her comfort zone.

He kind of liked being the confident one at the moment. Whether his confidence was due to her or to his own self-awareness, he wasn't sure. Whatever the reason, he didn't want to do anything to destroy it.

Jessica was too busy enjoying herself to give much thought to Thomas or her feelings for him. But as he reversed out of her driveway, she stood in the doorway and reflected on the past several hours. She'd meant what she'd said to him. If he didn't want to talk to her, she wouldn't force the issue. If it made her a bad journalist, so be it. All thoughts of her job disappeared after five minutes with him. She liked him. He was patient and kind, and sexy as hell. He made her pulse race and her face heat in the most delicious way. She liked spending time with him, listening to his stories. And his kisses? Wow. Her body still hummed every time she thought about them. She'd melted into him, he'd clutched her to him as if he were afraid she'd disappear, and their tongues had danced the hora, complete with music running through her brain. Her legs wobbled, and she sat on the bottom step in the foyer, reliving their kiss. Warm, firm, bone-melting.

"Ugh!" She shouldn't think of Thomas that way... He was the forbidden older crush from her childhood. He wasn't Jewish. And she wasn't staying here. Their lives were too different. She needed to remember they were having fun, which meant enjoying herself when they were together but not thinking about him when they were apart.

No matter how amazing his kisses were.

"There you are," her mother said from behind her. "I thought I heard you come inside."

Jessica turned. "I didn't mean to disturb you."

"You didn't. Where'd you go?"

"Thomas and I went shopping and to trivia night at the diner."

"You've spent a lot of time together."

Her mom's tone was neutral, but Jessica's hackles rose. "I need to interview him for my article."

Her mother smirked. "And trivia night helped you?"

"It was fun." She hoped her mom wouldn't see any reaction in her expression.

"Well, you seem to be having a lot of fun with him."

"I am. Is that a problem?" The last thing she wanted to do was to argue with her mom, but maybe it was time to get this issue out in the open.

"Fun is good. I hope you're careful." Her mom clasped her hands together, whitening her knuckles.

"Careful how?" Jessica's mind flashed to when she'd started high school and her dad had explained the need to be "careful" around the senior boys. Surely, her mother wouldn't repeat that cautionary tale.

"He's older than you are."

Apparently, she was. "I'm not a kid anymore, Mom. A four-year age gap isn't significant enough to be a problem."

However, as the words left her lips, she recognized the argument she'd made to herself when she'd first come home and noticed how attractive Thomas was. But from her mother, it sounded ridiculous. Who cared how old they were? They were both adults.

"True, but you're at different stages of your lives. He's settled here, you're in the city…"

Was she? If she truly lost her job, she wouldn't be settled anywhere. And Browerville was only forty-five minutes from New York. "You're settled here, with me in the city, and I still see you," she said. "Besides, it's nothing serious."

"It's for the better, since he's not Jewish."

And there was the crux of her mother's issue. Jessica's jaw dropped. Although she'd suspected it, hearing the words voiced out loud jarred her. "Mom, I can't believe you'd have an issue with his religion. Our family has never been religious. You socialized with his parents. How can you dislike him because he's Christian?"

"He and his family have been our neighbors for years, and they're wonderful people. I don't dislike him because of his religion."

Her mom's face was pinched. "There are enough conflicts between two people who come from the same background. When you add in a different religion, you add a lot more problems. Are you ready?"

"Or you create solutions that enable you to lead by example. Haven't you always taught us that?"

Her mother sighed and picked at lint on her trousers. "Yes, of course. It's…difficult, especially with all the hate there is in the world right now, against us, to risk extra conflict."

Jessica paused. She wanted to yell at her mother for narrow-mindedness and fear. But at the same time, she couldn't. Because the anti-Semitism she'd seen and experienced was real, and she understood some of the fear. But it didn't mean she planned to hide under a rock and never have anything to do with non-Jews. If anything, it galvanized her to get more involved with people of other cultures and religions and economic backgrounds. Because the only way to fight hate was with love.

She wished she could make her point to her mother. But she'd been raised in a different time, and if Jessica had this discussion, she needed to be prepared. Maybe it was time to talk to the rabbi. In the meantime, she needed to tell her mother something.

"I think you're way ahead of yourself. All we're doing is having fun. We're not serious."

"This is the time you need to consider things before you become serious and someone gets hurt."

She needed to meet with the rabbi—soon. "I won't get hurt, Mom. I promise."

Instead of continuing the argument, her mom stared at her. The seconds ticked by and Jessica braced herself for something. But whatever her mother thought—if she thought anything at all—she kept it to herself and kissed her forehead. "Please be careful."

Jessica exhaled, grateful for the temporary reprieve. "I will."

Her mom went upstairs and left Jessica to think about Thomas once again. But this time, the reasons she'd thought of earlier, the ones that prevented them from getting together, seemed superficial, especially after her mother had voiced them. She climbed the stairs to her room and planned to make time in her schedule to meet with the rabbi.

She and Thomas were having fun. There was nothing wrong with it. They were both adults, and neither one would get hurt. She was determined to enjoy herself with the sexy subject of her article. And after it was written, well, she'd worry later.

* * *

The next day, the lawn displays she'd ordered arrived and she and her dad went outside to arrange them. She admired the design.

"Looks good," her dad said. "I have to admit, I didn't think I'd like them, but I do. You know," he said, his voice filled with amusement, "if this journalism gig doesn't work out, you could always be a decorator."

Jessica's stomach lurched at her father's words. The pleasure she'd gotten from decorating disappeared. She tried to smile at him, but suspected it wasn't successful.

"Thanks, Dad. I'm glad you like it."

Her dad kissed her and went into the house. Jessica wandered the yard, lost. She had three days until the museum re-dedication and awards ceremony. She wasn't used to inactivity and it bothered her. Usually, she chased leads, wrote copy, researched. But there was nothing left to do except cover the ceremony and talk to Thomas.

She texted her friends. Meet for lunch?

Sarah responded right away. If we can make it at one, yes. Aaron's?

Works for me, Caroline texted.

See you there! Jessica responded.

Feeling a little better, she looked over toward Thomas's house and wondered what he was up to. Could she walk over and knock on his door? Would it be weird? Yes. But if she went home, she'd have to deal with her mother, and worse, her mother would have talked to her father by now, and he'd have additional reasons why she and Thomas should "be careful." They had turned this into something bigger than it needed to be, and the more they protested, the more she needed to defend him.

"Argh!"

"Problem?"

The sound of Thomas's voice made her jump.

"What are you doing here?" Fun together didn't include an ability for him to read her mind, did it? Because it was creepy and unfair.

"I live here."

Bewilderment changed to understanding. She'd wandered onto his property.

"I was distracted."

"Thinking about anyone I know?" His voice was tinged with humor.

"Everyone who will lose to my amazing decorating skills."

She stared at his neck as he looked over her shoulder at her front yard. He'd nicked it shaving. Her gaze traveled lower to where the burn scars peeked above the collar of his shirt and over his jawline to the curve of his ear. She blinked at the sound of his voice and forced herself to pay attention.

"—unfair of you," he said. "How do you know you'll win?"

"I didn't make it this far without confidence," she said.

His admiring glance made her blush.

"I think your parents get some of the credit."

She scowled. "Okay, fine."

"Uh-oh, problem?"

She shook her head. "I don't think they realize I'm old enough to make my own decisions."

"It's what happens when you come home. How long are you here, by the way?"

"It's a little up in the air right now." She'd avoided an answer the last time he'd asked.

"Flexibility must be nice."

That was one way of looking at it. But if she told him about the precariousness of her job, he might think she was trying to get him to talk to her. "Unless they're going to continue to give me advice on my personal life, in which case it will be a super short visit."

He leaned forward. "What kind of advice? Always carry a condom on you?"

"No, but that's a good one. They're way ahead of themselves, with how different you and I are, and warning me about the difficulty different religions can present."

"What?" He looked incredulous.

"I know, right? There's no need to worry. Next thing you know, they'll ask me which religion we'll raise our kids in!"

"Tell them Wiccan to get a reaction."

She clapped. "Perfect."

He ran a hand over his hair. "I can't believe they're worried about that. Imagine if they knew I was an alcoholic."

Jessica whipped around at the same time Thomas's eyes grew wide. For a minute, time stood still, like the long pause in the synagogue after the last blast of the shofar sounded. The air grew heavy. In the space, fear, shock, horror and embarrassment flashed across his face. And then nothing.

"Thomas?"

Her pulse pounded in her ears. One part of her was in shock. The other tried not to say anything she'd regret. But a million questions floated through her mind.

He raised his chin and straightened his posture.

"Can we talk about this?" she asked.

This wasn't a conversation two neighbors could have on the border of their property. It wasn't something two people "having fun" together should have, either. But it was out there, and it needed to be addressed. Except, he was silent.

Finally, he broke the silence. "No."

She wished he hadn't. "Thomas."

"It's my private life, Jessica. I don't want to discuss it with anyone. Not even you."

She wanted to argue with him. To remind him he was the one who'd brought it up, who'd mentioned it in the first place. To find out what had happened. Her reporter instincts were on high alert. But her humanity fought for control. He hadn't meant to say anything, and she didn't want to embarrass him.

But it was too late.

His neck and face were red. He looked past her. To an outsider, it looked as if he studied her lawn ornaments. She knew better, though.

"It's okay, Thomas. There's nothing to be ashamed about."

He spun on her and his eyes flashed. "I don't need your pity or your advice. In fact, I don't want to talk to you at all."

He stormed off, leaving Jessica in the middle of their yards, alone.

"My parents are freaking out over my interfaith wedding, Dr. Nelson wants to sing my undeserved journalism praises to the world, and Thomas won't talk to me, which kind of makes my parents' concerns moot, but there you have it." Jessica flopped onto the chair at a corner table in Isaacson's Deli and gave a dramatic sigh.

Caroline and Sarah exchanged worried glances.

"Uh-oh," Sarah said.

"Want to give us the more realistic version?" Caroline asked.

"Yes, but first I need to get food," Jessica said.

The three of them walked to the counter and placed their orders, brought their food to their table and got themselves settled.

"Okay, tell us what happened, without the drama," Sarah said.

"Well, first of all, both of my parents are concerned about my relationship with Thomas because he's not Jewish."

"Is that a concern you share?" Sarah asked. "And how worried are they?"

"Look, I get it," Jessica said. "After the Holocaust, most Jews worried about intermarriage and losing more Jews, but today? Many intermarriages are successful, and there is much more freedom when it comes to celebrating different religions. As for me, I've dated lots of Jewish men and haven't found anyone I clicked with. It's not to say I wouldn't click with anyone Jewish, but if I find someone I fall for, and he doesn't happen to be Jewish, I'm not sure I'm against it. I'm not sure I *should* be against it."

The more she thought about Thomas, the more Jessica pictured the two of them together. Even if she fought against it at the same time.

"So, do you see yourself with Thomas? Are you two moving that fast?" Caroline asked.

Jessica shrugged. "I like him. When we're not fighting about my article, which is the only disagreement we've had, we click. He's talked to me about Hanukkah and I've talked to him about Christmas."

"Are you serious about him?" Sarah asked.

"It hasn't been long enough to be serious," Jessica said.

Caroline raised an eyebrow. "There's no time limit when it comes to being serious. If you care for him, you need to consider what's important to you. If you don't mind dating someone who isn't Jewish, you need to have a discussion with your parents and explain your point of view. You're old enough to make your own decisions about intermarriage."

"Intermarriage! We're barely dating."

"Have you talked to Thomas?" Sarah asked.

They hadn't discussed it. In fact, the only relationship thing they'd discussed was keeping it fun. Fun was what Jessica had wanted at first. Or thought she'd wanted. But the more time she spent with Thomas, the less interested in a no-strings relationship she became. And wasn't that the perfect example of a person planning and God laughing. Not that she was so religious to think God would take the time to laugh at her. However, everyone needed a good laugh now and then, and she was adding to God's fodder.

A more disturbing thought entered her mind. Her parents might be right, though *not* about not dating someone who wasn't Jewish. Although her Judaism was important to her, she'd never wanted to eliminate an entire group of people based on religion. No, her parents were right about the complications someone of another religion added to the relationship.

If Thomas wanted a relationship with her.

Gah!

She was also going crazy having an entire conversation in her mind when her friends were sitting right there.

She focused her attention on them. Worried looks flashed across their faces.

"I'm not sure what happened there," Caroline said, "but you looked possessed."

"If I believed in exorcism, I'd have called for one," Sarah agreed. "You moved your hands and your eyes and your mouth. It's like you had a conversation with someone who only you could see."

Jessica's face heated. "Sorry, not intentional."

"As in, you couldn't help it?" Caroline asked. "Maybe I should call a doctor instead."

"Of course, you shouldn't." Jessica reached for her can of soda.

Sarah beat her to it. "You sure caffeine is a good idea? I'm not sure your brain needs any more boosts of energy right this second."

"Ouch, that's mean." Jessica held her hand out for her can of diet Coke.

Sarah gave it to her, and Jessica took a gulp. The fizz refreshed her, and her thoughts crystallized.

"I was playing in my mind a whole bunch of things."

"Like?" Caroline asked.

"Like, I think I do want a relationship with Thomas." Saying it out loud made her realize the truth of the words. And for the first time, the idea of a relationship didn't scare her or fill her with dread.

Now her friends looked at each other with smiles.

"I knew it was a matter of time," Sarah said.

"No one gets over a crush like that when they meet the person in real life," Caroline added.

Jessica took another bite of her bagel sandwich. "Don't get excited. We talked about not wanting one. And after…" She couldn't betray his secret. "Well…after our argument today, I don't know if he wants one with me. Plus, he hates journalists."

"What will you do about your article?" Sarah asked.

Now she pushed her plate away. "I don't know."

"For what it's worth," Sarah said, "you shouldn't have to sacrifice your morals or make yourself uncomfortable for your job."

Caroline nodded. "You might want to think about how far you want to push Thomas, and what you're willing to risk," Caroline added.

"I know." Sarah rested her chin in her hands. All she had done was make a mess of her life. Her friends were right.

"Okay, wait, back to the relationship topic please," Caroline said. "What made you two argue?"

Jessica bit her lip. "I can't tell you. It's not that I don't love you two, and I trust you to keep my secrets, but this one isn't mine. It's his. And he didn't want to tell me. It slipped out."

Sarah reached across the table and squeezed Jessica's arm. "It's okay. I understand."

"Me too," Caroline said.

Exhaling, Jessica nodded. "Thank you."

"Other than the argument, did he say anything else?" Caroline asked.

"No, he stared at me—or rather, glared—and walked away. I didn't have time to let him know his secret was safe with me or give him my reaction to it or anything."

"Have you tried to call or text him?" Sarah asked.

She picked at her bagel and tore it into little pieces rather than bite into it as usual. Her stomach was revolting against food and her brain was trying to process all the information. Sadness, confusion and sympathy battled each other. Aaron was lucky she didn't vomit his delicious bagel concoction on the linoleum floor. Or she was—she didn't think he'd forgive her for making a mess and scaring away customers, even if she was his girlfriend's best friend.

"I did. Several times. My calls go straight to voicemail and my texts show delivered but not read. I don't know what to do." She groaned. "Why couldn't I have fallen for an easy guy with no drama?"

"You tried and decided relationships weren't for you," Caroline said.

"I always thought it was odd you said you wanted to elope," Sarah added.

"You know me. I'm not into drama or gossip or any of that stuff," Jessica said.

The other women shook their heads. "Maybe he's not into it, either," Caroline said.

Sarah added. "I guess it'll be complicated, though, keeping your personal and professional lives separate. Are you sure you can? Come to think of it, why can't you write the article without him? Don't you have all the information you need?"

Caroline nodded. "Yeah, couldn't it focus on the museum itself and not on his rescue?"

"I think it will seem odd, since there's an award ceremony I'm supposed to cover." Jessica pulled up short. Bile rose in her throat. Did she want to write this story? If she could get Thomas to agree to a relationship, did she want to risk it and pursue the story? And regardless of their relationship, she didn't want to expose his alcoholism. It wasn't the kind of reporter she wanted to be. How could she get out of covering the story?

"You have a look," Sarah said. "What are you thinking?"

Before Jessica had a chance to answer, Sarah's roommate, Emily, approached their table.

"Hey, girls, what's up?"

"Emily, you're home!" Caroline rose from her seat and gave her a hug. "How was your trip?"

Sarah pulled another chair over for her roommate and Emily sank into it with a sigh. "Chicago was crazy. I had no time to do anything other than work the entire time. But they gave me the rest of the week off. Maybe we can all catch up?"

They all nodded before Sarah looked at her watch. "Yes, to catching up, but I've got to run off to work now. See you tonight, Em!"

"Me too," Caroline said. "I've got a class to teach."

Emily turned to Jessica. "What's new with you? How long are you home for?"

Jessica filled her in on her job, but left out most of the Thomas information. Although Emily was a close friend, something prevented Jessica from telling her everything.

"You and Thomas?" Emily elbowed Jessica. "He's stunning. How lucky are you to talk to him for your story."

Jessica's skin heated. She tried to avoid Emily's gaze, but her friend reached across the table and poked her.

"I haven't yet decided if it's luck or the universe is playing one big fat joke on me, but you're right, he's stunning." Her heart rate increased as she thought about him.

Emily frowned. "I admire the way you're able to compartmentalize work and play. My company won't let us date other employees because of all the issues it can cause."

"Well, as I told Caro and Sarah, there's no relationship at the moment, no matter how much I might want one. If and when the time comes, I'll let you know how good at compart-mentalizing I am."

Emily scoffed. "Don't brush off the compliment. There aren't a lot of people I admire."

"Thank you. I appreciate it."

"Besides," Emily said, "you haven't talked about your personal life, or anyone in it, for a long time. I think it's great you and Thomas might be a thing."

Emily was right. It had been a long time since she'd been with a guy in any meaningful way.

"Thanks. I'm glad you're home, but I've got to go to work," Jessica said. She rose and gave Emily a hug. "I've missed you. Are you here for Christmas?"

Emily nodded. "I don't travel again until January. Let's make sure to all get together before you leave."

"Definitely."

Chapter Ten

Crap. Of all the people to tell he was an alcoholic, he'd picked the one person who could ruin his life. Thomas pounded another nail into the wall before berating himself for his carelessness. He examined the drywall to make sure he hadn't cracked it and then added crown molding, this time in a much gentler fashion. But underneath it all, he fumed.

He hadn't meant to blurt out what he'd said. Her mom's reaction to his not being Jewish had surprised him, and it popped out. Did all Jewish people feel this way or was it her mom? He'd never know now because he couldn't talk to Jessica again. She was a reporter, here to cover a story about him, and he was forced to give her the silent treatment.

Damn it.

It didn't matter how attracted he was to her, or how much he enjoyed her company. It didn't matter that she was the first woman in a long time he'd started to feel close to. He needed to forget his feelings for her and move on.

Giving up hammering, since he was afraid he'd do more damage than good, he pulled out the boxes of decorations. The first box he opened was his mom's collection of the homemade ornaments he and his brothers and sister had made as children. The handprints made him smile. His hand now engulfed the entire ornament. He remembered his mother's joy-filled face when he'd given it to her, and how she had hung all of them in a place of honor on the tree.

But dredging up childhood memories also brought memories of Jessica to the fore, including the summer she'd been sixteen. He'd been around twenty and home for a short visit, but it was also the first time, he'd started to notice her as more than the pesky kid next door. He remembered discounting the thought as soon as it had first entered his mind, but for years after, he'd looked forward to his first glimpse of her upon returning home. His attraction to her grew from there. Had he not gotten carried away with alcohol, would he have been able to start something with her earlier? He'd never know.

It was another part of his life he'd altered due to his inability to control his drinking. He shook his head. He needed to call his sponsor but hated to disturb the guy when it wasn't an emergency. He wasn't at risk of a drink. He needed help getting his thoughts in order.

He texted Carl.

Got time for lunch?

You okay?

Not about to drink, if that's what you mean. Just want to work out some stuff in my mind.

Yeah. Usual spot?

12:30?

See you then.

Thomas then added some of his favorite ornaments to the tree and packaged the rest for his siblings. They'd want them in their own homes, and it was stupid to leave them in a box in his basement. He got ready for lunch.

He beat Carl to the diner by six minutes. He'd memorized the fare, despite its typical diner-size menu, but his mind needed something to think about other than Jessica or what she'd learned. He scanned the offerings, trying to decide between ham and eggs and a sloppy Joe, when Carl sat across from him in the booth.

"Are you thinking about venturing past your usual Reuben sandwich?" he asked, eyes wide in shock.

Thomas strummed his fingers on the table. "It's never too late to change. A wise person I know once told me that."

"Uh-oh, trying to butter me up before we talk. This is serious."

Carl flagged the waitress. "I'll have the rigatoni and garlic bread special."

"And I'll have a Reuben with extra fries."

His sponsor smirked, before he folded his arms on the table, leaned forward and pinned Thomas with his stare.

Thomas used to squirm under those intense blue eyes, wondering if he could see into his soul. But now, he tried to restrain his laugh. Carl was maybe five feet tall and scrawny. To those who didn't know him, he looked like a child pretending to be the bad guy.

"What's up?"

It's what he liked about Carl. He didn't beat around the bush. He forced Thomas to confront his concerns and talk through how to attack them.

"Jessica knows I'm an alcoholic."

"Good, you told her."

"Not on purpose." He summarized what happened.

Carl remained silent the entire time.

"What happened next?" Carl asked when Thomas finished.

"That's it. I haven't talked to her since."

"Why not?"

"Because she's a reporter. I'm not about to beg her not to print I'm an alcoholic in the paper. It's not like she'd listen anyway. And I'm pissed."

Carl remained silent.

"What, you're not going to say anything?"

He made a face. "I don't think you're done yet."

"She used me to get the information she needed for her story, and I fell for it. I can't talk to someone who'd do that."

"How do you know she'll print it? For that matter, how do you know she used you to get the information? From the sound of it, what you told her slipped out."

"It hasn't 'slipped out' with anyone else."

"How many people other than your family have you told your history to?"

"No one."

"Okay, maybe it means you trust her."

"She tricked me into it."

Carl raised an eyebrow. "Is that how you want to look at it?"

Thomas fumed and remained silent.

"You told her you wouldn't discuss the fire, right?"

Thomas nodded.

"And from what you said, she didn't mention anything. How did she try to gain your trust for the article?"

Carl was great when it came to helping him think logically. Unfortunately, he also required Thomas to consider hard issues and come to conclusions he didn't always like.

"Maybe she was trying to soften me up, so I'd agree to let her interview me."

"Or maybe she enjoyed your company. You said she used to follow you around when she was a kid. Her interest in you isn't out of the blue."

What Carl said made sense.

"I still feel betrayed, though. It doesn't make sense, but it's how I feel."

Carl nodded. "I get it. But what if the betrayal isn't because of what she heard but because of what you did?"

Thomas leaned against the booth. "Are you saying I'll feel this crushing guilt for the rest of my life?"

"No, but it might rear its ugly head at unexpected times. And you'll have to figure out a way to deal with it."

Once their food arrived, they ate in silence for a few minutes.

"Look, it's up to you what you do about her. But, ultimately, if you have a relationship with her, she'll need to know your history."

"Yeah, but the entire town doesn't."

They continued to eat in silence.

"Any thoughts about your future?" Carl asked when he'd finished.

"I might have an idea," Thomas said. The chief's suggestion to apply to be a fire instructor at the academy had stuck with him. The more he thought about it, the more he liked the idea. But he wasn't ready to share it yet.

"One you're willing to share?"

"Not yet."

Carl nodded. "Okay. You let me know when you are."

"You're awake early," Jessica's mom said the next morning, as she nursed her coffee. "Want to help me make latkes?"

"Oh, yes! But I have a meeting with the rabbi, I have to speak to Dr. Nelson's class, and run to the library to do some research. Can it wait until I return?"

"Wow, that's a lot for one day." Her mom eyed her. "Everything okay?"

Jessica didn't often meet with the rabbi, and she suspected her mom was curious, but this wasn't something she wanted to share. At least, not yet. "Yeah, I'm fine."

Her mom looked at her watch. "What time will you be finished, do you think?"

"Maybe around two?"

"Sure. Say hello to Dr. Nelson for me."

Giving her mom a thumbs-up, Jessica jogged out to her car and drove to the temple. Other than the holidays, Jessica hadn't been there since her high school youth group days and seeing the parking lot empty—other than employees' cars—jarred her. Climbing out of her vehicle, she wiped her hands on her black slacks, took a deep breath and entered the building. She greeted the temple administrator, who ushered her into the rabbi's office.

"Jessica, how nice to see you," the rabbi said, her tone warm.

"I appreciate your taking the time to meet with me."

"How are you? What are you doing now?"

Jessica continued the small talk for a few moments and when she couldn't wait any longer, she got to the reason for her appointment.

"I'm interested in a man," she said, "but he's not Jewish." She held her breath and waited for the rabbi's response.

But there was none, so she continued.

"And my parents aren't thrilled, although they like him as a person. My friends ask me if it's important to me or not, and I just… I don't know. I've always been taught I should marry someone Jewish—and I know it's premature to talk about marriage at this point—but I'm not sure how I feel about it. Excluding someone based on their religion is wrong, regardless of who it is."

"And so, you've come to me," the rabbi said.

"Yes."

"Tell me, is he understanding of your religion? What I mean by that is if he's respectful."

Jessica nodded. "Yes, he's interested in what we do and why, just as I'm interested in his. He's Catholic."

"Have you known him long?"

"He's my next-door neighbor. But he's older than I am. We didn't socialize when I lived here full-time."

"But he and his family know your family, and I'd assume, know you're Jewish."

"Yes."

The rabbi steepled her hands in thought for a moment before she responded.

"You know, one of the things we're supposed to atone for is judging others. And it includes judging other Jews for intermarriage."

Jessica's eyes widened.

"I'm sure you've heard, whether from your parents or others, preserving the Jewish faith is paramount, and intermarrying dilutes the effort. However, I'd like to contradict the idea and say there are many ways to ensure the Jewish faith continues. It doesn't have to be by marrying someone Jewish. Or, in your case, dating."

"Really?" Jessica asked.

The rabbi nodded. "Did you know about seventy percent of non-Orthodox Jews intermarry?"

"I didn't."

"Did you know intermarriage is as old as the Bible itself? Everyone thinks about Ruth…but what about Esther? Her intermarriage saved the Jewish people."

"Why does everyone frown on it?"

The rabbi shrugged. "Everyone has different feelings about it. But there's no universal prohibition of intermarriage in the Torah, only against certain ancient tribes. It was Ezra who introduced the idea that intermarriage was forbidden. The story of Ruth is often seen as a response to his edict, since she becomes the grandmother to King David and our future messiah."

"What you're telling me is you don't disapprove of it," Jessica said.

"It's not my decision who you love, Jessica. But I don't think it's an either/or situation, and I don't believe intermarriage is the terrible thing some people believe. In fact, it's often the non-Jewish parent who encourages the Jewish identity in a family. I do believe the Jewish community should stop passing judgment on this topic. Non-Jews who we welcome into the community may not be children of Israel, but they are builders of Israel. If you look at things in this light, you might come to a conclusion more consistent with your thoughts."

Jessica stood. "You've given me a lot to think about." She held out her hand to the rabbi.

The rabbi shook it. "I'm glad. Come talk to me again if you need."

Jessica thanked her and said goodbye, resolving to have another conversation with her mom.

Next, she went to the high school. Dr. Nelson had left a note at the front desk and they let her in, gave her a visitor's pass and led her to the classroom.

She knocked on the door.

When Dr. Nelson looked toward the doorway, her face brightened. She let Jessica in before she turned to her students.

"Can I have your attention, please?" She waited until everyone was focused on her.

"Today we have a special guest. A former student of mine who went into journalism. I suggested she return and tell you about what it's like to have that kind of career."

"Geez, even after we graduate, we can't get away." A kid in the back of the class spoke and made everyone laugh. Dr. Nelson's eyes twinkled, but her expression remained solemn.

"'Geez' is not the correct way to start the sentence, Jeremy. You should know better."

A mixture of sympathy and awe swelled in Jessica. While

she might have thought the same thing as the student, she'd never have had the guts to say the words out loud.

He nodded and looked at her with what she hoped was interest.

She swallowed before stepping forward. "Hi, my name is Jessica Sacks. I graduated eleven years ago from Browerville High. Dr. Nelson was my teacher, and yes, I survived."

The students looked at each other, and Dr. Nelson cleared her throat.

Jessica looked over at her. "Sorry, he started it."

Now the class relaxed.

"Anyway," Jessica continued, "I work for a newspaper in Brooklyn called the *Brooklyn Daily Herald*. Or I did, until they fired me."

The class gasped.

"You might wonder why I'm here today. To be honest, I wondered the same thing myself."

A few kids in the class snorted, and Jessica smiled, waiting for them to stop.

"But Dr. Nelson convinced me the lessons I'm learning now might help you on your journey. I thought I'd tell you what I do, what happened to cause me to lose my job, and what I'm doing to try to get it back. As well as answer questions, of course."

The class was well-behaved—Dr. Nelson required them to be—but their attention was focused and a few leaned forward in their seats while Jessica told them about her job and what had happened to get her fired.

A boy in the front row raised his hand. She pointed to him.

"Wait. You got fired for one mistake?"

She nodded. "I did. I apologized, the paper ran a retraction, I wrote the person a letter, but in the end, the publisher didn't care. The guy is a major advertiser and threatened to pull his business if I remained on staff."

"But you said you're trying to get it back," a girl in the second row added.

"Please raise your hands, class," Dr. Nelson said.

"I am. I think." She ignored the pit in her stomach. Now wasn't the time to decide. "My editor called me afterward and asked me to cover a local story here. Since I was coming home anyway, I agreed. And she said if I wrote it well, she might be able to get me my job back." The more she talked about it, the worse her mood.

A boy in the third row started to speak then raised his hand. Jessica nodded to him.

"Yes?"

"Why did you answer your phone in the first place? If someone fired me, I'd never talk to them again."

Other students in the class nodded.

"You know, there's a big part of me that feels the same way," Jessica said. "But the problem is, as an adult, you can't always react without thinking of the consequences. You can't always hold a grudge. Sometimes, you have to be the bigger person. I didn't want to answer the phone, but I did anyway. Maybe she was calling because I forgot something. Maybe she wanted to apologize. I didn't know."

Another student raised a hand. "Would you do it again?"

"Answer the phone? Yes. Agree to the article?"

Knowing what she knew now... "Probably not," she said. "I also believe in knowing your own self-worth. It's a tough concept to learn, and I'm not sure I've mastered it yet. It's complicated, because it's not the same as arrogance, and it can be easy to inflate when you're angry at the other person. But I do believe that, after ten years, my editor should know my worth and shouldn't need me to prove anything."

The words popped out of her mouth, but she recognized the truth behind them.

Another girl raised her hand. "What will you do now?"

"It's the million-dollar question," Jessica said. "Because I love journalism. Dr. Nelson is the one who inspired me to pursue it in the first place." She smiled at her former teacher, who returned it. "I love writing, putting my soul on the page, reading something over and knowing I said what I meant to say. And I don't want to give it up. But someday I'd like to write something different, something more 'me.'"

The boy who'd asked the first question raised his hand again. "Why didn't you do it first?"

"Great question. You know, when we're in school, we're told we have to know what we want to do with the rest of our lives. But I don't think anyone knows the answer to the question—or not most people at least. We start with something that sounds interesting, or we start with someone who will hire us. And along the way, we figure it out. I think it's a much more effective way to determine our path. When I graduated, I didn't know who I was, never mind how I could know if a job was 'me' or not. Ten years later, I'm still not sure, but I'm closer to finding out. There's nothing wrong with moving around and trying new things, no matter how old we are."

Dr. Nelson raised her hand, prompting an outburst of laughter.

"Jessica, what would be your one piece of advice to my class?"

Jessica paused a moment. "Learn how to write. Focus on the grammar and the technique, and all the rules. Yes, even the annoying ones. Once you know them, you can do anything, but only if you're good. So, get good."

The bell rang and, as the class left, a few students stopped to thank her. When they exited, the classroom was empty.

Dr. Nelson gave her a hug. "I told you it would go well," she said. "They listened to you *because* you made mistakes. You're more relatable to them because you've experienced what they're afraid of and survived."

"It did go better than I'd anticipated," Jessica said. "And it was good for me too."

"I thought it might be. Thank you for taking the time today. And please let me know if there's anything you need. I'm happy to help in any way I can."

Jessica thanked her and assured her she'd be in touch.

Leaving the high school, she let the ideas the talk had fostered percolate in her mind. In the meantime, she drove to the town library. She'd spent much of yesterday afternoon—after leaving Emily—searching the internet for any evidence to link Thomas's drinking to the night of the fire. But there was nothing. She'd been ready to give up, convinced Thomas had nothing to worry about, until she remembered a piece of advice one of her journalism school mentors had given her. Never be afraid of going old school. In this case, old school meant the library.

She approached the librarian behind the research desk. "Can I see the local Browerville news articles on the museum fire? And…any police blotter articles going back six months from then."

The librarian led her to the computer, where she pulled all the articles about the fire.

"When you're finished with these, you can do a search for 'police blotter' and read the ones that interest you."

Jessica thanked her and scanned through the articles. Like the search she'd done at home, the articles didn't mention alcohol. It wasn't until she looked at pages and pages of police blotters that she found a brief mention—six months before the fire, Thomas was cited for disorderly conduct outside a bar.

She paused. Instead of encouragement, her stomach dropped. Her hand on the mouse was like lead and with every click an urge to duck or wince overcame her. Now she'd found something concrete. Did she want to investigate further? It wasn't her business if it didn't relate to the fire.

There wasn't proof, but had she expected there to be? It's not like someone was going to write a tell-all *Thomas Carville is an Alcoholic*.

Her heart thudded in her chest. It's what her boss wanted her to do. Sure, she was writing about the museum rededication, and Thomas's heroic saving of Eric Payne, but by delving deeper into this story, she'd out him. Everything he'd worked hard to overcome, everything he'd done to save himself and others, his disease would supersede what he'd suffered during the rescue. It wasn't fair. She was an investigative journalist, true, but not a salacious one. What was the purpose of humiliating him in this story? It wouldn't change anything, other than turning her into the kind of journalist she didn't want to be.

Pushing away from the library's computer, she thanked the research librarian once again and called Alice.

"I think this story will be better without Thomas," she said when her boss answered.

A gasp greeted her. "I'm sorry, what?"

Jessica took a deep breath. "I'm not able to interview Thomas Carville for the story. But we can turn it into a museum-focused piece and—"

"No," Alice said. "Jessica, this is your one chance to get your job back. Harvey has finally calmed. But he won't run any old story, not from you. You said Thomas won't talk to you. I want you to find out why. I want the story ASAP."

Alice hung up before Jessica could respond.

Now what? The more she thought about Thomas, the less she wanted to write the story. Her job was on the line, but all of a sudden, the job she thought she'd wanted didn't appeal to her. Her friends were right. There were many other types of journalism. Maybe it was time to consider other options.

She wanted a relationship with Thomas. She wasn't sure what he wanted, or if he would speak to her again, but publishing this article wouldn't solve either issue. She'd never had to balance out her feelings for a subject with her need to find the truth. The more she pursued this story, the less she wanted to know. Was her job worth hurting Thomas? Did she want to lose him again? She needed to make Alice understand. Moaning, she drove home.

Inside her mom's kitchen, the ingredients were laid out on the counter. There were a lot of them.

"Are we expecting the town to join us?" Jessica asked as she shed her coat and washed her hands.

"Of course not," her mom said. "I'd have bought twenty pounds of potatoes instead of five."

"Oh, man, guess there will be plenty for me to share with my friends."

"Always."

She joined her mom at the counter and began to peel potatoes, letting them rest in cold water.

"How was your day?" her mom asked.

"Interesting." She wanted to tell her mom about her conversation with the rabbi, but she was a little afraid to bring it up out of the blue. She needed a better lead-in to the conversation.

"Wonderful. How's your article? The museum ceremony is in two days, right?"

"Yes, but I don't think an interview with Thomas is a good idea."

"Really?" Her mother gave her a long look. "Is it because of your feelings toward him?"

Jessica studied her mom's expression. It was neutral but stiff, like she restrained herself from commenting. That meant her mom didn't approve of any feelings Jessica might have but didn't want to say anything. It was the perfect opening to tell her about the rabbi's take on intermarriage and dating outside one's religion.

"I hope not." She dumped the potato peels into the wastebasket at her feet. "But, regardless, I think the direction of the story needs to change. Now I have to convince my boss to accept it." If only she knew how.

"So, you do have feelings for him." Her mom pursed her lips.

"It's complicated," Jessica said. "But I think I do."

"Is that wise?" Her mother spoke with care, as if she were trying to avoid a landmine.

Jessica understood the feeling. She was doing it too. Putting aside the potatoes, she turned to her mom. "I talked to the rabbi this morning and she gave me an interesting perspective."

She waited for her mom's reaction.

"And what was it?"

"She believes welcoming non-Jews into our lives can help ensure Jewish continuity."

Her mother's eyebrows rose and Jessica hurried to explain in more detail what the rabbi had said. It was an opinion different from that of her parents', and it would take them a while to digest it all. But she hoped her mom might try to look at it from another direction.

"What do you think of the rabbi's opinion?" her mom asked when Jessica finished.

"It's not something I'd ever considered before."

Her mom nodded.

"But it does address my issue of exclusion," Jessica added.

"What do you mean?"

"It never felt right to me to say I couldn't care about someone just because they weren't Jewish. To me, it sounded like someone disliking me *because* I'm Jewish. The rabbi's take makes more sense to me, gives me more hope."

Her mother paused. "To be honest, I'm not sure how I feel. I was raised a different way, but the rabbi gave an interesting perspective. I need to think about it before I form any other opinions."

Jessica exhaled a deep breath. Her mom's response was

more than she'd hoped for. And if she was honest with herself, she needed to think more about the rabbi's argument as well.

"I understand, Mom. Thank you."

Her mom nodded. "Let's keep talking about this, though."

Jessica gave her mom a hug. "Please."

"Back to your article, is your boss okay without an interview with him?"

Nope. "She might be, if I get the right kind of hook. I'll talk to her again after we make the latkes."

Luckily, they were ready to grate the potatoes in the food processor, a task too noisy for conversation.

Saved by the grater, an unsung Hanukkah miracle, Jessica thought to herself as she loaded the small appliance with sliced potato chunks. She adjusted the blade and turned it on, watching the potatoes shred. When the container filled, she emptied it into the bowl and repeated the process until all the potatoes were shredded. Meanwhile, her mom added the eggs, flour, salt and pepper, and mixed everything together.

Without the noise of the motor, her mother was able to continue the conversation.

"I hope you're successful finding another angle to the story."

Jessica squeezed her hand around the bowl. "I hope so too."

Her mom heated the oil in the fry pan before dropping rounded forkfuls in to fry.

"Is it in your best interest to change the story idea? I mean I know this isn't your usual story. Aren't you supposed to cover the story you're assigned?"

For a moment, Jessica wondered if her mom knew she'd been fired from her job.

"Yes, but I think the story will be better with my change in focus," she said as her mom flipped the latkes in the pan. "Sticking to the museum reopening is stronger. I've interviewed a number of firefighters. I'm sure it will be fine."

She needed to improve her pitch. It sounded weak to her own ears. Her mom arched an eyebrow but remained silent.

When the first batch of latkes was finished, they put them on paper towels to drain the excess oil, before repeating the process.

Jessica needed to think of a way to change the subject with her mom before they veered into something she couldn't avoid. Like how she'd been fired. She blew on one of the latkes and popped it in her mouth.

"Ow, id's hoth, bud good." She rushed to the sink for a drink of water.

Her mother handed her a paper towel. "You do this every time I make them. You never let them cool but put them in your mouth right away and burn yourself."

Jessica wiped her lips. "I know. But it's worth it."

Her mother wrapped her arm around her and gave her a squeeze. "I love how you still love latkes. I'm glad our holiday traditions are important to you."

"Are you kidding?" Jessica returned her mom's hug. "I will never stop loving them. And I've discovered other ways to eat them, not just with applesauce or sour cream. Have you tried lox with them?"

Her mom added more potatoes to the splattering oil. "I don't know," she said. "I'm a purist. I like mine plain, no matter what other variations are popular."

"I guess you've never eaten celery root latkes, either?"

"No but let me get this straight. I fought with you for eighteen years to eat anything green, and now you tell me you eat green latkes. With actual vegetables in them? Who are you and what did you do with my daughter?"

"Not only do I eat those, but I tried ones with zucchini too."

"Okay, I'm done." Her mother took off her apron and handed Jessica the spatula. "I failed as a mother if all it took was adding vegetables to latkes to get you to eat them."

Jessica laughed and flipped the latkes. Her mom returned and they continued the traditional version in silence.

They spent the next forty-five minutes making the latkes, chatting in between about her mom's job, gossip about friends, and the latest books they'd read. When all the latkes were finished, they set them to cool.

"Promise me something," her mother said, washing her hands at the sink.

"What is it?"

"Whatever decision you make, whether it's about your personal life or your work, you think about the ramifications and stay true to yourself. I'd hate for you to decide something based on your current condition without any thought for the future."

Jessica wiped the stovetop and counters to get rid of all the oil, although it would be days before the smell would disappear. "I am thinking of my future, Mom. You might not agree with what I decide, but I'm not rushing into anything."

She thought about Sarah, and how she'd lost herself along the way while pursuing her career. Luckily, her friend had found herself and a new career she loved.

"And I have no intention of being true to anyone *but* me. I promise."

Her mom gave her a long, silent look before hugging her. "I love you."

"I love you too."

Thomas looked out his window the next morning at the snow-covered front yard. The white stuff had fallen overnight and would make decorating outside much harder. Maybe he should take it as a sign he shouldn't bother with the town contest, the decorating, or any holiday festivities. He took a big swig of coffee. He'd agreed to participate. He wouldn't cancel, no matter how much he might want to. And the lights wouldn't hang themselves. With a sigh, he bundled up, grabbed his ladder and went outside, letting Reggie run around as he worked.

He couldn't help looking over at Jessica's yard. Her Hanukkah decorations were complete with hanging menorah lights and lawn dreidels. Part of him wanted to see what the house looked like lit up at night. Another part of him urged him to forget everything about her. As his neighbor, though, it was hard. As someone who had gotten under his skin, made him want to explore a relationship with her further, it was impossible.

"Need some help?"

A male voice shook him out of his reverie and he tried to clear the fog. Jessica's dad stood a few feet away.

"I didn't see you there," Thomas said. "I'm good, though. Thanks."

Mr. Sacks smiled. "No consorting with the enemy, huh? Or just want to keep the old guy off the ladder?"

"I plead the Fifth, sir."

"Fair." He turned and waved. "Take it easy."

Thomas nodded before he readied his lights for hanging, though the process worked better with a helper and it was slow going alone. If he and Jessica were on better terms, he might have taken Mr. Sacks up on his offer, although he'd never ask the older man to climb the ladder. Since he was trying to avoid Jessica, Thomas couldn't turn around and ask her father for help.

If he were on better terms with her, maybe she'd have helped him. The thought of staring at her perched on the ladder, her ass in tight jeans or leggings, made him sweat. It didn't matter how attracted to her he was, he needed to stay away.

By the time he finished the lights, his numb fingers were stiff, though his hands were sheathed in gloves. Deciding he was done, he returned inside to warm up.

A knock on his door interrupted him as he was finishing lunch.

"Liam, what the hell are you doing here?"

"Nice way to greet your brother," Liam said. "Good to see you too."

Thomas peered outside. "Where's Erin? Are you here alone?"

He nodded. "With the museum rededication and awards ceremony tomorrow, I thought you might need some company."

Thomas froze. His heart galloped in his chest. He looked at his brother, whose face shone with sincerity and understanding. He searched, but there was no pity, and a part of him relaxed. With relaxation, though, came guilt. "I appreciate your being here more than you'll know, but I'm not going to the ceremony. I think you wasted a trip."

His brother folded his arms across his chest. "Whether or not you're there, I'm staying."

A weight lifted from Thomas's shoulders. "Thank you."

His brother looked around. "Getting ready for Christmas. Looks good. And the house looks great."

Thomas nodded. "With all of you coming home for the holiday, I figured it should look like Christmas."

"Great, I can help while I'm here."

"How long are you staying?"

"A couple of days. Erin and the kids say hi, by the way."

"It'll be good to see them. I have something for you."

He handed Liam the ornaments from their childhood. His brother's face softened with nostalgia. "These are great. I remember making this one in second grade, I think." He held up his handprint. "I came home with more paint on my clothes than on the ornament. But Mom loved it."

Thomas swallowed against the lump in his throat.

"Erin will appreciate my adding these to our tree. Thanks." He clapped Thomas on the back, and Thomas led him into the kitchen.

"I'm finishing lunch. Want anything?"

"I'd love a sandwich."

Thomas pulled out cold cuts and bread and watched while his brother made himself lunch. Liam had always had a huge appetite, and Thomas remembered him stacking his sandwiches so high, he could barely fit them in his mouth. Now it seemed he'd outgrown the habit, as his roast beef sandwich was of a more reasonable size.

"Football?" His brother took a bite of his sandwich and pointed toward the family room.

Thomas lead the way and turned the Giants game on. Big Blue was winning three nothing.

"Won't last," his brother said.

Thomas shrugged. "I'll take it while I can."

They watched the game in silence, punctuating bad plays or calls from the refs with groans and cheers when their team pulled out a win in the final two minutes.

When it ended, Thomas turned off the TV.

"So what do you do around here for fun?" Liam asked.

Thomas nodded at the dog. "Take Reggie for walks or to the dog park. Fix up the house."

"You've got to be kidding me." His brother's look of shock made Thomas shift on the sofa. "What about friends?"

"I haven't seen the guys since I left the department."

"Why not?"

Thomas stared out the window. Snow began to fall again, and the fading light from the early sunset reflected his solitary and stark demeanor.

"It's easier," he said. "Easier to remain sober, easier to avoid discussing the fire." As he spoke the words, he realized how much he'd changed. He'd always been the active one, the person who was up for anything at any time. Surrounded by friends and family at all times, he'd thrived in the thick of things. It was one of the reasons he'd taken to being a firefighter so well. There was a brotherhood, a camaraderie, he'd valued. A sense of belonging.

He missed it.

His brother sighed before he went into the kitchen. "You want something to drink?"

"Water."

Liam returned with a can of soda and a bottle of water. Tossing the bottle to Thomas, he joined him on the couch again.

"Have I told you how much I admire you?"

Thomas's heart thudded. Not his brother too. He opened his mouth to protest, but Liam continued.

"It has nothing to do with rescuing the old man. Relax. I admire you because you admitted your disease and fight the battle every day. It's impressive."

"Thank you." Calm washed over him.

"But I hope when you're more secure in your disease, you figure out a way to reclaim some of what you lost, especially your social life. Because I don't want to see you alone and miserable, or cut off from doing the things you used to like to do."

Thomas swallowed, his throat thick with emotion. His brother put into words what he'd been feeling, but in such a graceful way he couldn't get offended or angry. Instead, he gave him a hug.

"Thanks, Liam."

He had to figure things out, but he'd wait until after the ceremony.

Chapter Eleven

Jessica approached the Browerville Museum ten minutes before the ceremony was due to start. With her iPad and purse,
she walked over to the front of the building where chairs were
arranged in front of a podium inside a heated tent. As she
scoped out her seat, she spotted the mayor with people from
the museum, as well as members of the fire department.

For a moment, her hopes soared as she looked for Thomas,
but they crumbled when she realized he wasn't there. She hadn't
expected him. But still, her chest ached with disappointment.

While she waited for the ceremony to begin, she studied
the edifice of the museum. Made of large gray stone, it hid
most of the effects from the fire. But there was still some soot
darkening around the windows. From the news reports, the
inside had suffered the most damage, as it was made of wood.

The ceremony began with speeches from the museum
staff, the mayor, who mentioned the award would be mailed
to Thomas later, and the fire chief. An architect in charge of
the renovation showed renderings of the improved spaces when
the repairs were complete, and the museum director displayed
photos and information of upcoming events.

When the ceremony was over, Jessica asked for a few
quotes from people for her article and took a tour of the parts
of the building reopened to the public. But something was
missing. She hoped it wasn't just Thomas. She'd written plenty

of articles in the past where, as hard as she'd tried, she hadn't been able to score interviews with every subject she desired. The articles had still been good pieces of journalism, and a few had won small awards. It wasn't the lack of Thomas's inclusion that made this article ring hollow. She wasn't sure what the problem was.

Returning home, she sat at her desk in her bedroom and tackled the piece, starting, stopping, rearranging…and still it wasn't right. She loved putting all of the information together, figuring out the story she wanted to tell, and how best to appeal to readers. But no matter how many times she played around with it, it didn't work.

She dialed her boss, taking a deep breath as the woman answered.

"Alice Clark."

"Hi, it's Jessica."

"Hey, how's the article coming? The ceremony was today, right? How did our hero firefighter do? You got him to talk to you, right?"

Jessica squirmed. "It's why I'm calling you. I'm having a little difficulty writing everything up."

"How hard is it to talk about the terrible fire, the destruction of the museum, and the hero who saved the day? It's like a fairy tale, only make sure it sounds professional. Not to mention why he was reluctant to talk to you—there's something there. You have to dig deeper."

"No, I've got the fire and the destruction. And the ceremony was today, you're right. It's the hero firefighter I'm having trouble with."

"How much trouble can one firefighter be?" Her boss's voice had that clipped tone Jessica hated. "I've told you, if he won't talk to you, find out why and write about that."

Jessica stifled her reaction. Her boss wouldn't see the

humor. She wasn't sure she did, either. "Well, he refused to attend the ceremony, and he still won't talk to me."

"Not acceptable. We can't have a story about a hero firefighter without the hero firefighter. You've dealt with plenty of reluctant sources before. This one shouldn't pose you any difficulties. I don't understand why you're reluctant to do your job, Jessica."

"I tried to talk to him, but I can't force the words from his mouth. I don't think we need him. I think we can make it work—"

"Jessica, there is no 'try' in journalism and I don't want you to 'think.' You get the story or you get scooped. Or kiss your career goodbye, in this case. Do I need to remind you?"

She was about to argue. To beg Alice for more time or for a different angle. But all the frustration and guilt and fear burst forth and she didn't want to argue or beg. She wanted to heal. And she didn't think healing was possible with this job.

"You know what? I don't think I'm the right person for this story." If she finished this one and they let her have her job back, what would happen the next time? How much of herself would she have to sacrifice to do her job?

"You can't say that now, Jessica. The ceremony already took place. You've worked on the story for weeks."

"And I've felt horrible about it the entire time. I'm done." Unlike last time, when Alice had first fired her, the idea of losing her job didn't terrify her. For the first time, peace enveloped her.

"Done? You think you're done because you feel uncomfortable? Grow up, kiddo. If you want a job in journalism, you need to learn to move past your feelings and report the story."

Jessica shook her head, though she couldn't be seen. "That's where you're wrong, Alice. I don't have to move past my feelings. I can use them and create work that resonates with people at the same time. Maybe it won't be hardcore journalism, but it will be something I'm proud of. I can't write this story the way you want it. Instead of turning in something you'll hate, I'm going to resign." Something swelled inside her; a kind of hysterical joy she recognized. It was pride.

"After the second chance I gave you? You're going to leave me high and dry?"

Withholding everything she could have said, things that would make her no better than Alice, Jessica responded. "High and dry? You gave me this assignment because you wanted me to prove my worth, though I've worked for you for years, and you promoted me. You should be aware of my worth and you should have fought for me harder. It's a small story and one the *Brooklyn Daily Herald* wouldn't have a reporter cover. You can get coverage of the ceremony anywhere. If I have to prove my worth to anyone, it will be to me. I'm worth more than this. And I can't live with myself if that is the kind of article I write."

Alice disconnected the call without another word. And, for the first time since being fired two and a half weeks ago, Jessica was free.

"Good for you, kid." Her dad's quiet voice made her jump.

"You heard me?"

He nodded. "Your door was open."

"You heard everything?"

"Enough. How come you didn't tell me and Mom you got fired?"

Jessica stared at the floor. "I was embarrassed."

"In front of us? Why would you be embarrassed? We're your parents."

"I didn't want you disappointed in me. They fired me."

"Everyone makes mistakes, Jessie. The key is what you learn from them. You should know that. Tell me, will you go through with it?" He tipped his chin at her phone. "Quitting?"

She took a deep breath before she answered. "Yeah, I am.

What they want me to write is wrong. I won't do that to someone I care about…or anyone, for that matter. I can't."

"There you go. You learned something. I'm proud of you. Will you look for something else? New York City or out here?"

She held her hand up. "Whoa, it's been all of two minutes max. I don't know anything other than what you overheard. It's a little premature for me to have a plan to move forward. But I will. I need a little time."

He walked forward and kissed her. "You're right. And I'm proud of you for defending yourself and for doing the right thing. And now you have to tell your mother."

She basked in his praise for a moment, knowing she faced a lot of tough decisions ahead. "I know. I'll do it right away."

She followed her dad downstairs and sat next to her mom in the living room.

"I need to talk to you," she said.

"About what?"

Jessica took a deep breath before she confessed everything. Writing the original story, making a big mistake, getting fired, and being given a second chance.

"I'm sorry I didn't tell you first. I should have. I'd never been fired before, and I didn't know what to do with it."

Her mom gave her a hug. "That's why we're here. To help you figure out what to do when you're unsure. Or at least to listen to you."

"I know."

"Good."

Jessica told her mom about quitting.

"I'm glad. I didn't like the idea of you making Thomas the subject your story, and your boss didn't seem to want to let you off the hook. It's better for everyone this way. You'll look for a new job after the new year?"

Jessica nodded. "I have to figure out where that might be."

"Well, as I'm sure your dad told you, you're welcome to stay here for a while."

"Thank you. I'll try not to overstay my welcome."

Thomas woke the next day, let Reggie out, and turned on the coffeepot. He stared out the window and watched Jessica's house.

What did her article say? He assumed she'd spoken to the chief and to Mr. Payne. Probably to staff as well. Had he been mentioned? He assumed he had been, due to the rescue, but what else had she mentioned? His alcoholism? If she had, everyone knew about it now.

He took a breath and poured himself some coffee. The aroma wafted through the kitchen, waking him before the caffeine hit his veins. He thought about what it meant to have the town know his failure. It would be awkward. Uncomfortable. But he didn't delude himself into thinking he was the only alcoholic in town. And he had a support system in place. He'd get over the shame and embarrassment. Eventually.

His brother's footsteps pounded down the stairs.

"Yo, what's the plan today?"

"Don't have one," Thomas replied.

"Let's go into town."

"No."

"Why not? You're not hiding out in your house. The best way to confront your demons is head-on."

So much for the pep talk he'd given himself.

"I've done it for months. I can take a few days to myself."

His brother clapped him on the back as he poured himself a cup of coffee. "Nope, you need to get out there now. We're going into town and buying Christmas presents."

"I already did." *With Jessica.* He gritted his teeth at the memory.

"Well, I didn't, so you're going to come with me."

"Liam."

"Thomas."

He glared at his brother, but Liam busied himself doing heaven knew what, and Thomas got no satisfaction out of it. Goddammit.

"Now that we've been introduced, get your ass in gear and let's go," Liam said.

What galled Thomas the most wasn't his brother's attitude. It wasn't the thought of unnecessary shopping. It was the fact that he was right.

With another glare and the emphasis of a certain finger, Thomas got himself ready to go into town.

The ride was silent and the closer they neared, the tighter Thomas's stomach knotted. Liam pulled into a spot in front of Aaron's deli.

"What are we doing here?"

"Parking, dumbass."

"In front of Isaacson's Deli?"

"Amazing, I know. But, occasionally, the parking gods smile at us and we get a spot right in front of where we need to go."

"You said we were shopping."

Liam looked at him like he'd grown another head. "Do you like to shop on an empty stomach?"

"That's a stupid question. I don't like to shop." *At least, not without Jessica.* He pulled up short. Why did he keep thinking about her?

"We need fuel before we go."

"And, of course, you picked the busiest place in town." Thomas climbed out and slammed his brother's car door a little harder than necessary.

Liam didn't reply, but led the way into the deli, which, as usual, was packed.

Fan-damn-tastic.

Standing in line among the chatter, Thomas tried not to pay attention to anyone else's conversations. But he couldn't help overhearing snatches. And he strained for sounds of his name. There was nothing. Parents talked about hockey practice, kids jabbered about school and toys, and other people talked about who knew what. Nothing that concerned him.

As he waited his turn, he looked around. No one avoided eye contact. No one glared or sighed with pity.

Who'd have thought an entire deli hadn't read the news this morning?

By the time Thomas reached the counter, his stomach unknotted and his appetite returned.

"Hey, Tommy, how are you? Missed you yesterday."

Thomas's spine stiffened as he turned to one of his buddies from the firehouse.

"Hassan, good to see you." He forced the words past his dry throat. "How are you?"

The man grinned, his deep brown face gleaming. "Wonderful. Amayah is pregnant, due in the summer."

"Fantastic! Congratulations to you and Amayah." He clapped his friend on the back, placed his order of a cinnamon raisin bagel with egg, and introduced his brother.

"Liam, Hassan. A good friend of mine from the station. Liam's my older brother."

"Nice to meet you." Liam held out his hand. "And congratulations on your news. I have a five-year-old son and a six-month-old daughter. You're in for a treat."

"Thank you." Hassan grabbed his take-out order. "It's good to see you, Tommy. Hope you'll stop by for a visit soon."

He nodded. "I'll try."

Thomas grabbed their trays of food as Liam led the way to a table.

He flicked the back of Thomas's head as he sat.

"Ow, what was that for?" Thomas glared at him.

"Making sure you're alive after interacting with someone. And you are."

Thomas wanted to wipe the self-satisfied smirk off his brother's face, but they were in public and he didn't want to cause a scene. He grumbled as he took a bite of his breakfast.

"What?" Liam leaned forward and cupped his ear. "'You were right.' Is that what you said?"

Now he wanted to give his brother the finger, but that would be worse. But when they returned to his house, he would give his brother a pounding.

Much to his dismay, Liam sat across from him, eating a bagel, egg and cheese, and grinning like a sloppy lunatic.

They finished eating, Thomas plotting how to get even with his brother while trying not to acknowledge that, maybe, Liam was right.

Outside, he smacked his brother on the ear.

"Ow!" He rubbed his ear. "What the hell was that for?"

"You had egg on you."

"So, you smacked me?"

Thomas smiled, the first time all day. "Two birds, one stone."

"Asshole."

Thomas followed his brother without a word. He couldn't remember if he'd ever gone Christmas shopping with Liam, but the guy spent more time than anyone he'd ever known examining possibilities, only to decide to wait to see if he found something else he preferred before he returned to the original object. As a result, they hit almost every retail store on Main Street.

Thomas had never paid much attention to stores in the past. He wasn't a fan of shopping, and his focus tended to be on smoke alarms, emergency exits and fire hazards, anyway. But he wondered if all the stores in the state had moved to Browerville, because he couldn't recall spending this much time in town. If the gifts weren't for his niece and nephews, he'd object.

Still, he'd never known his brother to be so friendly. It wasn't that Liam *wasn't* friendly, but he'd never gone to great lengths to seek someone out. Today, it seemed like everywhere they went, they ran into someone from their childhood Liam needed to greet, or a talkative shop owner who wanted to chat with Liam. And, no matter how much Thomas wanted to avoid people, his brother drew him into every scenario.

The first few times it happened, he cringed, waiting for someone to say something about yesterday's ceremony. The last few times, he faced his bewilderment.

Did no one attend the event? Maybe people didn't know he was the firefighter who'd rescued Mr. Payne.

But as they left the last store, Liam's Christmas list finally achieved, he spotted a newspaper dispenser. The *Browerville Sentinel*'s front page showed a photo from the event. It wasn't Jessica's paper, but maybe her story was run by smaller ones. In color. With shaking hands, he deposited his money, opened the door and snagged a paper.

His brother waited next to him.

He stared at the photo of the mayor, the fire chief and the museum director together, with a pair of giant scissors, ready to cut the ribbon.

He read the caption, listing their names and titles, stating the event, and referring readers to page three.

His hands sweated so much, the ink bled onto his skin and his fingers left prints on the paper.

He turned to page three and read the article. Then he read it again. He was about to read it for a third time when Liam spoke.

"Well, what's it say?"

"Nothing."

* * *

Jessica knocked on Emily and Sarah's apartment door and entered when they yelled, "Come in!" She stopped on the threshold, wide-eyed.

"If the town offered an 'interior apartment' decoration category, you two would win."

Her two friends had strung white running icicle lights around the ceiling perimeter of their living room, giving the room a waterfall effect. In one corner was Emily's Christmas tree, decorated in red and white balls. In the opposite corner, on a table covered with a blue tablecloth, was Sarah's menorah, along with wooden dreidels scattered about its surface, mingled with gelt, gold-foiled chocolate.

"It's beautiful," she added.

Emily smiled. "I'm glad you like it. And I think you're right. The town should definitely offer an apartment award."

Sarah nodded. "Especially because we've combined the two holidays."

The mention of combining holidays resonated with Jessica. Granted, her two friends were roommates, but there wasn't any competition between the two displays. One wasn't more prominent than the other. And the two women appeared to have found a respectful way to celebrate both holidays at the same time. Perhaps she could learn something from her two friends.

Caroline arrived as Jessica still twirled in place, taking everything in.

"Wow," Caroline said. "Um, I might need some motion sickness medication." She winked as she said it. "I'm joking, of course."

"Well," Emily added. "The room is a little small for running lights, but for now, it works. If anyone is bothered, we can always turn them off."

"In the meantime, take off your coats and relax for a bit before we have our cookie extravaganza," Sarah said.

Everyone settled, poured themselves glasses of spiced cider, and sat down to chat.

"This was such a great idea," Jessica said. "I think we should make this a yearly event."

"Does this mean you'll be home every Hanukkah?" Sarah asked.

Jessica shifted in her chair. "I resigned from my job. I have no clue what I'm doing next week much less next year."

The other ladies cheered, and Sarah nodded her support.

"What happened?" Emily asked.

"I couldn't cover the ceremony the way my boss wanted me to." She looked away. "There's a lot you all still don't know—and believe me when I tell you how much it means to me you're not pressing me for details." She took a deep breath. "But I didn't want to expose Thomas just to entice readers to a juicy story." She entwined her fingers together. "I hated trying to decide if betraying Thomas was worth it." When the others nodded, she continued. "I resigned."

"Good for you," Caroline said.

"So now you'll pursue a relationship with him?" Sarah asked. "For real this time?"

Jessica squirmed. "I thought we were talking about my job."

"Don't play stupid. It's not a good look," Caroline said. "Especially with us."

Her cheeks heated. "Sorry." She let out a huge sigh. "I want to. I know I have feelings for him, but I don't know what they are for sure. It hasn't been long enough to figure out yet, other than I want to spend time with him. Of course, the problem is he still won't talk to me."

"Have you tried to get him to talk to you?" Emily asked.

Jessica nodded. "There's only so much I can do—without throwing myself on him—to force him to talk." She moaned.

"I hate this limbo. It's one of the reasons I've never wanted a serious relationship."

"That's what you've always said, but I've never believed you," Caroline said. "I think you're afraid of it."

Anger built inside Jessica as she turned to her friend. "Excuse me? What right do you have to say that to me? I'm not afraid of a serious relationship."

"We're best friends, and we can say anything to each other," Caroline said, not backing down. "And I think at least a part of you is afraid of having the kind of relationship your parents have."

Jessica hated to admit that she was right.

"You know, love or relationships don't have to be the same for everyone," Caroline added. "Maybe it's something you can make your own, like your vision of yourself as a bride."

Some of Jessica's anger lessened as she considered her friend's words. "Maybe," Jessica said. "But I don't know if I'm there yet with Thomas."

Sarah leaned forward. "What made you decide not to cover the story and risk exposing him to whatever it was you were afraid of?"

Biting her lip, Jessica looked around the room. Her friends watched her, compassion and curiosity mixing in their expressions. Her neck grew warm and she pulled the collar of her sweater away from her skin. "I don't want to be the person who betrays someone's trust. It was one thing when I thought he was modest. I was able to justify the story because I thought he'd be glad when everything came to light." She paused as shame came over her. "That sounds horrible."

Emily gave her a hug.

She rested against Emily's shoulder and continued. "It's like… I was doing something for the greater good. Like you, Sarah, with your work helping fight anti-Semitism, or you, Caroline, helping the seniors, or you, Emily, advertising important causes. At least, it's what I tell myself when I'm investigating a big story and have to figure out ways to get the information people don't always want to tell me. But those stories expose corporate greed or someone doing something wrong or illegal. This was a hometown story, and my motivation was to get my job back. There wasn't some major news to be told, or some illegal activity to be exposed. And I realized my actions could hurt someone. It's not who I want to be."

"And it doesn't hurt you care for Thomas," Sarah added.

"Or are perhaps starting to fall in love with him," Caroline said.

"How can I fall in love with someone I've barely spent any time with?"

"Jess, you've been in love with him since you were thirteen," Sarah said. "It might not have been real, but your feelings were still involved. They've matured and changed shape over time."

Jessica's heart ached and she frowned. She'd never believed people's hearts ached when they cared for someone, but here she was, proving herself wrong. "Maybe." Jessica whispered her answer. "But how do I justify falling for someone who isn't Jewish when anti-Semitism is on the rise?"

Emily cleared her throat and Jessica covered her mouth. "I swear I mean no offense, Em."

Her friend—the only non-Jew among them—nodded. "I know you didn't. I can't justify your actions from a Jewish perspective, but there's something to be said for mixing with others, especially during difficult times. Look at me," she said. "Not only aren't I Jewish, but I'm not white, either. And while I will never suggest my job is to educate you, I think the four of us have done a good job in understanding each other's perspectives because of our lifelong friendship."

Everyone nodded.

"You won't lose something by dating someone who isn't Jewish, Jess," Caroline said. "If anything, you might help."

"Provided you both do the work and have the hard conversations," Sarah added.

Jessica nodded. "We've started to discuss our differences. Or we had."

"You did the right thing," Caroline said.

"Except he wants nothing to do with me, and I'm unemployed. I lost the guy and the job, and have no chance to further those conversations," Jessica said. "Yay me."

"Maybe you didn't lose him," Sarah said. "Maybe you can get him back."

"How?"

"Let him know you didn't write the story," Caroline suggested.

"He won't speak to me, Caro," she said. "He doesn't answer my calls or texts. And the last time I tried to catch him at home, he avoided me for days."

"Well, we'll have to brainstorm," Sarah said. "But maybe could we do it while we eat cookies? Those sugar cookies are staring at me."

Emily laughed. "I could move them, you know."

"No, I'd like a break," Jessica said. "Let's eat."

They all grabbed paper plates decorated with snowflakes and piled them with the different sweets everyone had brought. As they all exclaimed over their favorites, Jessica paused for a moment, relishing the close relationship she had with these women. They'd been here for each other since they were children. If she wanted to try to make a success of her and Thomas, maybe she should listen to them.

Chapter Twelve

When Thomas woke the next day and opened the front door to take Reggie out, a newspaper sticking out from under his mat stopped him. He bent to pick it up and frowned.

He didn't have newspapers delivered. From what he saw on his morning walks, the paper deliverer's aim was about as reliable as a toddler learning to throw for the first time, making it unlikely his newspaper would land under his front mat even if he had it delivered, which he didn't. And the paper was old. Well, it didn't look old, but the date was two days ago.

Despite Reggie's whine, he walked into the house.

"Liam, did you buy the paper?" He held it out.

"No. Why?" His brother scanned the newspaper and handed it to him. "Not me."

Unable to ignore Reggie any longer, Thomas tossed the paper onto the counter and walked the dog outside. He glanced at Jessica's house. Would she have delivered it to him?

When she'd first arrived, she'd left a Post-it note on his door. He glanced behind him. Nope, none on the door. Maybe she'd dropped the paper off to him, but he would have thought she'd include a note. It seemed like a Jessica thing to do.

Not that he knew her well enough to be sure.

He recalled their conversations. His chest ached as he remembered her voice—sarcastic yet soft, able to find the funny yet show compassion. She'd always asked him questions, but instead of his usual avoidance, he'd answered them. He'd confided more of himself to her than to anyone. It's what confused him. She was supposed to write the story about the fire.

Back inside, he took up the newspaper again and turned its pages, searching for an article. He found one, but it didn't have her byline. Frowning, he scanned it, looking for any mention of her name. There wasn't any.

Maybe she wrote for a different paper.

Then why was this one on his doorstep? It couldn't be a delivery mistake, since the date was two days old.

He turned on his computer and went to the paper's website, searching for her name. He came up empty.

"Well, Reg, it looks like we've got paper to make a fire." With that, he crumped the pages and set them in the fireplace, ready for later when he'd like it.

His brother came into the kitchen, duffel in hand. "I'm going home, but I'll see you in two weeks for Christmas."

Thomas gave him a hug. "Thanks for coming."

"Anytime. But I still think you should talk to her. If only to find out what happened to her article."

His stomach churned. "I think it's time I let it go."

Liam stared at him for a few moments in silence. "You ready?"

"Look, we went into town, and no one said anything. The *Browerville Sentinel* didn't print anything about me. There's only so many times I can beat myself up before I get sick of me."

"I think it's as close to 'You were right, Liam,' as I'll get."

"Damn straight."

"Glad to hear it." His brother put his hand on the knob and turned to him. "But be sure you've done everything you need to do to move past this. I'd hate for you to miss out on something you might regret."

Thomas didn't have to be a rocket scientist to know Liam

meant Jessica. He waved his brother on and walked into the living room. He stopped, his gaze drawn to the newspaper in the fireplace.

There was something he was missing. He picked up what was left of the paper and read the continuation of the story.

Mr. Payne's name jumped out at him. He read what was there.

"…and I was an idiot to do what I did and put people's lives at risk. Luckily, it all worked out, but I'd like to thank the Browerville Fire Department, especially Thomas Carville, for rescuing such a foolish old man."

Thomas frowned before sorting through the wadded-up pages for the beginning of the article. He read it, but nothing in the article provided any further information.

What the hell was Payne talking about?

He paced the room. There were a few things left on his list of people with whom he needed to made amends, and this guy was one of them. But he'd put it off out of fear—fear of reprisal, fear of getting sued, fear of admitting what a complete mess he'd made of his career, the only career he'd ever wanted. He couldn't live with fear anymore, especially if he wanted answers. It was time to confront his past.

Before he could second-guess himself, he searched his desk for the man's phone number. The chief had given it to him when he'd left the hospital.

"Call him," she'd said. "Often talking to the victims we save heals us too."

He'd scoffed at the idea, but he hadn't thrown away the information. It was here, somewhere…

"Found it," he whispered. With a deep breath, he called Eric Payne.

The call went to voicemail. "Hi, Mr. Payne. This is Thomas Carville. I, ah, don't know if you remember my name, but I'm, ah, the firefighter—" shoot, how did he refer to himself?

"—from the fire at the Browerville Museum. I'd like to talk to you if you have a minute." He gave his phone number and hung up before he could say anything stupid. Geez, it was like asking a girl on a date when he was a teenager.

Speaking of girls and dates, he needed to figure out what to do about Jessica. Because, as much as he'd like to avoid her for the rest of his life, it wasn't possible.

His cell phone rang, startling him, and he looked at the number on the screen. That was fast. He cleared his throat. "Hello?"

"Do I remember you? I'm old, not senile, Mr. Carville. Of course, I remember the man who saved my life."

Thomas sank into the nearest chair and gripped the phone hard. Shards of guilt pierced him. The man's voice was scratchy.

"How are you, sir?"

"Not bad." He coughed. "I'd be better if I'd seen you in person the other day, or if you'd returned any of my other calls. I wanted to thank you."

He closed his eyes. "You've already done that."

"Not enough."

Thomas shook his head. The gratitude ate at him. "After what I did, it's more than enough. You're still suffering the effects of smoke inhalation."

"If you hadn't rescued me, I'd be suffering the effects of death. Why are you beating yourself up about this?"

Thomas cleared his throat. "I wasn't at my best when I reported for duty."

There was a pause. "Were you sick? Sleep deprived?"

Thomas blew out a breath. "I was…not sober."

He waited. Whatever happened next—yelling, being hung up on, a lawsuit—he deserved.

"Neither was I."

Thomas didn't know what to say. He didn't know what he could say. The state of a victim didn't matter. It wasn't his business, either. But the silence on the other end demanded he say something.

"It doesn't matter, sir. You deserved to be rescued by someone who was competent—"

"Bull."

"Excuse me?"

"Bull."

Repetition didn't help. Maybe there was something wrong with this man. Thomas contemplated calling a doctor.

"I don't understand."

The man wheezed. "I know." He coughed again. "Look, you rescued me just fine."

"Except I didn't. There were many things I could have done differently if I wasn't drinking."

"And if I wasn't drinking, I would have noticed the smoke sooner. I think we both learned our lesson, don't you think?"

Now he was confused. "Lesson?"

"I don't know about you, but the fire forced me to confront my disease," Eric said. "I've been sober eight months and twenty-seven days."

Whoa. Similar to his own journey.

When Thomas didn't respond, Eric continued. "How about you?"

"Nine months and fourteen days." He rattled the numbers off. He was as aware of them as he was the air he breathed. Each day a new checkmark. But Eric, too?

"Good for you."

Thomas expelled a deep breath. "I'm sorry you suffered because of me."

"But that's the thing. I didn't. I shouldn't have been there in the first place and wouldn't have been if I'd been sober and paying attention. You rescued me. Would it have been a little less messy if you'd been sober? Probably. But it wasn't your fault, and if you're blaming yourself, stop."

As if it were that easy. "What are you doing now?" Thomas asked. "Have you returned to work at the museum?"

The man coughed again before barking a laugh. "No. I'm done. I've made amends with my daughter and hope to move closer to her soon."

"That's wonderful," Thomas said. "I'm happy for you."

"She heard about the fire, and we've been working on our relationship ever since."

"You're lucky."

"I know, which is why I'm going to give you a piece of advice. Don't let one screw-up spiral into something bigger. You were drunk. You got help. You're good now—at least, I think you are. Stop looking back. Fix what you can and move on. And, again, thank you for saving my life. Because no matter how you feel about it, I'm grateful every minute of every single day."

They ended the conversation.

Gratitude. Thomas had been overcome with guilt for what he'd done. He hadn't considered gratitude. Everywhere he looked there were things to be grateful for. His heart stuttered. He'd almost missed all of it.

The house, filled with memories from his childhood, which was now his. He wandered through its rooms, in various stages of completion and decorated for Christmas, waiting for his family to join him. He was lucky to have a supportive family who hadn't abandoned him when he was at his lowest. Hell, his brother had made an extra trip home to keep him company. And he'd see them all again, including his brother, to celebrate together.

His dad lent quiet support no matter what trouble Thomas got into, never excusing his behavior, but always letting him know he was there if he was needed.

Of course, despite Thomas's needs, he'd never thanked him for it. He wondered if he knew, and shame coursed through him.

He walked onto his deck and looked out at the trees that surrounded the property. He was done with shame and guilt. Sure, he needed to take ownership of his faults and his mistakes, but he was human, and if he made mistakes others could forgive, it was time he forgave himself.

He replayed in his mind the conversation with Eric Payne. The man had thanked him. He thought himself lucky. Well, hell, Thomas was lucky too.

Mr. Payne wasn't planning to sue him or to run him out of town. That in itself was a relief. His station buddies had never condemned him, either, though they must have known. He scoffed. He hadn't hidden his drinking as well as he'd thought he had. Of course, they'd known about it. And they still called him. He resolved to return their calls.

Hell, never mind return their calls, he should visit them at the firehouse, like they'd suggested.

Before he could change his mind, he grabbed the keys to his truck. Change started now.

Jessica walked over to Thomas's house, newspaper tucked under her arm. His truck had pulled out of the driveway fifteen minutes ago, at which point she'd gotten another local paper—this one reported on the entire county, not just Browerville. She'd double-checked the coverage of the museum rededication and awards ceremony and, like the *Browerville Sentinel*, it recorded straight event coverage, making no mention of Thomas's history. Once again, the byline wasn't hers. After tucking the paper under his doormat, she returned to her house.

She had to assume he'd see the paper. Would he understand why it was there or check for articles about the ceremony? How long would it take him to realize she hadn't written an article? And would he care?

Her reminders on her phone dinged. Rent was due in a week. She opened her bank account and calculated how long she could last without a salary. Not long. Living at home, while helpful, didn't enable her to save much money, what with socializing with her friends and holiday shopping. She needed to figure out a job right away.

Closing herself into her room with the door shut so no one would bother her, she opened her computer and pulled up her résumé. After making sure it was updated, she drafted cover letters to the executive editors at New York newspapers. She updated her profile on the online jobsites and paused. She loved her Brooklyn apartment, but her lease ended in a few months. If she was to consider moving, now was the time.

Her friends and family were here, but the idea of moving home didn't appeal to her. Especially since her relationship with Thomas was going nowhere. Coming home on weekends whenever she wanted sounded more appealing. However, she didn't want to eliminate an entire area code's worth of job opportunities. She searched for newspapers and magazines in New Jersey and added them to her list as well. She looked at online opportunities. If this experience had taught her anything, it was the need to open herself up to more than what was in front of her.

She pushed away from her keyboard, wondering what things would have been like if she hadn't been desperate to get a second chance with the *Brooklyn Daily Herald*. She wouldn't have gotten to know Thomas. With a smile, she remembered their conversations and how they'd joked with each other.

Goose bumps rose on the nape of her neck thinking about their amazing sex. It hadn't been planned, but she hadn't been sorry afterward. Though it had been spontaneous, and they hadn't been in a relationship, he'd been considerate, making sure she got as much enjoyment out of it as he had. For the first time in who knew how long, she understood why people searched for relationships. She'd always been a no-fuss kind of woman, which was why her dream was to elope. But when it came to relationships, she didn't want drama, didn't want to live her life chasing after something if it wasn't right. She wanted a man—if she were honest with herself, she wanted Thomas—but she wouldn't spend her life wondering what-if. She was going to continue to live her life, build her career, and enjoy herself. And if someone came along, great.

At least, that's what she'd always told herself. But ever since Thomas had stopped speaking to her, she'd spent all her time wondering about how to win him back. It was like she was thirteen again, mooning over someone who didn't know she existed. She didn't like falling into that trap, but she didn't know how to stop it. The rational side of her said to keep going. The emotional side said not to give him up.

She returned to her job search. Without employment, she'd lose her apartment. That meant finding a job with a salary she could live off of was her number-one priority.

She called Dr. Nelson.

"Jessica, I was just thinking about you," her mentor greeted when Jessica said hello.

Dr. Nelson's voice always made her smile. "You know, when I was your student, that statement would have scared the pants off me."

"I don't know why," she said. "You were my star student."

"Yes, but you always challenged me. And as a teenager, the last thing I wanted was too much attention."

"Well, I hope you've outgrown that insecurity. You're too intelligent to cringe at attention."

"Yes, ma'am." Jessica nodded. "Are you free for lunch?"

"For you, always. Why don't you come to my house, and I'll order salads from Bunny's Buffet?"

Jessica knew better than to argue with Dr. Nelson. She agreed and, thirty minutes later, knocked on her mentor's door.

"Jessica, darling!" The woman gave her a hug in the doorway of her condo before she stepped backward and led her into a book-lined sitting room that opened into a dining area.

"Our lunch will be here soon. In the meantime, tell me how you are."

Jessica took a deep breath before everything poured out in a rush—her job, her time home, Thomas.

Dr. Nelson let her speak without interruption.

As Jessica finished, the doorbell rang.

"Saved by the bell," Jessica said with a sigh.

"Oh, no, you're not," Dr. Nelson replied. She answered the door, paid the delivery guy, and brought their food to the glass table. "Sit while I get plates."

Although she wanted to help, Jessica hadn't yet contradicted her former teacher. She unpacked the salads, folded the bag and moved it out of the way.

Dr. Nelson returned with plates and the two women served themselves from the selection of salads she'd ordered— Mediterranean, pasta, and Caesar.

When lunch was served, the older woman put her napkin on her lap and turned to Jessica.

"You've experienced quite the upheaval in the past few weeks, I see."

"I believe that's an example of understatement," Jessica said.

Her smile broadened. "That's why you were my star student," she said. "You grasped concepts with ease and learned how to use them."

"I could do with a little less of art imitating life."

"Wrong metaphor, but I understand and sympathize with you. Where have you applied for jobs?"

Jessica listed the outlets she'd sent her résumés to, and the woman nodded. "I happen to know the senior editor at *Newsmonth* and the managing editor at *Shattering the Glass*.

I'd be happy to put in a good word for you at both places, if you'd like."

"I'd appreciate anything you're willing to do."

Dr. Nelson excused herself and returned a moment later with her phone. Jessica gasped when the older woman began to text. Dr. Nelson looked at her, eyebrow raised. "Are you surprised I text?"

"Yes, although I shouldn't be. Nothing about you surprises me anymore."

For the first time in Jessica's memory, her mentor laughed hard enough to bring tears streaming down her face. Jessica stared at her, unsure what to say or do. She was in unchartered territory here—Dr. Nelson was known as a stickler for proper grammar usage, was one of the most intelligent people she'd ever known and wasn't usually into bantering and joking around. Yet, here she was, pushing away from the table and holding her sides as if she'd splinter apart any second.

Meanwhile, their salads sat partially eaten. Should she continue to eat? Wait for the woman to recover? Offer to send for help?

Finally, Dr. Nelson recovered enough to sip a glass of water—elegantly, of course—and speak.

"Oh, my goodness, I haven't laughed like that in ages," she said. She shook her head. "As a teacher, I always cultivated this foreboding air—slightly untouchable, possibly supernatural, definitely not one to be trifled with. And the majority of my students greeted me in awed disbelief, which I'll confess, did not bother me in the slightest. It ensured they behaved and did what I told them to do. But there were always a couple—and you're one of those—who I thought understood me, at least as much as I'd let a student understand me. And, over the years, as you and I have grown closer, I assumed you'd lost that fear of me. To find out you still feel that way…well, it was a shock to my system, to say the least."

Jessica ate a forkful of salad. "There is nothing that will convince me you're ordinary, no matter how long or how well I know you. Therefore, nothing you do should surprise me, although I occasionally forget that fact."

"I guess it's related to your discomfort calling me by my first name."

Jessica nodded and took a sip of her water. "Correct."

Dr. Nelson tapped her manicured nails on the table. "I know which battles to fight," she said. "This isn't one of them. Anyway, returning to our subject. I have several contacts in careers related to English, and I'm happy to recommend my favorite student to them. As soon as I hear, I'll let you know."

Her phone chimed and a look of supreme satisfaction—similar to the looks she'd given Jessica and some of her classmates when they'd written a paper she'd liked—crossed her face. Moments such as these made Jessica think her former teacher was ageless.

"Here we are, just in time. Consuela Fernandez is the managing editor of *Shattering the Glass*, the online magazine I mentioned earlier, and one I think you'd find interesting. She likes to focus on women in various industries, politics, literature, et cetera, and I think you'd be a great fit. I'll send you her contact information, and you can reference me in your cover letter."

Jessica's phone buzzed with the information. "Thank you, Dr. Nelson. I appreciate your help."

"You're welcome. I'll send you the other person's contact information when she responds to my message. Now, let's enjoy the rest of our lunch while you fill me in on all the juicy details about your life."

Thomas gritted his teeth as he sat in his truck in the parking lot of the fire station. He'd entered this building a million times before, including a couple of weeks ago, with less trepidation. Yet somehow, today, he was filled with more anxiety. Maybe because, for the first time, he was going to confront what had happened with complete honesty.

About damn time.

He spent an extra twenty seconds yelling at himself to grow a pair—silently, since he didn't want to risk anyone hearing him—before he opened the door and walked across the lot. The wind was bitter today, and he rushed inside.

Even Mother Nature wanted him to get this over with.

He looked at his watch. Just in time for the house's monthly meeting, the one day per month when all the firefighters, regardless of their schedule, were together. At least he'd only have to do this once.

Inside the building, he jogged upstairs and slipped onto a chair at the rear of the conference room, the meeting already in progress. Christmas decorations cheered the drab room. A few of the other firefighters nodded to him, but most of them directed their attention to the chief. Thomas kept his hands fisted in his jacket pockets. His knee bounced as he waited for Chief Gordon to speak. When she finished with the day's business and with information about the house's Christmas party, and as always, asked if there were any questions, he raised his hand.

She lifted her eyebrows in surprise. "Nice to see you, Ace."

Thomas flinched at the use of his nickname. His scars itched. "Can I have a minute to speak, Chief?"

She glanced at the other firefighters in the room. "Since there aren't any questions, sure."

With a deep breath, he rose and walked to the front of the room. He stared out at the faces of his friends, people he'd risked his life for and with, and who did the same for him. He owed them everything, and now he owed them the truth.

He cleared his throat. "Hey, I know you all have better things to do than listen to me chat away…" He paused as they chuckled. "But I'm long overdue giving you an explanation for my behavior."

He waited for the room to quiet. "Nine and a half months ago, we all responded to a fire at the Browerville Museum. You all know the scene—you were all there. You all remember the choking black smoke, the risk to the historical objects as well as the people, the burning timber, the chaos. We've all seen plenty of similar instances. What made this one different, though, was me."

He looked around at the quizzical faces.

"I was drunk. Although it wasn't my first time drinking at work, it was the first time I'd responded impaired to a scene. The alcohol affected my response times, my judgment, and my ability to be a responsible member of your team. Ultimately, it caused my burns and almost cost Eric Payne his life."

His team stilled, even his good friends. He'd hidden it better than he'd thought. Guilt swamped him, but he continued.

"Many of you have wondered why I won't return. Or, at least, you did before now. Although I'm nine months and fifteen days sober, I recognize a big part of this job is trust. Trust in oneself that you can run toward the fire, not away, and trust in your team that they have your back. While I've never doubted any of you, you won't be able to say that about me. I've betrayed your trust, not only by drinking on the job, but by not telling you I struggled in the first place. It's also why I haven't answered your voicemails or texts. Because I couldn't without telling you my truth."

Thomas took a deep breath.

"I don't want to put anyone in jeopardy again. I don't know if you can forgive me, but I want you all to know I'm sorry. I'm sorry I put you in danger. I'm sorry I lost your friendship. And I'm sorry I didn't trust you all enough to ask for help."

With nothing left to say, he stepped away from the podium, walked to the rear of the room and exited.

The old Thomas, the one who'd lived in shame for more than eight months, would have left the station. This time, he stood outside the door and waited until the meeting was over. Because, while he didn't want to cause a scene inside, and he wasn't sure he could handle everyone's anger while standing behind the podium, his friends and team members deserved a chance to talk to him after the meeting. Despite his desire to leave, he stayed.

The first people to leave the room were two women. They exited, heads bent toward each other, talking. When they saw him, they straightened, looked at him, nodded, and walked away.

The two women weren't people he knew, and he assumed they'd joined the department while he was gone. Their reaction didn't bother him.

Rick, Ed and Hassan came out next.

Rick and Ed kept walking, but Hassan stopped.

"Tommy," he said. He gave Thomas a hug. "That was quite a statement you made in there."

Thomas swallowed. "Ruffled a lot of feathers." He glanced at the other men walking away.

Hassan nodded. "Give them time. None of us was expecting it. I don't know what to think, either, but you were brave to come clean here."

"Should have done it from the beginning."

"Yeah. But give everyone time to adjust. Including me."

"I will. You know where to find me if you want to talk. Or anyone else."

Hassan nodded. "I do." He hugged Thomas again. "Take care of yourself."

"You too."

The fire chief came out last. "My office, Thomas."

She was a small woman, but she held her own against the machismo found among the male firefighters. Before ascending to her position, she'd been as strong, or stronger, than many of the men, pulling her weight and developing trust among her team members. As a chief, she was fair. But Thomas recognized the tone. While it had never been used on him before, those team members who'd been its recipients hadn't fared well.

He straightened and followed Chief Gordon into her office. She closed the door and shut the blinds. Thomas appreciated, yet feared, the privacy.

Without a word, she walked to her desk, opened a drawer and pulled out an envelope. He recognized it. It was the resignation letter he'd given her two and a half weeks ago.

She showed it to him.

"I think it's time I accept this," she said. "And I want you to understand why."

He was a drunk, and he'd almost killed a man. He nodded.

"I'm not accepting this because you're an alcoholic. Your sobriety is something to be proud of, and it shows you've accepted your disease. This job it tough. The stress is insane. I'm not here to judge you. I'm proud of you for addressing your problem and admitting it here."

She paused, and he nodded.

"However, you put every other team member here in jeopardy with your actions. It happened on my watch, and as chief, I can't gloss over it, even if I empathize with you. You were irresponsible and broke trust, and in this job, trust is everything."

"I understand," he said. "I didn't come here expecting my job back."

"I know. With your public acknowledgment of your actions before the fire, it will be safer for you in the long run if I've accepted a resignation letter dated prior to today. It enables me to be supportive of you rather than have to initiate disciplinary actions. Understood?"

"Yes, Chief."

He started to exit the room, but she stopped him as his hand touched the doorknob.

"Thomas?"

"Yes?"

"Good luck."

With a nod, he exited her office. Outside, the firefighters on duty were in the lounge, watching TV, reading, playing cards. They quieted as he walked past them.

"Hey, Tommy," Rick called.

"Yeah?"

Rick walked over to him and shook his hand. "What you did in there took guts," he said. "You didn't have to come clean. You could have let it go. I don't condone what you did, but I don't see any reason to pile on you any more than you've already piled on yourself."

The other guys in the room nodded.

"Be safe, okay?" Rick said.

"Thanks." Thomas raised his hand in a wave, and left, lighter than he was before. Now it was time to implement his next step.

Chapter Thirteen

Jessica was delivering the third local paper to Thomas the next day when his front door swung open and Thomas himself appeared in the doorway.

"Caught you," he cried.

He stepped onto his front porch, clad in worn jeans and a T-shirt, arms crossed in front of him. His entwined arms accentuated his chest and arm muscles, and made her lady parts clench, despite the scowl on his face. His jeans showed off his thigh muscles. Why was it only assholes were gorgeous?

She stuck the newspaper under his doormat and turned around.

"You're not going to say anything?" he asked.

She spun around, noticing the goose bumps on his biceps. Excellent. He needed a good cooling off period.

"You told me not to talk to you. And you haven't returned my calls or texts."

"Jessica, this is ridiculous."

She put her hands on her hips. At least she wouldn't strangle the man.

"You're right, it is. I've learned a lot about myself these past few weeks. I don't need to endure work that embarrasses me, and I don't need to suffer men who treat me like you do, no matter how much I might care for them. Goodbye, Thomas."

"Jessica, wait."

She clomped down his porch stairs, stopping at the bottom, although her brain screamed at her to keep walking. She stilled, her back to him.

"You're going to keep giving me newspapers?"

"No, I'm not some dog playing fetch. This is the last one. Your actions might have been heroic, but the ceremony isn't making national news. And I proved my point, even if you're too thickheaded to get it."

She didn't want to talk to him anymore. Well, she did, but what was the point? They were going to argue. He hated journalists. Though she was out of a job, she would always be a journalist. What kind of human knowingly put themselves in the path of someone who hated them, and continued to do so? Certainly not her. Her friends might be die-hard romantics and want the two of them to get together, but here in real life? Not happening.

Waving behind her—to ignore him would be rude—she returned home. There. She was done. She'd proved to him she hadn't written the article. Or at least, when he read this last paper, he'd know. And now she would file him into her childhood memories and let him stay there.

Yeah right.

Her conscience needed to shut up. There was a reason why people said you could never go home again. He was proof. Much better to leave him as her childhood neighbor crush than try to force him into some mold of the perfect man. Because he wasn't. And no matter how hard she might want him, he never would be. And he'd never want her.

Her dad greeted her at the door, her phone in his hand.

"Hey, this thing has been ringing the whole time you were gone."

"I can't believe I forgot it." She took it from him. "Sorry."

Taking the phone from him, she scrolled through the missed calls. Three were from numbers she didn't recognize, but they'd all left voicemails. She played them, attention rapt.

"Dr. Nelson works fast," she told her dad. "I've got three editors who want to see my résumé." She opened her email. "And one of the papers I contacted prior to lunch with her also liked my résumé and asked for writing samples."

Her father nodded. "I'm not surprised. Good for you."

Upstairs in her room, she responded to the email with answers to their questions and writing samples. Taking a deep breath, she returned the calls.

Twenty minutes later, she called Dr. Nelson.

"Apparently, I'm not the only person a little afraid of you," she said when her mentor answered the phone. "Because all three of the editors you contacted called me to schedule interviews. I don't know how to thank you."

"Don't thank me until you've signed an employment offer. And while I may have nudged them a little, they checked you out and were impressed enough to get in touch with you. I pointed them in the right direction."

"Well, I appreciate it. And even if they don't hire me right now, I'm thrilled to be on their radar."

"Positive thinking, my girl. It's the only way this works."

"Well, talent might help, too," Jessica said.

"You've got plenty of that anyway."

Thanks to Dr. Nelson's hype, Jessica hung up the phone with a smile. She pulled articles she was proud of and moved them into computer folders, proofread her résumé one last time, and organized everything for her first interview. Then she went downstairs.

Her mom was in the kitchen, polishing the family menorah. It was silver with room for nine candles, one for each night of Hanukkah, plus the shamash, or helper candle, to light the others.

"Oh, I have to find mine," she said.

Her mom tipped her chin toward the table. "No, you don't. I pulled it out for you already."

Jessica kissed her cheek. "Thank you. Do you have candles, or do you need me to buy them?"

"I always have extras, but I'd love you to buy a couple of fresh packs and some wrapping paper."

Grabbing her keys and phone this time, Jessica took the car into town, pulling into the grocery store parking lot. The large windows in the front had been painted with winter scenes, and inside, the endcaps of each aisle offered holiday specials. Jessica grabbed two boxes of candles and two rolls of blue and silver paper. She checked out and returned home.

As she pulled into the driveway, she forced herself not to glance over at Thomas's house. It had been her standard practice since forever. She'd always checked to see if he was home or if she could see him. But now that she was finished with him, she needed to change her ways. Not looking over there was a good start.

"The grocery store carried cute things this year," Jessica said as she entered the kitchen. "Not a huge selection, but cute nonetheless."

Her mom sighed. "It helps that Hanukkah and Christmas are at the same time. I remember one year Hanukkah occurred right around Thanksgiving and when I asked for gift boxes at stores, the salespeople looked at me like I was crazy."

"Is that why you wrapped my gifts in food boxes?"

"Made the surprise last longer." A sly grin crept across her mom's face.

"Guess there's an upside to stores' lack of preparation. Because, let me tell you, I was mighty confused when I unwrapped a brownie box only to find my favorite book inside."

Jessica and her mom smiled at their treasured memory.

"Did you know—"

"Wait," Jessica said. She held up her hand. "Don't tell me anything else. I don't want my childhood ruined."

"But—"

"Nope." She shook her head. "Next, you'll tell me you made your latkes from a mix. I don't want to hear it."

"A mix?" Her mom's mouth dropped in horror. "Your grandmother would have killed me. I make my latkes from scratch, and you know it. You've helped me."

Jessica shrugged. "You need to leave me with my memories."

For the first time in nine months, Thomas slept through the night and woke refreshed. No nightmares of the fire woke him, no guilt swamped him, and no fears of what today would bring overwhelmed him. For the first time in nine months, Thomas was at peace.

He whistled as he jogged down the stairs. Reggie jumped from his dog bed, cocked his head to the side, and bounded over to him.

Thomas scratched the dog behind his ears. "You notice it, too, huh?" He clipped on his leash and took him for a walk through the neighborhood. He waved to Mr. Rappaport pulling out of his driveway, yelled a hello to the young mother walking her baby in a stroller, and nodded at someone else walking their dog on the opposite side of the road.

At home, he made himself coffee, fed Reggie, and called his sponsor.

"You were right," he said when Carl answered the phone.

"This is new. Tell me why."

"I talked to Eric Payne, the guy I rescued, and my firefighter buddies. Payne doesn't blame me at all. My buddies... well, it'll take them a while to forgive me I think, but knowing how they feel, or maybe because I know how they feel, a huge weight has lifted off me."

"Darn it."

"Excuse me?"

"You started out by telling me I was right, so I don't get to tell you I told you so."

Thomas grunted but chuckled along with Carl as he laughed.

"Man, it is good to hear you laugh," Carl said. "And I'm glad you feel better, all kidding aside."

"I owe you one."

"Nope," his sponsor said. "You did this on your own. I advised you, but it was up to you to follow through. Like it was your decision to get sober. Own it."

Thomas mulled over his sponsor's words. "Okay." Air escaped his lungs and, with it, more peace came over him.

"So what's your plan now?" Carl asked.

"I'm going to look into becoming an instructor."

"Hallelujah!"

"What does that mean?" Thomas asked.

"It means I'm glad you recognize you have something worthwhile to contribute."

Thomas considered his sponsor's words. He was right. It had taken him a long time to get to this point, but he possessed the confidence he thought he'd lost.

He ended the phone call and planned his day. His family was arriving soon to celebrate Christmas. He made a list of everything he needed to finish—decorating, grocery shopping, wrapping gifts and finishing his outdoor decorations for the contest.

The contest.

It had lost its luster once he and Jessica had stopped speaking to each other. He needed to fix things with her too.

Sitting at his computer, he searched for her byline. She'd written a lot of articles in her ten-year career. Not that he should be surprised. He scanned them. The breadth and depth of her coverage impressed him. Not only had she written human-interest stories early in her profession, she'd written investigative pieces about illegal dumping, union disputes and police corruption. He whistled under his breath.

But as hard as he searched, he couldn't find the Browerville Museum rededication and awards ceremony or the fire or him.

He wondered why someone with her credentials would be reporting on this small story to begin with.

The more he searched, the more questions he had. Like, her last byline was early November. What was she doing in the meantime?

He checked the masthead of the *Brooklyn Daily Herald*. She wasn't listed. Plenty of journalists were freelancers and weren't listed. Yet the paper registered three other investigative reporters. What made her different?

He rested his elbows on his desk and his chin in his hands. Why did he torture himself over her? Why couldn't he drop it, like he'd done any time he'd seen her? She was his neighbor, nothing more.

Except, he suspected she was something more. A lot more. And therefore he needed to know everything. He had to stop assuming things about her, stop running away from partial truths or half-told information and follow the trail until he got to the end.

He pulled out his phone, prepared to text her, but stopped. This was worth more than a text. More than a phone call. They needed to meet in person. He needed to see her face when she answered his questions, and she needed to see his.

Before he could invent an excuse as to why he should wait, he pulled on a jacket and strode across their yards to her front door.

He knocked, stuffing his hands in his pockets as he waited for her to answer.

Her dad answered.

He hadn't expected that. He was transported to his childhood when kids would show up at a house, ring the doorbell and ask if someone could come out to play. Except, he'd never showed up at her house, hadn't ever asked her to play. She'd been the one to ask to join his friends.

"Hey, Thomas, how are you?" Mr. Sacks asked.

"Good." He retreated a step. "The house looks great."

Mr. Sacks craned his neck to look next door. "Yours does too. Guess the contest will be a nail-biter."

Thomas nodded. "Is Jessica around?"

"No, she's out on an interview." Pride shone on his face. "I don't know how she does it, but leave it to my girl to find job openings during the holidays." He paused. "Can I give her a message for you?"

Job interview? "No, I'll catch her later. Thanks."

Mr. Sacks waved and shut the door, leaving Thomas to walk home, deep in thought. Why had she been working on a story about him if she hadn't had a job?

He returned home and leaned down to greet Reggie. "You know, Reg, I won't make any assumptions or try to answer my own questions this time. I need to find out from Jessica what's going on. See, you can teach an old dog new tricks."

Reggie woofed in agreement before licking Thomas's face.

Wiping it dry, he texted Jessica.

Can we talk when you're free?

He'd give her the rest of the day to answer before chasing her again.

"You are looking at the Senior Editor for Women's Issues at *Shattering the Glass*," Jessica cried, walking into her parents' family room.

"You got the job!" Her mom jumped off the sofa and rushed over to give her a hug. Her dad followed.

"I knew you could do it," he said. "When do you start?"

"January second. And the position is remote, since the company is based on the West Coast, so I can keep my apartment and work from home."

"Oh, honey, that's wonderful! You won't miss colleagues to talk with?" her mom asked.

"They have weekly video conferences with the different departments and all kinds of digital ways to collaborate, so remote people feel part of the community. I think there are several in-person regional meetings in New York City, and I don't know what else, which is a long way of saying I don't think so."

Laughter bubbled in her chest at the prospect of her new job and responsibilities. With all of the women's issues in the United States, Consuela Fernandez, her new boss and managing editor of *Shattering the Glass*, believed in the importance of devoting an entire team to those subjects, and Jessica was thrilled to be a part of it.

"We need to celebrate," her dad said. "Pick where you'd like to go tonight."

Jessica bit her lip. "Could we go to dinner and come here for dessert? I'd like to invite Dr. Nelson over to thank her for her help, plus Sarah, Caroline and Emily..."

"That's a great idea," her father said. He looked at her mom, who nodded. "You two decide where to go, and I'll make my famous Bundt cake."

Jessica's mouth watered. Her dad's Bundt cakes were a family favorite on every occasion and holiday. He always tailored them to fit whatever they celebrated, even creating a kosher one for Passover.

He stopped on his way into the kitchen. "In all the excitement, I forgot. Thomas stopped by, looking for you this afternoon."

A little of Jessica's excitement disappeared. "Did he say what he wanted?"

Her dad shook his head. "Nope. He said he'd catch you later."

Great. "Okay, thanks." Right now, she wanted to enjoy her accomplishment. She joined her mom on the sofa.

"I'm proud of you, honey," her mom said.

"Thank you. I like the company's philosophy, and the fact they're expanding their coverage of women's issues is exciting. I can't wait to do something I love and make a difference."

"You're going to be great."

Jessica pulled out her phone to scroll through restaurant ideas. Thomas had texted her while she'd been in the interview, her phone on silent.

Can we talk when you're free?

She'd deal with him later.

After some back-and-forth, they decided on a local Indian restaurant they'd been to the previous summer. Her mom made reservations and Jessica called everyone to invite them to join them for dessert tonight.

Later, after they'd returned from the restaurant and her guests had arrived, Jessica stood before her friends and raised a glass of the wine Caroline had brought.

"Thank you all for joining me tonight. I'm lucky to have a loving family and supportive friends. I could not have found this job without your help."

Dr. Nelson and Jessica's friends shook their heads in denial, but she pressed on. "No, it's true. Sarah, Caro and Emily, you showed me I didn't have to compromise my morals or ethics to do what I loved. And, Dr. Nelson, while I got the job on my own merits, your recommendation helped speed the process and opened doors I don't know I would have been able to open on my own. Plus, you instilled a love of writing in me that exists to this day. Thank you, everyone."

The room erupted in applause. Jessica's face heated, which caused everyone to laugh, and Jessica to blush further.

"Okay, okay," she said. "It's time for dessert."

Jessica's mom and dad went into the kitchen to get the dessert and Dr. Nelson turned to the other women. "It's wonderful to see you all again. What are you doing for the holidays?"

"I'm going to my grandparents' for Christmas," Emily said.

"And where do they live?" Dr. Nelson asked.

"Pennsylvania. Do you have Christmas plans?"

Dr. Nelson nodded. "My son and daughter-in-law will arrive on Christmas Eve. We'll go to church and visit with some other family. I hope the weather cooperates."

Jessica's father entered the room with his homemade Bundt cake.

Jessica's mouth dropped. "Dad, that's fabulous. How did you do it so fast?"

The Bundt cake was white with black lines on it made to look like newsprint. On the top, the headline read, Amazing Daughter Finds Dream Job.

Her mom looked at him with pride. "He's talented."

All the girls exclaimed.

"You used to have the best birthday parties," Caroline said. "I remember I couldn't wait for cake time because your dad's creations were fantastic."

Her dad bowed his head. "It relaxes me. And don't worry, Jess, it's chocolate inside."

"That is a stunning cake," Dr. Nelson cried. "I never knew your father was a baker," she said.

"Only as a hobby," he said. "It's more fun that way."

Jessica joined everyone at the table as they ate dessert at chatted together.

"Will you make one of your cakes for Hanukkah?" Dr. Nelson asked Jessica's dad.

He shook his head. "No, I'll make donuts and fried Oreos. It's our family tradition." He turned to Jessica's friends. "Girls, what are you doing for Hanukkah?"

Jessica half listened as Sarah said she'd celebrate with Aaron and their families and Caroline talked about a big splash for

Jared's daughter. What were Thomas's Christmas plans? Was the tree decorated yet? Ugh, why did she spend her time thinking about him?

Her mom caught her glance across the table and gave her a quizzical look. She mouthed, *Are you okay?*

Jessica nodded. But deep inside, something wasn't right. She couldn't let the situation with Thomas remain like this. She should have called him this afternoon.

"Earth to Jessica," Sarah called. "You still with us?"

She started. "Yes, sorry. My mind wandered."

"Not surprised," Caroline said. "You've had a lot happen to you in a short amount of time."

"Too bad you don't have one of my 'What did you do over vacation?' assignments," Dr. Nelson said. "Think of all the things you could write."

"Oy, I think I'll focus on my new job's writing assignments, thank you."

"Well, I couldn't be prouder," Dr. Nelson said. "I can't wait to read your first piece. Do you have any idea what you'll cover first?"

"No," she said. But she did know what she had to *do* first.

Chapter Fourteen

Thomas put the final touches on the Christmas lights on his front porch and admired his work after the people next door left. For the next three days, judges would evaluate everyone's creative efforts. If he were in charge, he'd win. He'd chosen a candy-cane theme, with red and white lights on the house, front porch and trees in his yard. Plastic candy canes lined his walkway and driveway, and he'd tied a red-and-white bow on the wreath on his front door. Candy canes hung from the windows as well.

He looked over at Jessica's house. Her Hanukkah decorations were creative, and he would have liked for their bet to work out. Competing with her would have been fun, before things between had blown up. Lost in thought, he didn't notice her approach until she was all the way up to his driveway.

"Jessica?" He blinked, like he'd conjured her.

She was wrapped in her navy parka, her cheeks pink from the cold. She held a foil-wrapped plate in her hands.

She peered at him. "You look like you've seen a ghost."

"Sorry, I…didn't expect to see you."

"You texted me."

"I did."

She swallowed. "I feel like we always get off on the wrong foot. Let me start over. Hi."

Shock turned to satisfaction when she didn't leave. "Hi."

"My dad said you stopped by. I didn't see your text until much later, but I thought I'd come over now to see if you were around."

His heart pounded. "I'm here."

She nodded. "I see." She grew solemn again. "I'm sorry."

"I am too."

"Can we go somewhere to talk?" She held out the plate. "I brought these, and they're much better warm."

With a nod, he pointed to his front door and followed her onto the porch. Just holding the door for her made him feel better, as did watching the happy greeting Reggie gave her. He waited until she was inside before leading her into the kitchen.

"Something to drink? I've got hot chocolate."

"Perfect." She looked around as he heated the water. "You decorated."

He'd put a red-and-green cloth on the table and festooned the tops of the cabinets with garland. "Yeah."

"It's pretty." She put the plate on the counter and sat at the kitchen table, her hands wrapped around the mug of steaming hot chocolate he put in front of her.

Nodding at the plate, he asked, "What are these?"

"Jelly donuts. My dad makes them for Hanukkah every year. He's the family baker, and they're delicious."

Lifting the foil, he looked at the sugarcoated confections and took a whiff. His stomach growled. "He made these? They smell good."

"Help yourself."

She shook her head when he offered her one.

The sweet dough and the tangy jam mixed to form a delectable, decadent treat. "They're fantastic," he said. Unable to control himself, he wolfed the entire donut in a couple bites. When he finished, he started to speak, but she raised a finger.

"Me first?" She straightened and looked at him for the first time since they'd entered his house. "I'm sorry I betrayed your trust. When I first contacted you, I never expected you to be anything other than my story's subject. But the more time we spent together, the harder it was to keep personal and professional separate, and the line blurred."

He pushed his chair away from the table to lean his elbows on his knees. "I don't want to be the kind of guy who makes a woman choose between her career and him. But there are parts of my life I want to keep private."

"I know." She looked away for a minute, made fists with her hands, and met his gaze again. "Part of my job as an investigative reporter was to investigate all the things you didn't say. But the more I dug, the more guilty I felt. I wish I'd stopped right away, but I had so much on the line."

"And I wish I was honest with you from the start," he said. "And nicer."

"I wasn't honest, either. I screwed up an article a few months ago with a major advertiser at the *Brooklyn Daily Herald*. They fired me, but my boss offered me this article as a way to save my job. At first, they didn't know there was more to the ceremony. But the more updates I provided, the more my boss wanted me to get the story on you. I didn't like the angle they wanted me to cover, but again, I was afraid. I couldn't afford my rent, and if I lost my job, I'd have to move home."

Thomas reclined in his chair. He understood desperation, but at his expense? "You decided my embarrassment was worth it?"

She shook her head. "I'll admit it took me longer than it should have to do the right thing, but ultimately, I told my boss I couldn't write the story, not if it meant betraying you. I quit and kept my notes. I deleted them so my editor couldn't assign the story to someone else."

He exhaled. She hadn't even written the story. No one knew about his shame, other than those to whom he'd confessed. He expected a wash of relief, but none came. He poked and prodded his psyche, but it was at peace, the same peace he'd experienced since confessing to his colleagues.

"Please say something, Thomas."

Maybe the article didn't matter. Maybe he was no longer ashamed of his actions. Well, that wasn't true. He couldn't condone what he'd done, but his actions no longer controlled him.

"Thank you."

She opened and closed her mouth. She looked away.

Was that it? He didn't want to lose her again.

Her chest rose and fell. "You didn't mean it," she said.

"What?" He raised his eyes to her face, confused. Had he missed something?

"You didn't mean thank you, or if you did, it wasn't a serious one."

It took him a few seconds to follow her train of thought. "I meant it. Wouldn't have said it if I didn't."

"But you shook your head no."

Turning toward her, he put into words what ran through his brain. "I was thanking you, in all seriousness, for the decision you made. It couldn't have been easy, and I appreciate it. But I realized, even if you had published your story, I'd be okay."

"How? I would have exposed you and left you to clean the mess. It's not fair."

"No, it's not. But I've already told those closest to me what I did. I'm not proud of it. I'm an alcoholic, but I'm in recovery. I confessed to the guys at the firehouse and, while some of them avoided me, a lot of them came and talked to me. I can survive this. Yeah, would I have hated your article. But I would have survived."

She rose, and his stomach dropped. She couldn't leave, not when she'd returned.

"Don't go."

"I spent all my teenaged years waiting for you to say that." The corner of her mouth rose.

"It was never the right time. Now…"

"Now, I think we've spent too much time trying to make it work between us for all the wrong reasons. And in the process, I think we learned it's not meant to be."

His heart seized. He couldn't lose her.

"Don't say that. Don't think that."

"Thomas." Sorrow turned her green eyes mossy.

"Say my name again," he said.

Tears threatened to overflow. "Don't make this harder than it is."

"Harder than it is? For whom? Because I don't know about you, but I won't survive without you. I can make it through alcohol withdrawal, losing my friends, changing careers— anything. But losing you? That will kill me."

"You think this is easy for me?" She stepped away from him.

The growing space between them filled him with dread.

Her voice sharpened she spoke. "I've dreamt about you my whole life, wanted to be with you, even when I didn't believe in relationships. No one compared to you. And when I got you, I put my career before you. Clearly, we are not *bashert*."

He frowned. "Buh-what?"

"Meant to be."

Stepping forward, he closed the terrible distance between them, at least physically, and took both her hands in his.

"I like that word. You see, I think we are *bashert*."

"How can you think that?"

"Because, despite everything, we keep coming back to each other. We don't give up. You make mistakes, as do I. We're human. But the important thing is we keep trying, we *both* keep trying. Sometimes I'll screw up and sometimes you will. As long as we return to each other, that's what matters."

She squeezed his hands, and he took that as a good sign. "I need to be a journalist. I need a career I'm proud of."

"Good. Write whatever stories fulfill you."

"What will you do?"

He paused, allowing the germ of an idea to bloom. "I was asked to consider being an instructor, and I'm thinking about it."

Her eyes lit up. "I think you'd be great at it. Remember how you taught your sister to play softball? You were patient with her."

"How'd you know?"

"I watched, remember?"

He shook his head. "Oh, brother."

"It's what you love."

He nodded. "I have to be sure it doesn't make sobriety harder, because I won't mess it up for anything."

"What about the elephant in the room?" she asked.

He looked around. "What elephant?"

She punched his arm and, for the first time since their conversation had started, he thought they might have a chance together.

"Our different religions," she said. "You're Christian, I'm Jewish. Can we work that out?"

"I've learned a lot about myself and how to deal with people as a result of my sobriety journey," Thomas said. "And one of the things I've learned is, in addition to honesty, if you treat others with respect, and you behave with intent, a lot of difficult situations can be avoided."

"Kavod," Jessica said.

Thomas frowned, puzzled. "Excuse me?"

"It's the Hebrew word for respect."

He tried out the foreign word. *"Kavod.* I like it. If we *kavod*—" He stopped midsentence at Jessica's laugh.

"Sorry," she said. "I mean this with all due *respect,* but *kavod* is not a *verb.*"

With flared his nostrils, he continued. "You're lucky I like you. Anyway, if we treat each other and our differences with respect, and humor, we can figure out how best to do things."

She thought about what he said. "I've always been curious about your beliefs, and I'd love to show you my religious traditions as well."

"And I'd love to learn about yours and share them."

Her expression turned serious. "If we try to be together, though, you should know I need someone by my side who stands up for me, stands up *with* me, when I'm attacked."

He frowned. "Like if your job is dangerous?"

"No, like when anti-Semitic things happen. It's on the rise, and I need to know you're on my side."

"I'm always on your side," he said. "I don't stand for hate in any form, and I'll never let you confront it alone. I have a lot to learn, but I can promise you that much."

She nodded and her face flushed. "I hope I didn't hurt your feelings. I love how you tried to use the Hebrew word. It means a lot."

"I've got a much thicker skin than you think, and I don't mean these scars." He pointed to his neck. "Your laughter never offends me. If anything, I enjoy it."

"Good, but I'll still try to be more aware."

"Aware, hmm?" He leaned forward and nuzzled her neck. "I don't think I've been unaware of you for a while now."

Her skin was smooth and the scent of her shampoo—something clean and floral—tickled his nose. He nibbled her earlobe and licked the skin behind her ear before he kissed her. She shivered and he drew her closer.

"Oh?"

Her husky voice made him want to throw her over his shoulder and carry her to the bedroom.

"Really," he whispered.

"I think you need to show me," she said. "I haven't always received your message."

He turned to meet her gaze. He cupped his hands around her jaw before he placed light kisses on her eyelids, the bridge of her nose and her cheekbones.

"How's this?" he asked.

From there he moved to her neck. He pulled at the top of her sweatshirt and licked the crevice above her collarbone while sliding his hands down her upper arms, holding her in place.

"Or this?" he asked.

Grasping her hand, he brought it to his mouth, where he planted kisses on each finger before sucking each one. By the time he'd finished with all ten, he ached with need.

"And what about that?" His voice was rough with need.

"Stop talking." She reached for his neck and pulled him close. She pressed her mouth to his, and he responded, meeting her tongue and exploring deeper until the blood pounded in his veins.

Her hands massaged his neck, sending chills along his spine. He groaned, her mouth absorbing the sound. She arched against him, thrusting her breasts into his chest. He slid his hands around her waist, his thumbs against her ribs. He wanted to explore her body, taste her skin, see her flush, feel her heat.

Slipping his hands beneath her sweatshirt, he pulled away and looked at her questioningly. When she nodded, he raised it over her head and stared at her. Her pale pink lacy bra blended into the pink of her skin, and through the sheer silk, her nipples puckered. Before he had a chance to do more than look, she pulled the hem of his shirt out of the waistband of his jeans. One by one, she undid the buttons, following each opening with a kiss until his skin burned with desire. Exposed, he maneuvered his arms out of the sleeves.

Time stopped for an instant while they each watched the other.

"Are you sure about this?" he asked. "About us?"

"Do you forgive me?" she asked.

He nodded. "There's nothing to forgive. I understand why you did it and appreciate why you stopped. I'm sorry I doubted you."

Her wariness disappeared and desire sharpened her gaze. "Then I'm sure," she whispered.

She stood in front of him, splayed her hands on his chest and brushed the healed burn scars. Her proximity, mixed with the different levels of feelings as his damaged nerve endings reacted to her touch, made him shiver with anticipation. She took control, leading with her lips as she covered every inch of his arms, chest and back with kisses. When he tried to touch her, she stepped away, and he stood there, shaking, letting her have her way.

When he could stand it no longer, he grasped her upper arms and moved her in front of him.

"My turn," he growled.

Starting behind her left ear—he loved that soft spot—he trailed kisses down her neck, across her collarbone to the hollow between her breasts. He reached behind her and unclasped her bra, removing it with his teeth and taking each breast in his hand. He rubbed his thumbs over her nipples until they peaked and she dropped her head.

Unlike his, her skin was smooth and warm and soft. He pressed her close to him and inhaled the scent of her hair, feeling their hearts beat against each other, listening to her breathing.

"Come with me," he said and, when she murmured, he took her by the hand and led her to the bedroom.

Jessica's first thought when Thomas led her to the room was, *That is one massive bed.* It dominated the master bedroom. Now, the dark oak headboard and king-size mattress covered with a gray quilt beckoned.

He backed her against the mattress, used his booted foot to

spread apart her legs, and stood facing her, one thigh between hers. This close to him, his fresh, clean scent surrounded her. The button of his jeans pressed against her waist. He caressed her cheek.

"Okay?" he asked.

She nodded before lifting her hands and trailing them over his chest. As she went lower, his stomach muscles twitched. She smiled.

"Don't even think of tickling me." His voice was a combination of fierce warning and deep need.

"What will you do?" She pressed against him.

He grasped her buttocks and stared into her eyes. His were brown, but they'd darkened to black the more she touched him.

"I dare you," he said.

Well, that was a mistake. Splaying her fingers at his waist, she absorbed his heat, slowed her breathing, and gave him a false sense of calm. She tickled beneath his rib cage.

"Ah!" He yelled, a sound more like a gargle, and jumped away.

Before she could make her escape, however, he grasped her, swung her over his shoulder, and dropped her onto the bed.

Luckily, he preferred a soft mattress. It was her last thought before he climbed on top of her, pinned her arms above her with one hand and tickled her belly with the other.

She couldn't breathe. She writhed under him.

"Had enough?" he asked.

She couldn't answer.

He took pity on her and waited while she panted until she'd caught her breath. Now she knew what happened if she dared him. "That was mean," she said.

He shook his head. "No, that was deserved."

Before she could argue, he lowered his lips to hers and plundered her mouth. Disappearing into his kiss, her mind lost all ability to think. All she could do was kiss him. Her skin heated with desire, her hips moved against him, and the friction between them drove her wild. She didn't notice when he let go of her arms. With shaking fingers, she pulled at the waistband of his jeans.

He groaned, raised his hips, and they made quick work of removing the rest of their clothes. Naked, she wrapped herself around him, embracing him and feeling the different textures of their skin meeting as one.

Now, his kisses slowed, each one longer and deeper than the one before. Their breaths mingled and their noses brushed. She sighed, filled with the knowledge her dreams of this man were about to come true.

He pulled away. The sudden lack of body heat made her shiver. "Wait," she said, at once hating the desperation in her voice yet at the same time not caring if it meant he'd return.

"Just a sec, I need a condom." He pulled out a hidden drawer in his headboard area and grabbed a foil packet.

She didn't understand how he could be calm when her world was about to shatter from a combination of wonder and desire.

But his fingers trembled and he swore beneath his breath as it slipped from her grasp.

She held out her hand. "Give it to me," she said.

He handed the packet to her and she unwrapped it. She slid the condom on and his jaw tightened, his breath hissing as she glided it into place. Eyes hooded, he flipped her over, rising above her and staring at her. She reached for him, cupping his jaw and lifting her hips to meet him.

"Are. You. Ready?" He interrupted each word with a kiss.

"I've been ready for you forever," she whispered.

His pupils widened and he slid into her. He was large, larger than she'd remembered, yet somehow, exactly right.

Once inside, their bodies rocked together. She disappeared into the moment. His rough hands on her skin, the scent of his body and the sound of his breath—harsh, jagged, and deep—overcame her.

"Open your eyes," he whispered. "I want to see your pleasure."

She dragged them open. His cheeks were ruddy, the tendons in his neck taut. Her body tightened and pleasure spiraled higher and higher. She held on to his shoulders, slick with sweat, and buried her face in his neck. A kaleidoscope of colors burst behind her eyelids as she reached her peak and tumbled over. He froze, pumped once more and shouted his release.

Sated, they drifted to reality together, still touching, still wrapped in each other's arms.

Thomas rolled over once again, and Jessica settled against him, her back to his chest, feeling his heartbeat.

"What are you thinking?" he asked.

"For once, I'm right where I want to be."

He kissed the nape of her neck and pulled her closer to him. "I never knew how lost I was until you. I made it through so many things, but I don't think I could survive without you."

Her eyes filled with tears at his touching words. One dripped down her cheek and landed on his arm. He peered over her shoulder.

"What's wrong?"

"Absolutely nothing." She gave him a watery smile. "I think that might be the nicest thing anyone has said to me."

"Clearly, you've hung around the wrong people." He nuzzled her neck.

She sighed in contentment. "Not for lack of trying."

His throaty laugh vibrated against her. The sensation, like many other things about him, was new to her. She wondered what else there was to discover about him, and how long she'd get to try.

"I might have been a little slow in the past," he said. "But now that I've let you in, I won't let you go unless you beg."

Jessica twisted around until she faced him again. "Beg? I don't beg."

"Are you sure?" His eyes crinkled in the corners with a hint of daring.

"Quite," she said.

Once again, he flipped her onto her back and towered over her, his bulging arms on either side of her.

"I'm going to make a liar out of you," he said.

And as he lowered himself onto her, she knew he was right.

An hour later, Thomas was in the kitchen with Jessica, sated and starving.

She sat at his kitchen table, dressed in one of his T-shirts, while he stood at the stove whipping up cheese omelets. Reggie paced between the two of them. The only reason he didn't touch her was that he needed food for energy. That, and fire safety. Because, you know…the stove.

He'd been serious when he said he'd never survive without her.

"Are we okay now?" she asked.

He sprinkled a combination of cheeses over the eggs and lowered the flame before he turned to look at her.

"I am," he said. "Are you?"

She nodded.

He brought the pan to the table and served her before himself. Then he put the pan on the counter, dragged her plate next to his, and patted his lap. They fed each other the omelets, turning a basic food into one of his favorites.

"Your dad said you were out on an interview, and you said you'd gotten a new job." He wiped his mouth and pushed the plates away. He rubbed her back. "Tell me about it."

She wiggled around to get comfortable and made him hard again, but her clear ease with him filled him with peace. The last thing he wanted was for her to think he wasn't interested in her career.

"I'm going to cover women's issues for an online news site." Her speech quickened. "I'm excited to do something meaningful. Not that I didn't enjoy what I did before. It gave me great experience, but I want something more. Plus, I hated the way my editors pursued a 'get the most salacious story at all costs' mission. I've never been someone who wanted to succeed at the expense of others."

He couldn't help feeling some of Jessica's joy. It spread from her to him, giving him a glimpse of what a relationship with her would be like. He liked it.

"I think it's great," he said. "I'm happy you're doing something you feel good about." He reached for her hand, running his thumb across knuckles. "My family is coming in next week. What do you think about you and your parents joining us for Christmas Eve dinner?"

"Are you sure? I wouldn't want us to interfere with your plans."

"You'd never interfere. I'd like to think you're my girlfriend." He waited for her to acknowledge their status.

Her smile widened, and the last of his insecurity melted away. He continued. "And my girlfriend and her family should join my family for dinner."

"Even though we don't celebrate?"

"We're going to have to figure out a way forward with different holidays. I think this would be a good start."

She kissed him. Man, if this was what she'd do every time he included her family in something, he'd build an adjoining set of rooms for them all to move in.

The next day, Jessica defrosted her mom's latkes and brought her menorah into the kitchen. Her mom spread foil on the counter for both hers and theirs to be lit this evening. Tonight was the first night of Hanukkah, and Jessica was ready.

In the meantime, today the town council was going to judge the holiday displays. She bundled into a jacket and went outside to be sure everything was set for the contest. Glancing next door, she noticed Thomas doing the same thing.

She admired his long legs and broad shoulders as he walked to the property boundary.

With a nod toward her house he said, "May the best man win."

She bristled. "Or woman."

He acknowledged her correction. "Winner gets a gift, right?"

"Yup, but don't worry, I've got what I want all picked out already."

Eyebrows raised, he stuffed his hands in his pockets and rocked back and forth on his heels. "Do you now? Pretty confident, aren't you?"

"You're not?"

"Oh, I'm plenty confident." He stepped forward and touched her cheek. "I hate to disappoint you so soon after becoming a couple."

The morning air was cold. His breath came out in white puffs. Jessica leaned into his hand. Shivers ran down her neck. Was this what people meant when they talked about chemistry and zings and temptation? His touch was warm. What would kissing him in the cold be like?

"Ahem."

Her dad's voice startled both of them, but Thomas jumped. She withheld a reaction as she returned to reality.

"Hi, Dad." She kept her gaze trained on Thomas a moment longer before turning around.

"Mr. Sacks," Thomas said, his hands once again in his pockets.

"Thomas." Her dad nodded in his direction. "Jess, I'm running out for the last of your mom's Hanukkah gifts. Need anything?" He looked between the two of them, paused and continued. "From the store?"

Oh, God, her father did not say that. Trying hard to pretend his comment didn't affect her, all the while ignoring the weird, strangled sounds from Thomas, she plastered a slight bland expression on her face.

"Nope, I'm good. Thanks."

She held her breath while he returned to the garage. Only when his car door slammed and his brake lights turned on did she let out the huge breath in a long, slow, whistle.

"Your dad—" Thomas started to say, but Jessica held up a finger to shush him.

She watched his car reverse out of the driveway and waved as he passed by the two of them. When the vehicle was out of sight, she leaned against him.

"Oh my God, oh my God, oh my God," she wheezed. He patted her back, but his chest vibrated.

"Your dad—" He gasped. "I've never been so called out without being called out before. It's like I was a kid again. Oh, man, can you imagine what he would have done if we'd dated when we were kids?"

"I don't want to." She took a deep breath. "What are you doing tonight?"

"That's a change of subject. Nothing. Why?"

"Want to come over for the first night of Hanukkah?" If they were to learn to respect each other's traditions, she wanted to start right away. "We'll have lots of yummy treats."

He rubbed his stomach. "You know the key to my heart is my stomach," he said, "but don't you want to celebrate as a family?"

"You're welcome to join. How about after dinner?"

He nodded. "As long as I'm not intruding."

"You're not." She looked away before meeting his gaze. "I think it's important to share my holiday with you if we're going to date."

His expression softened. "I'd like that. I want to understand you and your faith better."

"Like I'd like to understand yours." His eagerness to learn gave her hope they could work together, and she hoped her parents would come around.

Three hours later, three judges drove to each of their houses. They spent about ten minutes walking around each yard and consulting with one another. They photographed the houses from various angles and waved goodbye as they left.

Around three thirty, Thomas knocked on her door and held a small, sealed envelope with snowflakes on it.

"Check your mailbox yet?"

She grabbed her coat, and he held it for her as she slid her arms inside. Slipping her feet into her boots, she accompanied Thomas outside. They walked to the mailbox at the bottom of her driveway in silence.

Who won? She thought about their bet and her heart quickened in anticipation.

She'd bought him a gift in case, and she'd give it to him today if he won. And if she won? Would she still give the gift to him? She looked sideways at his chiseled jaw. Warmth spread through her, the same one that occurred every time she realized they were together.

Of course, she'd give it to him. She might add to it later.

At the bottom of her driveway, she opened her mailbox and pulled out a similar envelope to the one Thomas held. She flipped it over. She squeezed it. When she held it to the light, Thomas reached for her arm.

"How about we open them?"

"On three?" she asked.

He nodded. "One."

"Two," she said.

"Three."

She tore open the envelope and pulled out a letter.

Thank you for entering the Browerville Annual Holiday Decorating Contest. You've helped add holiday spirit to our town. As a result of your entry fee, we have raised $13,000 for Arts in our schools! We couldn't have done it without you.
The Contest Committee

Behind the letter was a card.

Congratulations! You have won 2nd Prize in the Residential Category.

She gasped. "We won!"

Thomas gave her a hug, "Congratulations."

"What about you? How did you do?"

"Honorable mention."

"No way. Your decorations are beautiful."

He looked around. "It's not a big deal. It spurred me on to get out of my holiday funk. Now, when my family arrives, we'll look festive. Besides," he said, wrapping his arm around her, "now I get to give you a present."

"Tell me, tell me, tell me," she begged. "What did you get me? Will I like it? When can I open it?"

"What are you, five?" he asked. "Hanukkah doesn't start for a couple more hours. You can't open it yet."

"That's unfair. It's tied to the contest."

"Yes, but it's a holiday gift. It means you have to wait for the holiday. You're lucky you don't celebrate Christmas. You'd have to wait longer. Plus, I'd have to decide—do I give it to you for Christmas Eve or Christmas Day...?"

She pushed his chest. "Ugh." His chest was rock-hard, and her push did nothing to change his mind.

Did she want such a stubborn man? She glanced at the creases next to his mouth as he laughed, and she knew.

Yes.

Chapter Fifteen

That night Thomas rang Jessica's doorbell at seven thirty, after the family ate. The electric menorah in their window was lit with two candles—the one candle on the right and the tall candle in the middle. He smoothed his hair and wiped his free hand on his pant leg as nerves overwhelmed him. He hoped he wasn't intruding.

The door swung wide and Jessica's mom greeted him. "Hi, Thomas. Nice to see you!"

"Hi, Mrs. Sacks. Happy Hanukkah."

"Oh, thank you. Come in. Jessica told me you were stopping by."

He stepped into their foyer and handed Mrs. Sacks a box wrapped in silver paper.

Her eyes lit up. "Is this for me?"

Thomas nodded. "Happy Hanukkah."

She unwrapped the gift and opened the box of chocolate dreidels. "This is thoughtful, Thomas. Unnecessary, but thoughtful." She turned to Jessica as she entered the room. "Look what Thomas brought me."

Jessica smiled and Thomas's nerves lessened.

"Those look yummy," Jessica said. She started to take one and her mom swatted her hand away.

"Hey, these are for me. And maybe Dad, if he's in my good graces. You need to get your own."

"That doesn't seem 'holiday-spirit-like,'" Jessica said.

Her mom shook her head. "This holiday celebrates miracles. And the miracle of me sharing my chocolate has not yet occurred."

Jessica turned to Thomas. "Oh, boy. Come on into the kitchen. I'll show you our menorahs."

He followed her, admiring her cute ass down the hallway into the kitchen. Two menorahs sat on the counter.

"This one is mine." She pointed to a fused glass menorah dappled with blue and white glass that reminded him of the sky. "And this one is my parents'." Theirs was more traditional, made of ornate silver.

"I never realized there were different kinds," he said.

She nodded. "When I was a kid, I had one where each candle sat in a ceramic dreidel of a different color. When I got too old, I picked out this one."

"I like it."

"Thanks. Sit down? I have donuts, if you'd like. And latkes."

"I'll never say no to either of those things," he said. "But first, here's your gift. Or should I say 'prize'?"

"Oh, it's a prize. I beat you."

"Somehow I don't think you're ever going to let me live this down," he said, enjoying the banter.

"Well, at least not until next year's contest."

"Wait, we're doing this again?" he asked.

"Of course, we are. I'm going to win first place next year."

"How about we take one year at a time? Starting with your prize."

He held out the silver package, wrapped similar to the one he'd given her mom, but a different shape, and larger.

"It's a little fragile, be careful," he said.

"It's also heavy."

She unwrapped it and read the words on the outside of the box. "You bought me a fire truck?"

"Keep opening."

She opened the box and gasped. "It has a dreidel hanging from the ladder!" She threw her arms around him and squeezed. "I love it!"

He cupped her cheek. "I wanted to get you something that reminds you of me, but also shows my acceptance of you."

Her green eyes filled, reminding him of emeralds, all sparkly and full of light. "I think this is the most meaningful gift I've gotten. Thank you."

She kissed him, her lips soft and sweet. "I love this."

His chest filled. "I'm glad. I was nervous."

She pulled away. "Why?"

"I wasn't sure if you'd think it silly. There isn't a lot of Hanukkah merchandise out there, and to be honest, I kind of like that. It makes it seem more… I don't know. I didn't want to cheapen it." He flushed. "But when I saw it was a fire truck, I couldn't resist."

"You know," she said, a gleam in her eye, "you've set yourself a difficult task."

She kissed him again, deeper this time, and he had to focus on her words. "Why?"

"Because this gift will be impossible to top."

This time she licked his lips, and he groaned. "Why would I have to top it?" He forced the words out, his hands itching to lay her flat on the table.

"Because I'm going to win the contest next year."

He was about to respond when the doorbell rang. He groaned. "That's them, isn't it?"

"Yes, it is." She pulled back and ruffled her hair. "I need to put on lip gloss." Moving away from him, she rummaged in the kitchen drawer and applied the pale pink shimmer to her lips when her friends walked in.

He was glad he was toward the rear of the room to give himself a chance to adjust and observe.

"Happy Hanukkah!" Jessica cried and greeted the first couple into the room. "Sarah, Aaron, I'm glad to see you both." She hugged them and took a platter from Aaron's hands.

"My mom's *ruggelach* recipe," he said. "Sarah made sure I made chocolate for you, but there's raspberry and peach as well."

"Yum! You guys know Thomas, right?"

He stepped forward and shook hands with both of them. They gave him warm smiles. "Nice to see you," he said.

"Likewise," Aaron said.

"Jessica's talked a lot about you," Sarah said.

The comment didn't fill him with anxiety, but pleasure. "Good things, I hope."

Sarah nodded.

"Yes," said another voice. "I'm Caroline, and this is my boyfriend, Jared. And only good things."

"It's nice to see you two together," Jessica said. She placed a platter of jelly donuts on the counter. "How's Becca?"

Jared grinned. "She's home with my parents, who are thrilled to babysit. And the adoption should be official any day now."

Caroline squeezed his arm.

"Mazel tov," Jessica said.

"In the meantime," he continued, "it's nice to be here with all of you, and I appreciate all the food you brought with you, Aaron."

"I know, right?" a female voice added above the laughter. "Hi, I'm Emily." A woman stepped forward on her own, holding two bottles of wine. "And we *goyim* have to stick together," she said eyeing Thomas. "This is how we get fed."

"She's learning." Jessica laughed. "Nice use of Yiddish. Maybe you can teach my boyfriend here some too."

As everyone chatted, Thomas pulled Jessica close. "Boyfriend, huh?" He kept his voice at a whisper, though he could have spoken in normal tones and not have been heard over the group.

"Do you mind?"

"Not at all."

"Before we get this celebration started, can I say something?" Aaron's voice rose over everyone else's.

Thomas pulled Jessica to him, leaning her against his chest.

Aaron glanced at Sarah, who nodded and blushed.

Jessica gasped.

"I asked Sarah to marry me, and she said yes." Aaron stood tall and proud, and though Thomas didn't know him, happiness poured off the man like water from a fountain.

Shrieks of joy ripped through the air. Jessica's parents ran in and joined in the congratulations. Jessica pulled out of Thomas's arms and joined Sarah and Caroline in a group hug. As the woman oohed and aahed over the ring, Jared clapped Aaron on the back.

Thomas observed everyone, waiting for his chance to enter into the fray and offer his good wishes. The people here were a family of sorts, and he didn't want to intrude. At the first break in the excitement, when everyone seemed to pause for air, he stepped forward.

"Congratulations to you both." He offered his hand to Aaron and a smile to Sarah.

Aaron put his arm around Sarah, love oozing from his pores. "Thanks, guys. We couldn't wait to share our news with you."

"Let's all grab our goodies and sit," Jessica said. "We want to hear all the details."

She returned to Thomas's side while everyone else poured glasses of wine and fixed themselves plates filled with Hanukkah treats.

"I know it's a little overwhelming right now," she said to him, "with the engagement announcement, but I think you'll like them when you get to know them."

He met her gaze. Nothing mattered to him but her. "I already do."

She squeezed his waist before pulling away, a stricken expression on her face. "Will the wine bother you? There's going to be a toast…"

He shook his head. "No. You don't need to worry about me. I've got things under control, and you're not responsible for whether or not I drink. Trust me, I'm okay, and if I'm not, I'll tell you."

She kissed him and went to fill her plate. As he followed her, filling his own, as well, he marveled he'd found someone as special as Jessica. He could get used to this and, more importantly, he wanted to.

"I want to make a toast," Jessica's dad said, "before we leave all of you to your celebration. To Aaron and Sarah. We wish you all the joy and *nachas* you both deserve. *Mazel tov!*"

Everyone raised their glasses, including Thomas, who raised a glass of water. The clinks reminded him of happiness, and he looked around the room of smiling people. For the first time in a long time, he realized he was happy too.

"Sarah, your ring is beautiful," Jessica said as she munched on a latke with applesauce.

Sarah held out her hand. The round diamond was set into a platinum band with diamond chips on either side of the main stone. It was simple and stunning, and fit her friend's personality perfectly.

"I know, isn't it?" she said. "I love it. He did such a good job and surprised me."

"How did he propose?" Caroline asked.

"It was romantic," she said. "He invited me over to light the Hanukkah candles at his apartment. When I got there, he'd cooked a beautiful dinner, cleaned his apartment, and he gave me flowers. We chanted the prayers and lit the candles, and he was on his knees holding out a ring and telling me he wanted to spend every Hanukkah for the rest of our lives together."

Jessica drew her hand to her chest. "I love that."

Caroline, Emily and Sarah looked at her in shock.

"What?" she cried. "I do."

"You're the least romantic out of all of us."

Jessica shrugged. "Well, he got me."

The other women looked at each other and over at the men, who sat together talking. "Aaron didn't get you, but I think Thomas did," Sarah said.

Caroline and Emily nodded.

Jessica's face heated.

"Mmm-hmm." Emily flashed a knowing grin. "Go ahead, deny it. I dare you."

"Okay, fine. Maybe."

The women laughed.

She looked at her best friend. "And I'm excited for your wedding, Sarah. Have you decided on a date yet?"

"Fine, change the subject," Sarah said. But her smile showed how happy she was and, for the next ten minutes, the women discussed wedding ideas, until the men turned their focus to them.

"Okay, ready for dreidel?" Jessica asked.

Sarah, Caroline and Emily nodded. Aaron rubbed his hands together, but Jared and Thomas looked at each other.

"Care to explain to the newcomers?" Jared asked. "The only dreidel game I'm familiar with is with children."

Jessica nodded. "Yes, dreidel is a children's game, where you spin the top and, depending on the letter it lands on, you either win or lose pennies or M&M's or whatever. But since we're adults now—"

"—in theory," Aaron said dryly.

Jessica made a face at him while Sarah poked him in the ribs.

"Since we're adults now," Jessica continued, "we're upping the ante." She went over to the bookshelf on the other side of the room, where she'd stored a Hanukkah bag. Inside, she pulled out rolls of quarters. "Who needs?"

Thomas looked around confused, and she sat next to him. "Don't worry, I have quarters for you."

"I would have brought some if you'd told me," he said.

"I know, but your first time is on the house," she said.

She tipped her chin toward Caroline, who shared her roll with Jared. "See?"

"Gotcha."

"Everyone puts a dollar into the pot and keeps four dollars for themselves," she said. She passed out a small bowl of dreidels. They were of all sizes and colors and materials. Each person rummaged through, trying to find the "perfect" one. After several test spins—where Jessica also made sure Thomas knew what to do—they settled on their dreidels.

"Thomas, do you need any pointers?" Emily asked.

"Nah, I think I'm good," he said. "But thanks."

"Okay, let's review the letters," Jessica said. "*Nun* means none, *shin* means put one in, *gimel* means you get all, and *hay* means you get half." She pointed out the letters to Thomas. "Don't worry, I'll help you."

At the beginning of each round, they all put one quarter into the pot. One by one, they spun the dreidel, paying or winning money. The more they played, the rowdier they became. Jessica loved how everyone got into it, even Thomas, who, after a few rounds, was a pro.

She decided it was time to impress him. On her next turn, she spun the dreidel upside down, on its stick, rather than on the pointy end.

"Whoa, what are you doing?" Thomas asked.

Everyone around her nodded.

"Spinning my dreidel."

"Upside down?" he asked.

"There's no rule saying I can't."

"Show-off," he said as he nudged her.

The dreidel landed on *gimel*, and she swept the pile of money into her own collection.

"All right, now you need to teach me how to do that," he said.

The game paused while Jessica taught Thomas how to spin the dreidel upside down. Or, at least, she tried. He wasn't able to get his hand out of the way in time for the dreidel to land on the floor and spin. It kept falling over on its side. Thomas's growls of frustration grew until he gave up.

"I think you have to be Jewish for this one," he said.

"Or have smaller hands," she said.

He leaned close and whispered in her ear. "Do you really want me to have smaller hands?"

Her face heated. In fact, she was pretty sure her entire body did. She didn't want anyone to know what he'd said, so she buried her face in his shirt. His laughter vibrated in his chest.

"All right, enough, you two," Emily cried. "Are we finishing our game? And, Thomas, that was a cop-out answer."

"Yeah, I know," he said.

They finished the game. Emily won.

"Thirty-five dollars for me!" she announced with glee.

"Hmm," Caroline said. "Didn't you win last year too?"

Emily batted her eyelashes. "Maybe."

"I think it's rigged." Caroline gave her a pretend scowl. "But I love you anyway."

"Let's open gifts." Jessica eyed the pile in the corner.

They all distributed their gifts to each other.

"Who's opening first?" Emily asked.

"How about we start with the gift from me?" Sarah suggested. She pointed to the silver bags with blue tissue paper peeking from the tops.

Jessica pushed aside the tissue paper and pulled out a soft, pale gray cashmere scarf. Everyone's scarves were different shades of gray, blue or beige. She rubbed it against her cheek.

"This is beautiful," Caroline said.

"I love it," added Emily.

"And it's not black," Jessica said. She winked.

"I'm glad you all like it," Sarah said. "As much as I wanted to go with a color, I thought neutrals were more useful."

"Okay, my turn." Caroline pointed to the blue bags with dreidels in pastel colors.

Jessica reached into the bag and pulled out a running belt in a deep rose color. She looked over at her friends. Sarah's was blue and Emily's was neon green. Meanwhile, the guys' were black.

"This is perfect," Emily said.

Sarah nodded.

"I love mine," Jessica added.

"I figured even if you don't run—" she stared at Jessica "—you can use it carry your phone when you want your hands free."

Jessica nodded. "You have no idea how useful this would be while I interview someone. Or it will be in the future."

Caroline's gaze clouded. "I didn't mean to make you feel bad about your old job."

Standing, Jessica walked around and gave her a hug. "I swear, you didn't. I love it."

"Now open mine," Emily said.

Jessica returned to her seat on and took the small box wrapped in red-and-white paper. Unwrapping it, she pulled out a gift card to Hard As Nails.

"Please tell me you didn't get us those," Aaron laughed.

"Men can get their nails done, too, you know," she said.

Throats cleared. "Not these men," Jared said.

"Don't worry," Emily said, her voice raised over the others. The guys pulled out gift cards to the local bookstore.

"Thank God," Thomas breathed.

"Mani-pedi's!" Jessica cried. "Can we all go together?"

Emily clapped her hands. "That's what I was hoping for," she said.

Jessica and her friends pulled out their phones, and they searched for dates. She nodded when Caroline suggested a good one and added it to her calendar.

"Okay, girls, time to open my gift," she said as soon as she was able to get everyone's attention away from their calendars.

She'd chosen iridescent gold bags with blue paper—red paper for Emily. Inside were leather-bound notebooks and colorful pens.

Sarah gasped. "This is beautiful!"

"I love it," Caroline added.

"It's perfect," Emily agreed.

The guys exchanged a few more gifts—including one's from Jessica that she'd added Thomas' name to—and when everyone had opened everything, the party wrapped up. The four women hugged as the men made plans to get together later in the week.

Jessica gave everyone their coats and she and Thomas said goodbye to each person.

"Did you like my friends?" she asked when they had left.

He nodded. "I do. Aaron's great. And Jared too. He and Caroline have a kid?"

Jessica shook her head. "No, his brother and sister-in-law died in a car crash and named him the guardian of his two-year old niece. Well, two-and-a-half by now. He's just about finished with the adoption process. They moved here about six months ago to be closer to his parents."

"Ah, makes sense. That's a helluva responsibility. Good for him."

"He's a great dad, and Caroline is happy. I wouldn't be surprised if they get engaged soon too."

"Sarah and Aaron looked happy together."

"They're like the perfect couple," Jessica said. "I'm glad she came home and came to her senses." At Thomas's quizzical look, she continued. "She was about to get engaged to another guy in DC, but came to her senses before she made a huge mistake. And now she and Aaron can live the life they were meant to live."

He put his arm around her. "Good for them."

She turned in his arms, stood on tiptoe and kissed him. He moaned against her mouth, pulling away as she was about to suggest they go to her room.

"I should go. I need to put the finishing touches on everything for Christmas."

"When will I see you?" Jessica asked.

"You and your family are coming for Christmas Eve dinner, right?"

She nodded. "You're sure we can't bring anything?"

"Just yourselves."

He kissed her again, drawing it out and returning for more before he opened the front door and walked next door.

"You still have the hots for little Jessie Sacks next door?" Thomas's sister asked, an incredulous look on her face.

"When do we get to see her?" his brother asked.

"Pipe down, both of you," his father said. He turned to Thomas. "Is she the one who helped you decorate the tree?"

Thomas threw another log on the fire, keeping his back to his family as long as possible. Having a family in the house, along with spouses and kids, gave the place an energy he didn't know he'd missed.

Until they'd started quizzing him on his love life.

Although, come to think of it, he kind of liked that too. He swung around.

"Oh, look at that goofy smile." Liam pointed. "He's got it bad for her."

"You used to look at Erin the same way," his dad said.

Liam put his arm around his sister.

"Smart man," she said. "Thomas, I think it's great."

"Thank you," he said.

"Are you going to answer us?" his dad asked.

He groaned. He was starting to remember how much of a nuisance family could be.

"Little Jessie isn't little anymore, Dad. And I don't think she'd appreciate you referring to her that way. I invited her and her parents to dinner tonight. And—"

"Wait, this is serious," his dad said.

He nodded. "It is."

The older man rose and gave him a hug that belied his age. "Good."

"She's Jewish, right?" Debbie asked. "It's nice to have them join us tonight."

"Her family is a little worried about the difference in religion, but she and I have talked about it, and I want to show them how we can celebrate together and still respect our differences and similarities, without anyone sacrificing for the other."

Debbie's gaze softened. "That's wonderful."

Oh, boy, his sister was going to cry. Since when did she become emotional?

"What can we do to help?" his sister asked.

That night, as the sun set, Thomas and his sister surveyed the dining room. His mom's Christmas tablecloth, a red damask with glittery gold flossing woven through it. The china was hers, too, white bone with green fir boughs painted on the edges. Matching red napkins and his mom's good silver completed the look. In the center of the table, fir boughs with bells sat, making the room smell of pine.

In the kitchen, his dad and brother put the finishing touches on the main course—lamb chops and butternut squash and sausage-stuffed shells. Thomas prepared the spinach salad with goat cheese and beets and the rice pilaf ahead of time.

The Sackses would be arriving any minute now.

The doorbell rang, and he smiled, as if he'd conjured them on his porch by thinking of them. He rushed to answer, greeting and ushering them into the house as snow began to fall.

"Looks like you're going to get a white Christmas," Jessica's mom said as she shook off the snow from her hair and unzipped her coat. She stood on tiptoe and kissed Thomas's cheek. "Thank you for the invitation."

"We're thrilled you're here." He took their coats before winking at Jessica.

With everyone inside, he led them into the living room. The Christmas tree glowed in the corner, its lights and that of the lit fireplace, the only illumination in the room.

"It's beautiful," Jessica's dad said, walking over and admiring the tree.

"Thank you," Thomas said. "My mom saved a lot of these decorations. I thought, since the family was coming, they'd like seeing them used."

Jessica rubbed his back. "What about you? Do you like them?"

"I do. They hold wonderful memories." He turned to Jessica's mom. "You remember my family, right?"

Her mom smiled. "Of course. Tom, it's wonderful to see you again. How do you like living in Arizona?"

"Can't beat the weather," he said, "although I miss Thomas and the kids." He glanced toward the window. "There's nothing like a white Christmas."

Thomas gestured to the coffee table. "Please, enjoy some hors d'oeuvres. Can I get anyone anything to drink?"

At their nods, he walked to the bar table on which he'd put

a variety of sodas, water, seltzer and juices. He filled people's glasses with their requests before he pulled up a chair and joined everyone.

Thick red candles sat on the ends of the coffee table, the flames moving with the air currents as people sat and helped themselves to cocktail napkins.

Thomas pointed to the items on the table. "We have hummus and vegetables, kosher pigs in blankets…" He paused. "Though that might be an oxymoron."

Everyone laughed.

"There's bruschetta and soft pretzels with a cheese-and-beer dip."

"You can't expect us to eat a meal after this," Debbie said as she filled her napkin.

"No one comes to Christmas dinner to starve," he said.

Jessica's father looked over at his wife. "Honey, I think we'll fit right in."

Thomas observed everyone as they talked, filling each other in on their lives, exclaiming with the children over their excitement for the holiday, and finding points of commonality the two families could share. He made eye contact with Jessica, whose relaxed expression warmed his heart.

He rose and conversation lulled. "If I could have everyone's attention for a moment," he said. "Dinner is almost ready, but before we go into the dining room to eat, it wouldn't be right not to acknowledge something else happening this evening. Tonight is the last night of Hanukkah, and I thought it would be nice to light the menorah before we eat dinner."

He looked at Jessica's parents. "If it's all right with you?"

The two adults looked at one another before returning their attention to him. They nodded. A tremulous smile played on Renée Sacks's lips. Mitchell Sacks's hands trembled as he helped his wife up from her seat.

"What a wonderful idea," she said.

"Would you mind explaining Hanukkah to my family?" Thomas asked. "I want everyone to be able to understand." He held out a hand to Jessica. "If the two of us are to be together, we have to learn from each other, respect each other's differences, and embrace what makes us unique." He looked around the room. "I hope you will all join us."

Jessica stood and gave him a hug. "Thank you," she whispered.

As Jessica's parents gave a brief explanation of the holiday, Thomas led Jessica over to the menorah.

"It's beautiful," she said. The menorah was a simple clear Lucite block with rainbow-colored candleholders.

"I'm glad you like it. I figure the two of us bring color into this relationship. Why not reflect that in the menorah?"

He pulled out a box of white candles and Jessica placed nine candles in it, one for each night of the holiday, plus the additional candle used to light the others. When her parents finished explaining the holiday, they all gathered around the menorah while Jessica sang the prayer and lit the candles with the *shamash*. Everyone watched the flames flicker.

Thomas drew Jessica into his arms. "I don't know where this relationship will go, but I do know I love you. I want us to make this work. I can't promise to always understand, but I can promise to always try. I think our life can be much better together, with both of us bringing our love, traditions and respect into everything we do." He cupped her cheek and caught the tear that leaked from the corner of her eye.

She turned to face their families and said, "We'd like to know we have your support."

As one, everyone stepped forward and encircled the couple.

"You have my blessing, not that you've ever needed it," Thomas's father said, his face creased into a wide smile.

Jessica's parents looked at each other, spoke that silent conversation with one another that Thomas had always admired but never understood, and said, "We love you, and if this is who you want, we support you."

He looked into Jessica's eyes. "Ready?"

* * * * *